Celtic
Myths

Celtic
Myths

General Editor: Jake Jackson

Associate Editor: Laura Bulbeck

FLAME TREE
PUBLISHING

This is a FLAME TREE Book

FLAME TREE PUBLISHING
6 Melbray Mews
Fulham, London SW6 3NS
United Kingdom
www.flametreepublishing.com

First published 2014

22 24 23
9 8

ISBN: 978-0-85775-822-4

Contributors, authors, editors and sources for this series include:
Loren Auerbach, Norman Bancroft-Hunt, E.M. Berens, Katharine
Berry Judson, Laura Bulbeck, Jeremiah Curtin, O.B. Duane, Dr
Ray Dunning, W.W. Gibbings, H. A. Guerber, Jake Jackson, Joseph
Jacobs, Judith John, J.W. Mackail (translator of Virgil's *Aeneid*) Chris
McNab, Professor James Riordan, Rachel Storm, K.E. Sullivan.

A copy of the CIP data for this book is available from the British Library.

Printed and bound by Clays Ltd, Elcograf S.p.A

Contents

Series Foreword

STRETCHING BACK to the oral traditions of thousands of years ago, tales of heroes and disaster, creation and conquest have been told by many different civilizations in many different ways. Their impact sits deep within our culture even though the detail in the tales themselves are a loose mix of historical record, transformed narrative and the distortions of hundreds of storytellers.

Today the language of mythology lives with us: our mood is jovial, our countenance is saturnine, we are narcissistic and our modern life is hermetically sealed from others. The nuances of myths and legends form part of our daily routines and help us navigate the world around us, with its half truths and biased reported facts.

The nature of a myth is that its story is already known by most of those who hear it, or read it. Every generation brings a new emphasis, but the fundamentals remain the same: a desire to understand and describe the events and relationships of the world. Many of the great stories are archetypes that help us find our own place, equipping us with tools for self-understanding, both individually and as part of a broader culture.

For Western societies it is Greek mythology that speaks to us most clearly. It greatly influenced the mythological heritage of the ancient Roman civilisation and is the lens through which we still see the Celts, the Norse and many of the other great peoples and religions. The Greeks themselves learned much from their neighbours, the Egyptians, an older culture that became weak with age and incestuous leadership.

It is important to understand that what we perceive now as mythology had its own origins in perceptions of the divine and the rituals of the sacred. The earliest civilisations, in the crucible of the Middle East, in the Sumer of the third millennium BC, are the source to which many of the mythic archetypes can be traced. As humankind collected together in cities for the first time, developed writing and industrial scale agriculture, started to irrigate the rivers and attempted to control rather than be at the mercy of its environment, humanity began to write down its tentative explanations of natural events, of floods and plagues, of disease.

Early stories tell of Gods (or god-like animals in the case of tribal societies such as African, Native American or Aboriginal cultures) who are crafty and use their wits to survive, and it is reasonable to suggest that these were the first rulers of the gathering peoples of the earth, later elevated to god-like status with the distance of time. Such tales became more political as cities vied with each other for supremacy, creating new Gods, new hierarchies for their pantheons. The older Gods took on primordial roles and became the preserve of creation and destruction, leaving the new gods to deal with more current, everyday affairs. Empires rose and fell, with Babylon assuming the mantle from Sumeria in the 1800s BC, then in turn to be swept away by the Assyrians of the 1200s BC; then the Assyrians and the Egyptians were subjugated by the Greeks, the Greeks by the Romans and so on, leading to the spread and assimilation of common themes, ideas and stories throughout the world.

The survival of history is dependent on the telling of good tales, but each one must have the 'feeling' of truth, otherwise it will be ignored. Around the firesides, or embedded in a book or a computer, the myths and legends of the past are still the living materials of retold myth, not restricted to an exploration of origins. Now we have devices and global communications that give us unparalleled access to a diversity of traditions. We can find out about Native American, Indian, Chinese and tribal African mythology in a way that was denied to our ancestors, we can find connections, match the archaeology, religion and the mythologies of the world to build a comprehensive image of the human experience that is endlessly fascinating.

The stories in this book provide an introduction to the themes and concerns of the myths and legends of their respective cultures, with a short introduction to provide a linguistic, geographic and political context. This is where the myths have arrived today, but undoubtedly over the next millennia, they will transform again whilst retaining their essential truths and signs.

Jake Jackson
General Editor, London 2014

Introduction to Celtic Myths

THE CELTS LEFT A RICH LEGACY of myths, legends, customs and folklore, which are among the oldest and most enduring in Europe, though they did not form an empire and their kingdoms comprised a wide variety of countries and cultures. Perhaps because of this their identity remains controversial, and our image of them is reworked by each new generation of Celtic scholars. The mystery of the Celts arises from the fact that they left no written accounts of themselves. Consequently, our knowledge of them is based on indirect evidence provided by archaeology, linguistics and Classical commentaries.

The Mystery of the Celts

Celtic material culture emerged in Central and Western Europe in the first millennium BC. It is first encountered in the artefacts of the Halstatt period (700–400 BC), so-named after an important archaeological site in upper Austria. The origins of the culture are much earlier, however, in the later Bronze Age settlements of non-Mediterranean Europe and probably even earlier still in the first Neolithic farming communities c. 4000 BC. The La Tène period (fifth century BC to the Roman occupation c. AD 45), which is named after a site on the shores of Lake Neuchâtel in Switzerland, represents the full-flowering of the culture. Finds have been made over much of Europe from northern France to Romania and from Poland to the Po Valley. This evidence portrays a heroic and hierarchical society in which war, feasting and bodily adornment were important. In many respects this confirms the picture of the Celts painted by Classical writers from the sixth century BC onwards.

Hecataeus of Miletus and Herotodus, writing in the sixth and fifth centuries BC, recognized a group of peoples to the north of the Greek port of Massalia (Marseilles) as having sufficient cultural features in common to justify a collective name, 'Keltoi'. By the fourth century BC commentators had accepted the Celts as being among the great

Barbarian peoples of the world, along with the Scythians, and Libyans; they were said to occupy a large swathe of Western Europe from Iberia to the Upper Danube. Later, Mediterranean writers such as Livy and Polybius report that in the fourth and third centuries BC Celtic tribes spread south into Italy and east to Greece and Asia Minor, where they settled as the Galatians. The same writers record heavy defeats for the Celts by the Romans towards the end of the third century BC and the subsequent occupation of their heartlands in Gaul by the mid-first century BC. Nowhere do the ancients refer to Britain as a Celtic land and debate continues over the precision with which the label 'Celt' was applied by Classical writers.

Without their own accounts it is impossible to say whether the Iron Age tribes of Europe, including Britain, saw themselves as collectively 'Celtic'. It is true to say, however, that Caesar recognized similarities between Britain and Gaul, and there is ample evidence of the La Tène culture in the British Isles. In the absence of archaeological evidence to show a migration of peoples from Gaul to Britain, it seems likely that it was the culture which spread; the indigenous peoples simply became Celtic through social contact and trade. Thus, when we refer to 'the Celts' we are not referring to an ethnic group but a culture adopted across non-Mediterranean Europe between the sixth century BC and the fifth century AD. It is ironic that the Irish and Welsh literature to which we owe so much of our understanding of Celtic mythology originated among peoples who may not have seen themselves as Celts.

Gods and Heroes

The Celts were polytheistic. The names of over 200 gods have been recorded. It is likely that individual deities went under several titles, so there were probably fewer than this. The scene remains complex, however, and attempts to reduce the Celtic pantheon to a coherent system have met with varying degrees of success.

The Celts had gods for all of the important aspects of their lives: warfare, hunting, fertility, healing, good harvests and so on. Much of the difficulty in classifying them arises from the fact that very few were recognized universally. In much greater numbers were local, tribal and possibly family deities. Our knowledge of the Celtic pantheon is based on the interpretations of contemporary observers, later vernacular literature (mainly from Ireland and Wales) and archaeological finds.

Very little iconography in the form of wood or stone sculptures has survived from before the Roman conquests, although a vast amount of perishable material must have existed. The earliest archaeological evidence from this period is from Provence and Central Europe. At Roquepertuse and Holtzerlingen, Celtic deities were represented in human form as early as the sixth and fifth centuries BC. Roman influence witnessed the production of many more permanent representations of the gods; dedicatory inscriptions reveal a huge array of native god names.

Caesar identified Celtic gods with what he saw as their Roman equivalents, probably to render them more comprehensible to a Roman readership. He said of the Gauls that the god they revered the most was Mercury and, next to him, Apollo, Mars, Jupiter and Minerva. Lucan (AD 39–65), a famous Roman poet, named three Celtic deities: Teutates (god of the tribe), Taranis (thunder) and Esus (multi-skilled). Other commentators identify Teutates with Mercury, Esus with Mars and Taranis with Dispater (the all father). Inscriptions on altars and monuments found across the Roman Empire, however, identify Teutates with Mars, Esus with Mercury and Taranis with Jupiter.

It is to Christian monks that we owe the survival of the ancient oral traditions of the pagan Celts and a more lucid insight into the nature of their deities. Very little was committed to paper before the monks began writing down Irish tales in the sixth century AD. The earliest written Welsh material dates from the twelfth century. Informative though they might be, however, the stories are influenced by Romano-Christian thinking and no doubt the monks censored the worst excesses of heathenism.

The stories are collected in sequences which follow the exploits of heroes, legendary kings and mythical characters from their unusual forms of conception and birth to their remarkable deaths. Along the way we learn of their expeditions to the otherworld, their loves and their battles. Many of the Irish legends are contained in three such collections. The first, known as the *Mythological Cycle* or *Book of Invasions*, records the imagined early history of Ireland. The second, the *Ulster Cycle*, tells of Cú Chulainn, a hero with superhuman strength and magical powers. The third is the story of another hero, Finn Mac Cumaill, his son Ossian and their warriors, the Fianna. This is known as the *Fenian Cycle*.

The pagan character of the mythology found in Irish literature is very clear. The Welsh tales, collected mainly in the Mabinogion, are much later (fourteenth century) and are contaminated more by time and changing literary fashions.

Rites and Rituals

Caesar wrote that the Gauls burnt men alive in huge, wicker effigies. Lucan speaks of 'cruel Teutates, horrible Esus and Taranis whose altar is as bloody as that of the Scythian Diana'. Medieval accounts tell of men hung from trees and torn to pieces in honour of Teutates, and of victims burnt in hollow trees as sacrifices to Taranis.

How reliable or typical these horrific tales may be is a matter of judgement. It is to be expected that Caesar and the sycophantic Lucan might emphasize the cruelty of Celtic cults to justify Roman massacres and the systematic extermination of the druids. Equally, Christian historians had an interest in discrediting paganism.

Druids may be named after the oak, their sacred tree. They were highly esteemed in Celtic society not only as holy men but also as teachers, philosophers, judges, diviners and astronomers. There were no druidesses as such, although priestesses are reported to have stood alongside the druids as they tried to resist the Roman occupation of Anglesey (AD 60).

It was forbidden for the druids' secrets to be written down lest they be profaned and lose their power. Consequently, laws, histories, traditions and magic formulae, which took many years to learn, were lost to posterity.

Without authentic written records Druidism is shrouded in mystery and obscured by romanticism, but the writings of Classical observers, such as Caesar, give us some idea of Druidic customs. We know, for example, that they were a well-organized, inter-tribal group who met annually to confer and to elect a leader. They held their ceremonies in forbidding, sacred groves which were allowed to grow thick and wild, and they presided at sacrifices, some of which might well have been human. Druids taught that the soul does not perish after death but that it transmigrates or moves into a new body. Perhaps some of the victims were willing participants who saw themselves as dying for the good of the tribe.

Mistletoe, a perennial plant, was considered sacred by the druids. They saw the relationship between the plant and the trees on which it grew as similar to that between the soul and the body. Like the soul, mistletoe was thought to proceed from the gods.

The tolerance shown by the Romans to the religions of the vanquished did not extend to the druids. The emperors Augustus, Tiberius and Claudius all sought to eradicate them. They painted a grim picture of them as unsavoury figures associated with disgusting ritual practices. This persecution was probably born of fear rather than moral scruple. The druids were a powerful group and a potential focus for rebellion.

Certain Celtic deities were associated with particular places such as sacred groves, remote mountains and lakes. Springs were thought to be the homes of goddesses in the service of the Earth Mother, the source of all life. Sulis, for example, guarded the hot springs at Aquae Sulis (present-day Bath).

The Celts believed that their gods and goddesses had powers to heal and protect, and to influence the outcome of important and everyday events. Celts asking a favour of a particular deity would make a sacrifice. If they were appealing to a water goddess, they might throw valued possessions into the water. Archaeologists have made some of their most important discoveries of weapons and other Iron-Age objects in the mud at the bottom of lakes.

Saints and Survivals

The religious practices of the Celts survived well into the Christian era. This is shown by resolutions passed at Church councils in the sixth century AD and by the edicts of Charlemagne (AD 789) against 'the worshippers of stones, trees and springs'. Powerless to suppress the old beliefs, Christianity assimilated aspects of paganism.

This appropriation accounts for the large number of saints rooted in Celtic gods and heroes, the springs dedicated to saints or to the Virgin and the sanctuaries built on sacred mounds. Indeed, the Christian religion is a rich source for the study of Celtic spirituality.

From AD 432, St Patrick established a form of Christianity in Ireland to suit a society that was still tribal. Rural monasteries, where monks followed the teachings of their founders, varied from the urban system of churches and Bishops, which was favoured by Rome. This was a much more familiar approach for the Celts, whose structures centred on the family, the clan and powerful local leaders. This form spread to other Celtic countries until the Celtic and Roman Churches met at the Synod of Whitby (AD 664) where the Roman approach prevailed. Thereafter, many of the teachings favoured in Ireland and Britain were forced underground.

The Celtic church was distinctive in many ways which betrayed its ancient roots: its affinity with nature in all its aspects, for example; its respect for the seasonal festivals; the equality it afforded women; and the active participation of the congregation during worship.

The Christian church adapted stories of Celtic divinities as miraculous events in the lives of the saints. Many reflect the Celtic sympathy with nature and the ability of the gods to assume the shape of animals. St Ciaran, for example, trained a fox to carry his psalter; St Kevin had his psalter returned by an otter when he dropped it in a lake; and St Columba subdued the Loch Ness Monster. St Patrick was attributed the most miracles, many of which arise from his struggle with the druids; it was said he could take the form of a deer.

The four main religious festivals of the Celts that were absorbed into the Christian calendar were Samain, Imbolc, Beltaine and Lughnasa.

Samain (1 November) marked the end of the agricultural year and the beginning of the next. It was a time for important communal rituals, meetings and sacrifices, as well as being a period when spirits from the otherworld became visible to men. Under Christianity this celebration became Harvest Festival and All Souls Day. The eve of the festival, known today as All Hallows Eve or Halloween, was particularly dangerous.

Imbolc (1 February) was sacred to the fertility goddess, Brigit, and it marked the coming into milk of the ewes and the time for moving them to upland pastures. It was subsequently taken over by the Christians as the feast of St Brigid.

At Beltaine (1 May), people lit bonfires in honour of Belenus, a god of life and death. The festival was seen as a purification or a fresh start. It is likely, too, that the fires were used to fumigate cattle before they were moved to the summer pastures. Under Christianity it became the feast of St John the Baptist.

Finally, there was the festival of Lughnasa (1 August), which the Christians renamed Lammas. It honoured the sun god, Lugh.

Recurring Themes

The myths of the Celts, found in Irish, Welsh and Continental vernacular literature, have inspired the imagination of poets and storytellers from the twelfth century to the present day. Their archetypal themes and imagery, though cloaked in novel forms by each new generation, never lose their potency.

No Celtic creation myth has survived, although Caesar, among other ancient commentators, testifies that they did have one. The nearest we have is a collection of stories in the Book of Invasions (twelfth century), which provide a mythical history of Ireland from the Flood to the coming of the Gaels (Celts).

Love is a central theme in Celtic mythology; love between deities and between gods and humans. The love triangle is a recurring variation, often involving a young couple and an unwanted suitor or an older husband. The outcome is often tragic. Typical of this genre are the Welsh story of Pwll and Rhiannon and the Irish tales of Diarmaid and Grainne, and Deirdre and Naoise.

Sometimes the triangle involves the young woman's father, who is often represented as a giant. In these stories the hero is frequently set seemingly impossible tasks to complete before winning the daughter's hand. A primary example is the Welsh tale of Culhwch and Olwen. Here Culhwch seeks the help of Arthur and his band of warriors to complete a list of tasks which culminate in a hunt for the monstrous boar, Twrch Trwyth.

Another theme is that of sacral kingship and sovereignty, in which the coupling of the king and the goddess of fertility ensures prosperity in the land. The goddess sometimes appears as a hag who turns into a beautiful young woman following the ritual.

Magic is an essential feature of Celtic myths. It is commonly used as a means of escape, as in the case of Diarmaid and Grainne who evade Finn's huntsmen for years using a cloak of invisibility, borrowed from Óengus, a love god. A typical form of magic found in many of the myths is the Celtic deities' ability to transform themselves or others into a variety of creatures. For example, Midir, the Irish lord of the otherworld, turns himself and the beautiful Etain into swans to escape from the palace of Óengus. The skill is also commonly used to deceive and punish.

Cú Roi and Sir Bartilek are transformed into giants for the beheading game, to make them unrecognizable to Cúchulainn and Gawain. When Math returns home to discover that his foot-maid has been raped by his nephews, Gwydion and Gilfaethwy, he punishes them by turning them into a succession of animals, one male and one female, demanding they produce offspring every year.

Love and enchantment are intimately linked in Celtic tales: Oisin is enchanted by Naim's beauty; a love potion is the undoing of Tristan and Iseulte; Diarmaid is enchanted by Grainne; Naoise is enchanted by Deirdre.

Other common themes are the otherworld feast and the feast where dramatic events occur. Such a feast might include a seduction, as in the story of Diarmaid and Grainne, or a dispute, as in the tale of Briccriu's

Feast. In the latter, an argument over who should receive the choicest cut of meat leads to the contenders taking part in a game to prove who is the most courageous. This involves their submitting without flinching to beheading. Because he is the only one brave enough to go through with it, the Ulster hero, Cúchulainn, is spared the ordeal and wins 'the champion's portion'.

The Arthurian Legends

Tales of King Arthur and his Knights of the Round Table, which swept Europe in the Middle Ages and beyond, were designed to entertain.

But, like the Irish and Welsh legends, they were echoes of the mythology which must have existed in Ireland, Britain and Gaul at the time of the Roman conquests.

Early references to Arthur appear in a Welsh poem by Aneirin (sixth century AD), the writings of the British monk, Gildas (sixth century AD) and of the Celtic historian, Nennius (eighth century AD). A tenth-century Latin history of Wales lists his victories and his defeat at the battle of Camlan. There is no proof that Arthur actually existed, but it is possible that he was a Romanized *dux bellorum* (battle leader) who lived in Britain in the late fifth century and was famed for resisting the Saxons. By the Middle Ages he and his band had become firmly imbedded in the popular imagination, sharing many of the attributes of Finn MacCumaill and the Fianna.

Arthur had many faces before emerging as a Christian king, the epitome of medieval chivalry and the once and future saviour of his people. In early stories he is given the epithet Horribilis and is called a tyrant. The eleventh-century Welsh story, *Culhwch and Olwen*, the earliest, fully fledged Arthurian tale in a Celtic language, portrays him as a Celtic king and benefactor touched with magic. In later romances he is shown as flawed, falling into slothful states from which it is difficult to arouse him.

The popular image of King Arthur was begun by Geoffrey of Monmouth. His twelfth-century *History of the Kings of Britain* inspired the Norman poet, Wace, who wrote a more courtly version and introduced the Round Table. The French poet, Chrétien de Troyes, developed the story later in the twelfth century, adding novel elements from Continental sources and the songs of Breton minstrels. It was Chrétien who introduced the idea of courtly love and the earliest version of the Grail legend. In the thirteenth century, Layamon wrote a longer, English version, replacing love and chivalry with earlier Celtic traditions and Dark Age brutality. German contributions followed and, in the fourteenth century, the greatest single Arthurian legend in Middle English, *Sir Gawain and the Green Knight*, appeared. In the fifteenth century Thomas Malory published the *Le Morte d'Arthur*, which was to become the best-known and most complete version of the story.

The pagan roots of Arthurian legend are clearly evident in typical devices such as the band of warriors (the knights), the love triangle (Arthur, Guinevere and Lancelot), the search for a magic cauldron (the Grail), the beheading game (Sir Gawain and the Green Knight) and the otherworld (Avalon, Arthur's final resting place). Medieval authors, from Geoffrey of Monmouth to Malory, found inspiration in these themes, and wove them with other elements into a form which spoke to their courtly contemporaries. So powerful and archetypal is the imagery that it continued to enthrall succeeding generations. In the nineteenth century, English poets such as Alfred, Lord Tennyson (1809–1892) and Algernon Charles Swinburne (1837–1909) revisited the themes. In the twentieth century, further Arthurian interpretations and adaptations appeared in literature (T.H.White's *Once and Future King* – 1958) and in new media such as film and television. The latter range from the brutally realistic (John Boorman's *Excalibur* – 1981) to the ridiculous (*Monty Python and the Holy Grail* – 1974).

The Invasions Cycle:
Tales of the Tuatha De Danann and the Early Milesians

THE THREE STORIES which introduce this volume are based on tales selected from the Book of Invasions, otherwise known as the Mythological Cycle. This chapter begins after the conquest of the Fir Bolg by the Tuatha De Danann, the god-like race, whose name translates as 'the people of the god whose mother is Dana'. Three of the most outstanding stories have been chosen for this section, each of which has an especially powerful narrative impact.

The Tuatha De Danann are recorded as having originally travelled to Erin from the northern islands of Greece around 2000 BC. They possessed great gifts of magic and druidism and they ruled the country until their defeat by the Milesians, when they were forced to establish an underground kingdom known as the Otherworld or the Sidhe, meaning Hollow Hills.

Lugh [*Pronounced Lu, gh is silent, as in English.*] of the Long Arm, who also appears later in the Ulster Cycle as Cuchulainn's divine father, emerges as one of the principal heroes of the Tuatha De Danann who rescues his people from the tyranny of the Fomorians.

The Quest of the Children of Tuirenn, together with the sorrowful account of Lir's children, are undoubtedly two of the great epic tales of this cycle.

The Wooing of Etain which concludes the trio, was probably written sometime in the eighth century. The story unfolds after the People of Dana are dispossessed by the Children of Miled and for the first time the notion of a Land of Youth, or Otherworld, is introduced, a theme again returned to in the third and final Fenian Cycle.

The Quest of the Children of Tuirenn

❧

NUADA OF THE SILVER HAND rose to become King of the Tuatha De Danann during the most savage days of the early invasions. The Fomorians, a repulsive band of sea-pirates, were the fiercest of opponents who swept through the country destroying cattle and property and imposing tribute on the people of the land. Every man of the Tuatha De Danann, no matter how rich or poor, was required to pay one ounce of gold to the Fomorians and those who neglected to pay this tax at the annual assembly on the Hill of Uisneach were maimed or murdered without compassion. Balor of the Evil Eye was leader of these brutal invaders, and it was well known that when he turned his one glaring eyeball on his foes they immediately fell dead as if struck by a thunderbolt. Everyone lived in mortal fear of Balor, for no weapon had yet been discovered that could slay or even injure him. Times were bleak for the Tuatha De Danann and the people had little faith in King Nuada who appeared powerless to resist Balor's tyranny and oppression. As the days passed by, they yearned for a courageous leader who would rescue them from their life of wretched servitude.

The appalling misery of the Tuatha De Danann became known far and wide and, after a time, it reached the ears of Lugh of the Long Arm of the fairymounds, whose father was Cian, son of Cainte. As soon as he had grown to manhood, Lugh had proven his reputation as one of the most fearless warriors and was so revered by the elders of Fairyland that they had placed in his charge the wondrous magical gifts of Manannan the sea-god which had protected their people for countless generations. Lugh rode the magnificent white steed of Manannan, known as Aenbarr, a horse as fleet of foot as the wailing gusts of winter whose charm was such that no rider was ever wounded while seated astride her. He had the boat of Manannan, which could read a man's thoughts and travel in whatever direction its keeper demanded. He also wore Manannan's breast-plate and body armour which no weapon could ever pierce, and he carried the mighty sword known as 'The Retaliator' that could cut through any battle shield.

The day approached once more for the People of Dana to pay their annual taxes to the Fomorians and they gathered together, as was customary, on the Hill of Uisneach to await the arrival of Balor's men. As they stood fearful and terrified in the chill morning air, several among them noticed a strange cavalry coming over the plain from the east towards them. At the head of this impressive group, seated high in command above the rest, was Lugh of the Long Arm, whose proud and noble countenance mirrored the splendour of the rising sun. The King was summoned to witness the spectacle and he rode forth to salute the leader of the strange army. The two had just begun to converse amiably when they were interrupted by the approach of a grimy-looking band of men, instantly known to all as Fomorian tax-collectors. King Nuada bowed respectfully towards them and instructed his subjects to deliver their tributes without delay. Such a sad sight angered and humiliated Lugh of the Long Arm and he drew the King aside and began to reproach him:

'Why do your subjects bow before such an evil-eyed brood,' he demanded, 'when they do not show you any mark of respect in return?'

'We are obliged to do this,' replied Nuada. 'If we refuse we would be killed instantly and our land has witnessed more than enough bloodshed at the hands of the Fomorians.'

'Then it is time for the Tuatha De Danann to avenge this great injustice,' replied Lugh, and with that, he began slaughtering Balor's emissaries single-handedly until all but one lay dead at his feet. Dragging the surviving creature before him, Lugh ordered him to deliver a stern warning to Balor:

'Return to your leader,' he thundered, 'and inform him that he no longer has any power over the People of Dana. Lugh of the Long Arm, the greatest of warriors, is more than eager to enter into combat with him if he possesses enough courage to meet the challenge.'

Knowing that these words would not fail to enrage Balor, Lugh lost little time preparing himself for battle. He enlisted the King's help in assembling the strongest men in the kingdom to add to his own powerful army. Shining new weapons of steel were provided and three thousand of the swiftest white horses were made ready for his men. A magnificent fleet of ships, designed to withstand the most venomous ocean waves, remained moored at port, awaiting the moment when Balor and his malicious crew would appear on the horizon.

The time finally arrived when the King received word that Balor's fierce army had landed at Eas Dara on the northwest coast of Connacht. Within hours, the Fomorians had pillaged the lands of Bodb the Red and plundered the homes of noblemen throughout the province. Hearing of this wanton destruction, Lugh of the Long Arm was more determined than ever to secure victory for the Tuatha De Danann. He rode across the plains of Erin back to his home to enlist the help of Cian, his father, who controlled all the armies of the fairymounds. His two uncles, Cu and Cethen, also offered their support and the three brothers set off in different directions to round up the remaining warriors of Fairyland.

Cian journeyed northwards and he did not rest until he reached Mag Muirthemne on the outskirts of Dundalk. As he crossed the plain, he observed three men, armed and mailed, riding towards him. At first he did not recognize them, but as they drew closer, he knew them to be the sons of Tuirenn whose names were Brian, Iucharba and Iuchar. A long-standing feud had existed for years between the sons of Cainte and the sons of Tuirenn and the hatred and enmity they felt towards each other was certain to provoke a deadly contest. Wishing to avoid an unequal clash of arms, Cian glanced around him for a place to hide and noticed a large herd of swine grazing nearby. He struck himself with a druidic wand and changed himself into a pig. Then he trotted off to join the herd and began to root up the ground like the rest of them.

The sons of Tuirenn were not slow to notice that the warrior who had been riding towards them had suddenly vanished into thin air. At first, they all appeared puzzled by his disappearance, but then Brian, the eldest of the three, began to question his younger brothers knowingly:

'Surely brothers you also saw the warrior on horseback,' he said to them. 'Have you no idea what became of him?'

'We do not know,' they replied.

'Then you are not fit to call yourselves warriors,' chided Brian, 'for that horseman can be no friend of ours if he is cowardly enough to change himself into one of these swine. The instruction you received in the City of Learning has been wasted on you if you cannot even tell an enchanted beast from a natural one.'

And as he was saying this, he struck Iucharba and Iuchar with his own druidic wand, transforming them into two sprightly hounds that howled and yelped impatiently to follow the trail of the enchanted pig.

Before long, the pig had been hunted down and driven into a small wood where Brian cast his spear at it, driving it clean through the animal's chest. Screaming in pain, the injured pig began to speak in a human voice and begged his captors for mercy:

'Allow me a dignified death,' the animal pleaded. 'I am originally a human being, so grant me permission to pass into my own shape before I die.'

'I will allow this,' answered Brian, 'since I am often less reluctant to kill a man than a pig.'

Then Cian, son of Cainte, stood before them with blood trickling down his cloak from the gaping wound in his chest.

'I have outwitted you,' he cried, 'for if you had killed me as a pig you would only be sentenced for killing an animal, but now you must kill me in my own human shape. And I must warn you that the penalty you will pay for this crime is far greater than any ever paid before on the death of a nobleman, for the weapons you shall use will cry out in anguish, proclaiming your wicked deed to my son, Lugh of the Long Arm'.

'We will not slay you with any weapons in that case,' replied Brian triumphantly, 'but with the stones that lie on the ground around us.' And the three brothers began to pelt Cian with jagged rocks and stones until his body was a mass of wounds and he fell to the earth battered and lifeless. The sons of Tuirenn then buried him where he had fallen in an unmarked grave and hurried off to join the war against the Fomorians.

With the great armies of Fairyland and the noble cavalcade of King Nuada at his side, Lugh of the Long Arm won battle after battle against

Balor and his men. Spears shot savagely through the air and scabbards clashed furiously until at last, the Fomorians could hold out no longer. Retreating to the coast, the terrified survivors and their leader boarded their vessels and sailed as fast as the winds could carry them back through the northern mists towards their own depraved land. Lugh of the Long Arm became the hero of his people and they presented him with the finest trophies of valour the kingdom had to offer, including a golden war chariot, studded with precious jewels which was driven by four of the brawniest milk-white steeds.

When the festivities had died down somewhat, and the Tuatha De Danann had begun to lead normal lives once more, Lugh began to grow anxious for news of his father. He called several of his companions to him and appealed to them for information, but none among them had received tidings of Cian since the morning he had set off towards the north to muster the armies of the fairymounds.

'I know that he is no longer alive,' said Lugh, 'and I give you my word that I will not rest again, or allow food or drink to pass my lips, until I have knowledge of what happened to him.'

And so Lugh, together with a number of his kinsmen, rode forth to the place where he and his father had parted company. From here, the horse of Manannan guided him to the Plain of Muirthemne where Cian had met his tragic death. As soon as he entered the shaded wood, the stones of the ground began to cry out in despair and they told Lugh of how the sons of Tuirenn had murdered his father and buried him in the earth. Lugh wept bitterly when he heard this tale and implored his men to help him dig up the grave so that he might discover in what cruel manner Cian had been slain. The body was raised from the ground and the litter of wounds on his father's cold flesh was revealed to him. Lugh rose gravely to his feet and swore angry vengeance on the sons of Tuirenn:

'This death has so exhausted my spirit that I cannot hear through my ears, and I cannot see anything with my eyes, and there is not one pulse beating in my heart for grief of my father. Sorrow and destruction will fall on those that committed this crime and they shall suffer long when they are brought to justice.'

The body was returned to the ground and Lugh carved a headstone and placed it on the grave. Then, after a long period of mournful silence, he mounted his horse and headed back towards Tara where the last of the victory celebrations were taking place at the palace.

Lugh of the Long Arm sat calmly and nobly next to King Nuada at the banqueting table and looked around him until he caught sight of the three sons of Tuirenn. As soon as he had fixed his eye on them, he stood up and ordered the Chain of Attention of the Court to be shaken so that everyone present would fall silent and listen to what he had to say.

'I put to you all a question,' said Lugh. 'I ask each of you what punishment you would inflict upon the man that had murdered your father?'

The King and his warriors were astonished at these words, but finally Nuada spoke up and enquired whether it was Lugh's own father that had been killed.

'It is indeed my own father who lies slain,' replied Lugh 'and I see before me in this very room the men who carried out the foul deed.'

'Then it would be far too lenient a punishment to strike them down directly,' said the King. 'I myself would ensure that they died a lingering death and I would cut off a single limb each day until they fell down before me writhing in agony.'

Those who were assembled agreed with the King's verdict and even the sons of Tuirenn nodded their heads in approval. But Lugh declared that he did not wish to kill any of the Tuatha De Danann, since they were his own people. Instead, he would insist that the perpetrators pay a heavy fine, and as he spoke he stared accusingly towards Brian, Iuchar and Iucharba, so that the identity of the murderers was clearly exposed to all. Overcome with guilt and shame, the sons of Tuirenn could not bring themselves to deny their crime, but bowed their heads and stood prepared for the sentence Lugh was about to deliver.

'This is what I demand of you,' he announced.

Three ripened apples
The skin of a pig
A pointed spear

Two steeds and a chariot
Seven pigs
A whelping pup
A cooking spit
Three shouts on a hill.

'And,' Lugh added, 'if you think this fine too harsh, I will now reduce part of it. But if you think it acceptable, you must pay it in full, without variation, and pledge your loyalty to me before the royal guests gathered here.'

'We do not think it too great a fine,' said Brian, 'nor would it be too large a compensation if you multiplied it a hundredfold. Therefore, we will go out in search of all these things you have described and remain faithful to you until we have brought back every last one of these objects.'

'Well, now,' said Lugh, 'since you have bound yourselves before the court to the quest assigned you, perhaps you would like to learn more detail of what lies in store,' And he began to elaborate on the tasks that lay before the sons of Tuirenn.

'The apples I have requested of you,' Lugh continued, 'are the three apples of the Hesperides growing in the gardens of the Eastern World. They are the colour of burnished gold and have the power to cure the bloodiest wound or the most horrifying illness. To retrieve these apples, you will need great courage, for the people of the east have been forewarned that three young warriors will one day attempt to deprive them of their most cherished possessions.

'And the pig's skin I have asked you to bring me will not be easy to obtain either, for it belongs to the King of Greece who values it above everything else. It too has the power to heal all wounds and diseases.

'The spear I have demanded of you is the poisoned spear kept by Pisar, King of Persia. This spear is so keen to do battle that its blade must always be kept in a cauldron of freezing water to prevent its fiery heat melting the city in which it is kept.

'And do you know who keeps the chariot and the two steeds I wish to receive from you?' Lugh continued.

'We do not know,' answered the sons of Tuirenn.

'They belong to Dobar, King of Sicily,' said Lugh, 'and such is their unique charm that they are equally happy to ride over sea or land, and the chariot they pull is unrivalled in beauty and strength.

'And the seven pigs you must gather together are the pigs of Asal, King of the Golden Pillars. Every night they are slaughtered, but every morning they are found alive again, and any person who eats part of them is protected from ill-health for the rest of his life.

'Three further things I have demanded of you,' Lugh went on. 'The whelping hound you must bring me guards the palace of the King of Iruad. Failinis is her name and all the wild beasts of the world fall down in terror before her, for she is stronger and more splendid than any other creature known to man.

'The cooking-spit I have called for is housed in the kitchen of the fairywomen on Inis Findcuire, an island surrounded by the most perilous waters that no man has ever safely reached.

'Finally, you must give the three shouts requested of you on the Hill of Midcain where it is prohibited for any man other than the sons of Midcain to cry aloud. It was here that my father received his warrior training and here that his death will be hardest felt. Even if I should one day forgive you of my father's murder, it is certain that the sons of Midcain will not.'

As Lugh finished speaking, the children of Tuirenn were struck dumb by the terrifying prospect of all that had to be achieved by them and they went at once to where their father lived and told him of the dreadful sentence that had been pronounced on them.

'It is indeed a harsh fine,' said Tuirenn, 'but one that must be paid if you are guilty, though it may end tragically for all three of you.' Then he advised his sons to return to Lugh to beg the loan of the boat of Manannan that would carry them swiftly over the seas on their difficult quest. Lugh kindly agreed to give them the boat and they made their way towards the port accompanied by their father. With heavy hearts, they exchanged a sad farewell and wearily set sail on the first of many arduous journeys.

'We shall go in search of the apples to begin with,' said Brian, and his command was answered immediately by the boat of Manannan which steered a course towards the Eastern World and sailed without stopping until it came to rest in a sheltered harbour in the lands of the Hesperides. The brothers then considered how best they might remove the apples from the garden in which they were growing, and it was eventually decided among them that they should transform themselves into three screeching hawks.

'The tree is well guarded,' Brian declared, 'but we shall circle it, carefully avoiding the arrows that will be hurled at us until they have all been spent. Then we will swoop on the apples and carry them off in our beaks.'

The three performed this task without suffering the slightest injury and headed back towards the boat with the stolen fruit. The news of the theft had soon spread throughout the kingdom, however, and the king's three daughters quickly changed themselves into three-taloned ospreys and pursued the hawks over the sea. Shafts of lightning lit up the skies around them and struck the wings of the hawks, scorching their feathers and causing them to plummet towards the waters below. But Brian managed to take hold of his druidic wand and he transformed himself and his brothers into swans that darted below the waves until the ospreys had given up the chase and it was safe for them to return to the boat.

After they had rested awhile, it was decided that they should travel on to Greece in search of the skin of the pig.

'Let us visit this land in the shape of three bards of Erin,' said Brian, 'for if we appear as such, we will be honoured and respected as men of wit and wisdom.'

They dressed themselves appropriately and set sail for Greece composing some flattering verses in honour of King Tuis as they journeyed along. As soon as they had landed, they made their way to the palace and were enthusiastically welcomed as dedicated men of poetry who had travelled far in search of a worthy patron. An evening of drinking and merry-making followed; verses were read aloud by the King's poets and many ballads were sung by the court musicians. At length, Brian rose to his feet and began to recite the poem he had written for King Tuis. The King smiled rapturously to hear himself described as 'the oak among kings' and encouraged Brian to accept some reward for his pleasing composition.

'I will happily accept from you the pig's skin you possess,' said Brian, 'for I have heard that it can cure all wounds.'

'I would not give this most precious object to the finest poet in the world,' replied the King, 'but I shall fill the skin three times over with red gold, one skin for each of you, which you may take away with you as the price of your poem.'

The brothers agreed to this and the King's attendants escorted them to the treasure-house where the gold was to be measured out. They were about to weigh the very last share when Brian suddenly snatched the pig's skin and raced from the room, striking down several of the guards as he ran. He had just found his way to the outer courtyard when King Tuis appeared before him, his sword drawn in readiness to win back his most prized possession. Many bitter blows were exchanged and many deep wounds were inflicted by each man on the other until, at last, Brian dealt the King a fatal stroke and he fell to the ground never to rise again.

Armed with the pig's skin that could cure their battle wounds, and the apples that could restore them to health, the sons of Tuirenn grew more confident that they would succeed in their quest. They were determined to move on as quickly as possible to the next task Lugh had set them and instructed the boat of Manannan to take them to the land of Persia, to the court of King Pisar, where they appeared once more in the guise of poets. Here they were also made welcome and were treated with honour and distinction. After a time, Brian was called upon to deliver his poem and, as before, he recited some verses in praise of the King which won the approval of all who were gathered. Again, he was persuaded to accept some small reward for his poem and, on this occasion, he requested the magic spear of Persia. But the King grew very angry at this request and the benevolent attitude he had previously displayed soon turned to open hostility:

'It was most unwise of you to demand my beloved spear as a gift,' bellowed the King, 'the only reward you may expect now is to escape death for having made so insolent a request.'

When Brian heard these words he too was incensed and grabbing one of the three golden apples, he flung it at the King's head, dashing out his brains. Then the three brothers rushed from the court, slaughtering all they encountered along the way, and hurried towards the stables where the spear of Pisar lay resting in a cauldron of water. They quickly seized the spear and headed for the boat of Manannan, shouting out their next destination as they ran, so that the boat made itself ready and turned around in the direction of Sicily and the kingdom of Dobar.

'Let us strike up a friendship with the King,' said Brian, 'by offering him our services as soldiers of Erin.'

And when they arrived at Dobar's court they were well received and admitted at once to the King's great army where they won the admiration of all as the most valiant defenders of the realm. The brothers remained in the King's service for a month and two weeks, but during all this time they never once caught a glimpse of the two steeds and the chariot Lugh of the Long Arm had spoken of.

'We have waited long enough,' Brian announced impatiently. 'Let us go to the King and inform him that we will quit his service unless he shows us his famous steeds and his chariot.'

So they went before King Dobar who was not pleased to receive news of their departure, for he had grown to rely on the three brave warriors. He immediately sent for his steeds and ordered the chariot to be yoked to them and they were paraded before the sons of Tuirenn. Brian watched carefully as the charioteer drove the steeds around in a circle and as they came towards him a second time he sprung onto the nearest saddle and seized the reins. His two brothers fought a fierce battle against those who tried to prevent them escaping, but it was not long before they were at Brian's side, riding furiously through the palace gates, eager to pursue their fifth quest.

They sailed onwards without incident until they reached the land of King Asal of the Pillars of Gold. But their high spirits were quickly vanquished by the sight of a large army guarding the harbour in anticipation of their arrival. For the fame of the sons of Tuirenn was widespread by this time, and their success in carrying away with them the most coveted treasures of the world was well known to all. King Asal himself now came forward to greet them and demanded to know why they had pillaged the lands of other kings and murdered so many in their travels. Then Brian told King Asal of the sentence Lugh of the Long Arm had pronounced upon them and of the many hardships they had already suffered as a result.

'And what have you come here for?' the King enquired.

'We have come for the seven pigs which Lugh has also demanded as part of that compensation,' answered Brian, 'and it would be far better for all of us if you deliver them to us in good will.'

When the King heard these words, he took counsel with his people, and it was wisely decided that the seven pigs should be handed over peacefully, without bloodshed. The sons of Tuirenn expressed their gratitude to King Asal and pledged their services to him in all future battles. Then Asal questioned them on their next adventure, and when he discovered that they were journeying onwards to the land of Iruad in search of a puppy hound, he made the following request of them:

'Take me along with you,' he said 'for my daughter is married to the King of Iruad and I am desperate, for love of her, to persuade him to surrender what you desire of him without a show of arms.'

Brian and his brothers readily agreed to this and the boats were made ready for them to sail together for the land of Iruad.

When they reached the shores of the kingdom, Asal went ahead in search of his son-in-law and told him the tale of the sons of Tuirenn from beginning to end and of how he had rescued his people from a potentially bloody war. But Iruad was not disposed to listen to the King's advice and adamantly refused to give up his hound without a fight. Seizing his weapon, he gave the order for his men to begin their attack and went himself in search of Brian in order to challenge him to single combat. A furious contest ensued between the two and they struck each other viciously and angrily. Eventually, however, Brian succeeded in overpowering King Iruad and he hauled him before Asal, bound and gagged like a criminal.

'I have spared his life,' said Brian, 'perhaps he will now hand over the hound in recognition of my clemency.'

The King was untied and the hound was duly presented to the sons of Tuirenn who were more than pleased that the battle had come to a swift end. And there was no longer any bitterness between Iruad and the three brothers, for Iruad had been honestly defeated and had come to admire his opponents. They bid each other a friendly farewell and the sons of Tuirenn took their leave of the land of the Golden Pillars and set out to sea once again.

Far across the ocean in the land of Erin, Lugh of the Long Arm had made certain that news of every success achieved by the sons of Tuirenn had been brought to his attention. He was fully aware that the quest he had set them was almost drawing to a close and became increasingly anxious at the thought. But he desired above everything else to take possession of the valuable objects that had already been recovered, for Balor of the Evil Eye had again reared his ugly head and the threat of another Fomorian invasion was imminent. Seeking to lure the sons of Tuirenn back to Erin, Lugh sent a druidical spell after the brothers, causing them to forget that their sentence had not yet been fully completed. Under its influence, the sons of Tuirenn entertained visions of the heroic reception that awaited them on the shores of the Boyne and their hearts were filled with joy to think that they would soon be reunited with their father.

Within days, their feet had touched on Erin's soil again and they hastened to Tara to the Annual Assembly, presided over by the High King of Erin. Here, they were heartily welcomed by the royal family and the Tuatha De Danann who rejoiced alongside them and praised them for their great courage and valour. And it was agreed that they should submit the tokens of their quest to the High King himself who undertook to examine them and to inform Lugh of the triumphant return of the sons of Tuirenn. A messenger was despatched to Lugh's household and within an hour he had arrived at the palace of Tara, anxious to confront the men he still regarded as his enemies.

'We have paid the fine on your father's life,' said Brian, as he pointed towards the array of objects awaiting Lugh's inspection.

'This is indeed an impressive sight,' replied Lugh of the Long Arm, 'and would suffice as payment for any other murder. But you bound yourselves before the court to deliver everything asked for and I see that you have not done so. Where is the cooking-spit I was promised?

And what is to be done about the three shouts on the hill which you have not yet given?'

When the sons of Tuirenn heard this, they realized that they had been deceived and they collapsed exhausted to the floor. Gloom and despair fell upon them as they faced once more the reality of long years of searching and wandering. Leaving behind the treasures that had hitherto protected them, they made their way wearily towards their ship which carried them swiftly away over the storm-tossed seas.

They had spent three months at sea and still they could not discover the smallest trace of the island known as Inis Findcurie. But when their hopes had almost faded, Brian suggested that they make one final search beneath the ocean waves and he put on his magical water-dress and dived over the side of the boat. After two long weeks of swimming in the salt water, he at last happened upon the island, tucked away in a dark hollow of the ocean bed. He immediately went in search of the court and found it occupied by a large group of women, their heads bent in concentration, as they each embroidered a cloth of gold. The women appeared not to notice Brian and he seized this opportunity to move forward to where the cooking-spit rested in a corner of the room. He had just lifted it from the hearth when the women broke into peals of laughter and they laughed long and heartily until finally the eldest of them condescended to address him:

'Take the spit with you, as a reward for your heroism,' she said mockingly, 'but even if your two brothers had attended you here, the weakest of us would have had little trouble preventing you from removing what you came for.'

And Brian took his leave of them knowing they had succeeded in humiliating him, yet he was grateful, nonetheless, that only one task remained to be completed.

They lost no time in directing the boat of Manannan towards their final destination and had reached the Hill of Midcain shortly afterwards, on whose summit they had pledged themselves to give three shouts. But as soon as they had begun to ascend to the top, the guardian of the hill, none other than Midcain himself, came forward to challenge the sons of Tuirenn:

'What is your business in my territory,' demanded Midcain.

'We have come to give three shouts on this hill,' said Brian, 'in fulfilment of the quest we have been forced to pursue in the name of Lugh of the Long Arm.'

'I knew his father well,' replied Midcain, 'and I am under oath not to permit anyone to cry aloud on my hill.'

'Then we have no option but to fight for that permission,' declared Brian, and he rushed at his opponent with his sword before Midcain had the opportunity to draw his own, killing him with a single thrust of his blade through the heart.

Then the three sons of Midcain came out to fight the sons of Tuirenn and the conflict that followed was one of the bitterest and bloodiest ever before fought by any group of warriors. They battled with the strength of wild bears and the ruthlessness of starving lions until they had carved each other to pieces and the grass beneath their feet ran crimson with blood. In the end, however, it was the sons of Tuirenn who were victorious, but their wounds were so deep that they fell to the ground one after the other and waited forlornly for death to come, wishing in vain that they still had the pig skin to cure them.

They had rested a long time before Brian had the strength to speak, and he reminded his brothers that they had not yet given the three shouts on the Hill of Midcain that Lugh had demanded of them. Then slowly they raised themselves up off the ground and did as they had been requested, satisfied at last that they had entirely fulfilled their quest. And after this, Brian lifted his wounded brothers into the boat, promising them a final glimpse of Erin if they would only struggle against death a brief while longer.

And on this occasion the boat of Manannan did not come to a halt on the shores of the Boyne, but moved speedily overland until it reached Dun Tuirenn where the dying brothers were delivered into their father's care. Then Brian, who knew that the end of his life was fast approaching, pleaded fretfully with Tuirenn:

'Go, beloved father,' he urged, 'and deliver this cooking-spit to Lugh, informing him that we have completed all the tasks assigned us. And beg him to allow us to cure our wounds with the pig skin he possesses, for we have suffered long and hard in the struggle to pay the fine on Cian's murder.'

Then Tuirenn rode towards Tara in all haste, fearful that his sons might pass away before his return. And he demanded an audience with Lugh of the Long Arm who came out to meet him at once and graciously received the cooking-spit presented to him.

'My sons are gravely ill and close to death,' Tuirenn exclaimed piteously. 'I beg you to part with the healing pig skin they brought you for one single night, so that I may place it upon their battle wounds and witness it restore them to full health.'

But Lugh of the Long Arm fell silent at this request and stared coldly into the distance towards the Plain of Muirthemne where his father had fallen. When at length he was ready to give Tuirenn his answer, the expression he wore was cruel and menacing and the tone of his voice was severe and merciless:

'I would rather give you the expanse of the earth in gold,' said Lugh, 'than hand over any object that would save the lives of your sons. Let them die in the knowledge that they have achieved something good because of me, and let them thank me for bringing them renown and glory through such a valorous death.'

On hearing these words, Tuirenn hung his head in defeat and accepted that it was useless to bargain with Lugh of the Long Arm. He made his way back despondently to where his sons lay dying and gave them his sad news. The brothers were overcome with grief and despair and were so utterly devastated by Lugh's decision that not one of them lived to see the sun set in the evening sky. Tuirenn's heart was broken in two and after he had placed the last of his sons in the earth, all life departed from him and he fell dead over the bodies of Brian, Iucharba and Iuchar. The Tuatha De Danann witnessed the souls of all four rise towards the heavens and the tragic tale of the sons of Tuirenn was recounted from that day onwards throughout the land, becoming known as one of the Three Sorrows of Story-Telling.

The Tragedy of the Children of Lir

❧

DURING THE GREAT BATTLE of Tailtiu that raged on the plain of Moytura, the Tuatha De Danann were slain in vast numbers and finally defeated by a race of Gaelic invaders known as the Milesians. Following this time of wretched warring, Erin came to be divided into two separate kingdoms. The children of Miled claimed for themselves all the land above ground, while the Tuatha De Danann were banished to the dark regions below the earth's surface. The Danann gods did not suffer their defeat easily, and immediately set about re-building an impressive underground kingdom worthy of the divine stature they once possessed. Magnificent palaces, sparkling with jewels and precious stones, were soon erected and a world of wondrous beauty and light was created where once darkness had prevailed. Time had no meaning in this new domain and all who lived there remained eternally beautiful, never growing old as mortals did above ground.

The day approached for the Tuatha De Danann to choose for themselves a King who would safeguard their future peace and happiness. The principle deities and elders of the people gathered together at the Great Assembly and began deliberating on their choice of leader. Lir, father of the sea-god, Manannan mac Lir, had announced his desire to take the throne, but so too had Bodb the Red, son of the divinity Dagda, lord of perfect knowledge. It came to pass that the People of Dana chose Bodb the Red as their King and built for him a splendid castle on the banks of Loch Dearg. The new ruler made a solemn pledge to his people, promising to prove himself worthy of the great honour bestowed on him. Before long, the People of Dana began to applaud themselves on their choice. Their lives were happy and fulfilled and their kingdom flourished as never before.

Only one person in the entire land remained opposed to the new sovereign. Lir was highly offended that he had not been elected by the People of Dana. Retreating to his home at Sídh Fionnachaidh, he refused to acknowledge Bodb the Red, or show him any mark of respect. Several of the elders urged the King to gather his army together and march to Armagh where Lir could be punished for this insult, but Bodb the Red would not be persuaded. He desired more than anything to be reconciled to every last one of his subjects and his warm and generous spirit sought a more compassionate way of drawing Lir back into his circle.

One morning, the King received news that Lir's wife had recently passed away, leaving him grief-stricken and despondent. Many had tried, but none had yet managed to improve Lir's troubled heart and mind and it was said that he would never recover from his loss. Bodb the Red immediately sent a message to Lir, inviting him to attend the palace. Deeply moved by the King's forgiveness and concern, Lir graciously accepted the invitation to visit Loch Dearg. A large banquet was prepared in his honour and four shining knights on horseback were sent forth to escort the chariot through the palace gates. The King greeted Lir warmly and sat him at the royal table at his right hand. The two men began to converse as if they had always been the closest of friends, and as the evening wore on it was noticed by all that the cloud of sorrow had lifted from Lir's brow. Presently, the King began to speak more earnestly to his friend of the need to return to happier times.

'I am sorely grieved to hear of your loss,' he told Lir, 'but you must allow me to help you. Within this court reside three of the fairest maidens in the kingdom. They are none other than my foster-daughters and each is very dear to me. I give you leave to take the one you most admire as your bride, for I know that she will restore to your life the happiness you now lack.'

At the King's request, his three daughters entered the hall and stood before them. Their beauty was remarkable indeed, and each was as fair as the next. Lir's eyes travelled from one to the other in bewilderment. Finally, he settled on the daughter known as Aeb, for she was the eldest and deemed the wisest of the three. Bodb the Red gave the couple his blessing and it was agreed that they should be married without delay.

After seven days of glorious feasting and celebrating, Aeb and Lir set off from the royal palace to begin their new life together as husband and wife. Lir was no longer weighted down by sorrow and Aeb had grown to love and cherish the man who had chosen her as his bride. Many years of great joy followed for them both. Lir delighted in his new wife and in the twin children she bore him, a boy and a girl, whom they named Aed and Fionnguala. Within another year or two, Aeb again delivered of twins, two sons named Fiachra and Conn, but the second birth proved far more difficult and Aeb became gravely ill. Lir watched over her night and day. Yet despite his tender love and devotion, she could not be saved and his heart was again broken in two. The four beautiful children Aeb had borne him were his only solace in this great time of distress. During the worst moments, when he thought he would die of grief, he was rescued by their image and his love for them was immeasurable.

Hearing of Lir's dreadful misfortune, King Bodb offered him a second foster-daughter in marriage. Aeb's sister was named Aoife and she readily agreed to take charge of Lir's household and her sister's children. At first, Aoife loved her step-children as if they were her very own, but as she watched Lir's intense love for them increase daily, a feeling of jealousy began to take control of her. Often Lir would sleep in the same bed chamber with them and as soon as the children awoke, he devoted himself to their amusement, taking them on long hunting trips through the forest. At every opportunity, he kissed and embraced them and was more than delighted with the love he received in return. Believing that her husband no longer felt any affection for her, Aoife welcomed the poisonous and wicked thoughts that invaded her mind. Feigning a dreadful illness, she lay in bed for an entire year. She summoned a druid to her bedside and together they plotted a course to destroy Lir's children.

One day Aoife rose from her sickbed and ordered her chariot. Seeking out her husband in the palace gardens, she told him that she would like to take the children to visit her father, King Bodb. Lir was happy to see that his wife had recovered her health and was quick to encourage the outing. He gathered his children around him to kiss them goodbye, but Fionnguala refused her father's kiss and drew away from him, her eyes brimming with tears.

'Do not be troubled, child,' he spoke softly to her, 'your visit will bring the King great pleasure and he will prepare the most fleet-footed horses for your speedy return'.

Although her heart was in turmoil, Fionnguala mounted the chariot with her three brothers. She could not understand her sadness, and could not explain why it deepened with every turning of the chariot wheels as they moved forward, away from her father and her beloved home at Sídh Fionnachaidh.

When they had travelled some distance from Lir's palace, Aoife called the horses to a halt. Waking the children from their happy slumber, she ordered them out of the chariot and shouted harshly to her manservants:

'Kill these monstrous creatures before you, for they have stolen the love Lir once had for me. Do so quickly, and I shall reward you as you desire.'

But the servants recoiled in horror from her shameful request and replied resolutely:

'We cannot perform so terrible an evil. A curse will surely fall on you for even thinking such a vile thing.'

They journeyed on further until they approached the shores of Loch Dairbhreach. The evening was now almost upon them and a bank of deep crimson cloud hung lazily on the horizon above the shimmering lake. Weary starlings were settling in their nests and owls were preparing for their nocturnal watch. Aoife now sought to kill the children herself and drew from her cloak a long, pointed sabre. But as she raised her arm to slay the first of them, she was overcome by a feeling of maternal sympathy and it prevented her completing the task. Angry that she had been thwarted once more, she demanded that the children remove their garments and bathe in the lake. As each one them entered the water, she struck them with her druid's wand and they were instantly transformed into four milk-white swans. A death-like chill filled the air as she chanted over them the words the druid had taught her:

'Here on Dairbhreach's lonely wave
For years to come your watery home
Not Lir nor druid can now ye save
From endless wandering on the lonely foam.'

Stunned and saddened by their step-mother's cruel act of vengeance, the children of Lir bowed their heads and wept piteously for their fate. Fionnguala eventually found the courage to speak, and she uttered a plea for lenience, mindful of her three brothers and of the terrible tragedy Lir would again have to suffer:

'We have always loved you Aoife,' she urged, 'why have you treated us in this way when we have only ever shown you loyalty and kindness?'

So sad and helpless were Fionnguala's words, so soft and innocent was her childlike voice, that Aoife began to regret what she had done and she was suddenly filled with panic and despair. It was too late for her to undo her druid's spell, and it was all she could do to fix a term to the curse she had delivered upon the children:

'You will remain in the form of four white swans,' she told them, 'until a woman from the south shall be joined in marriage to a man from the north, and until the light of Christianity shines on Erin. For three hundred years you will be doomed to live on Loch Dairbhreach, followed by three hundred years on the raging Sea of Moyle, and a further three hundred years on Iorras Domhnann. I grant you the power of speech and the gift of singing, and no music in the world shall sound more beautiful and pleasing to the ear than that which you shall make.'

Then Aoife called for her horse to be harnessed once more and continued on her journey to the palace of Bodb the Red, abandoning the four white swans to their life of hardship on the grey and miserable moorland lake.

The King, who had been eagerly awaiting the arrival of his grandchildren, was deeply disappointed to discover that they had not accompanied his daughter.

'Lir will no longer entrust them to you,' Aoife told him, 'and I have not the will to disobey his wishes.'

Greatly disturbed by this news, the King sent a messenger to Lir's palace, demanding an explanation for his extraordinary behaviour. A strange sense of foreboding had already entered Lir's soul and, on receiving the King's message, he became tormented with worry for his children's safety. He immediately called for his horse to be saddled and galloped away into the night in the direction of Loch Dearg. Upon his arrival at Bodb's palace, he was met by one of Aoife's servants who could not keep from him the terrible tale of his wife's treachery. The King was now also informed and Aoife was ordered to appear before them both. The evil expression in his daughter's eye greatly enraged the King and his wand struck violently, changing Aoife into a demon, destined to wander the cold and windy air until the very end of time.

Before the sun had risen the next morning, an anguished party had set off from the palace in search of Lir's children. Through the fog and mist they rode at great speed until the murky waters of Loch Dairbhreach appeared before them in the distance. It was Lir who first caught a glimpse of the four majestic white swans, their slender necks arched forwards towards the pebbled shore, desperately seeking the warm and familiar face of their father. As the swans swam towards him, they began to speak with gentle voices and he instantly recognized his own children in the sad, snow-white creatures. How Lir's heart ached at this woeful sight, and how his eyes wished to disbelieve the sorrowful scene he was forced to witness. He began to sob loudly and it seemed that his grief would never again be silenced.

'Do not mourn us, father,' whispered Fiachra comfortingly, 'your love will give us strength in our plight and we shall all be together one day.'

A beautiful, soothing music now infused the air, miraculously lifting the spirits of all who heard it. After a time, Lir and his companions fell into a gentle, peaceful sleep and when they awoke they were no longer burdened by troubles. Every day, Lir came to visit his children and so too did the Men of Erin, journeying from every part to catch even a single note of the beautiful melody of the swans.

Three hundred years passed pleasantly in this way, until the time arrived for the Children of Lir to bid farewell to the People of Dana and to move on to the cold and stormy Sea of Moyle. As the stars faded and the first rays of sunlight peered through the heavens, Lir came forward to the shores of the lake and spoke to his children for the very last time. Fionnguala began to sing forlornly of the grim and bitter times which lay ahead and as she sang she spread her wings and rose from the water. Aed, Fiachra and Conn joined in her song and then took to the air as their sister had done, flying wearily over the velvet surface of Loch Dairbhreach towards the north-east and the raging ocean:

Arise, my brothers, from Dairbhreach's wave,
On the wings of the southern wind;
We leave our father and friends today
In measureless grief behind.
Ah! Sad the parting, and sad our flight.
To Moyle's tempestuous main;
For the day of woe
Shall come and go
Before we meet again!

Great was the suffering and hardship endured by the swans on the lonely Sea of Moyle, for they could find no rest or shelter from the hissing waves and the piercing cold of the wintry gales. During that first desolate winter, thick black clouds perpetually gathered in the sky, causing the sea to rise up in fury as they ruptured and spilled forth needles of icy rain and sleet. The swans were tossed and scattered by storms and often driven miles apart. There were countless nights when Fionnguala waited alone and terrified on the Rock of Seals, tortured with anxiety for the welfare of her brothers. The gods had so far answered her prayers and they had been returned to her on each occasion, drenched and battered. Tears of joy and relief flowed freely from her eyes at these times, and she would take her brothers under her wing and pull them to her breast for warmth.

Three hundred years of agony and misery on the Sea of Moyle were interrupted by only one happy event. It happened that one morning, the swans were approached by a group of horsemen while resting in the mouth of the river Bann. Two of the figures introduced themselves as

Fergus and Aed, sons of Bodb the Red, and they were accompanied by a fairy host. They had been searching a good many years for the swans, desiring to bring them happy tidings of Lir and the King. The Tuatha De Danann were all now assembled at the annual Feast of Age, peaceful and happy, except for the deep sorrow they felt at the absence of the four children of Lir. Fionnguala and her brothers received great comfort from this visit and talked long into the evening with the visitors. When the time finally came for the men to depart, the swans felt that their courage had been restored and looked forward to being reunited with the People of Dana sometime in the future.

When at last their exile had come to an end on the Sea of Moyle, the children of Lir made ready for their voyage westwards to Iorras Domhnann. In their hearts they knew they were travelling from one bleak and wretched place to another, but they were soothed by the thought that their suffering would one day be over. The sea showed them no kindness during their stay at Iorras Domhnann, and remained frozen from Achill to Erris during the first hundred years. The bodies of the swans became wasted from thirst and hunger, but they weathered the angry blasts of the tempests and sought shelter from the driving snow under the black, unfriendly rocks, refusing to give up hope. Each new trial fired the desire within them to be at home once again, safe in the arms of their loving father.

It was a time of great rejoicing among Lir's children when the three hundred years on Iorras Domhnann finally came to an end. With hearts full of joy and elation, the four swans rose ecstatically into the air and flew southwards towards Sídh Fionnachaidh, their father's palace. But their misery and torment was not yet at an end. As they circled above the plains of Armagh, they could not discover any trace of their former home. Swooping closer to the ground, they recognized the familiar grassy slopes of their childhood, but these were now dotted with stones and rubble from the crumbling castle walls. A chorus of wailing and sorrow echoed through the ruins of Lir's palace as the swans flung themselves on the earth, utterly broken and defeated. For three days and three nights they remained here until they could bear it no longer. Fionnguala led her brothers back to the west and they alighted on a small, tranquil lake known as Inis Gluare. All that remained was for them to live out the rest of their lives in solitude, declaring their grief through the saddest of songs.

On the day after the children of Lir arrived at Inis Gluare, a Christian missionary known as Chaemóc was walking by the lakeside where he had built for himself a small church. Hearing the haunting strains floating towards him from the lake, he paused by the water's edge and prayed that he might know who it was that made such stirring music. The swans then revealed themselves to him and began to tell him their sorry tale. Chaemóc bade them come ashore and he joined the swans together with silver chains and took them into his home where he tended them and provided for them until they had forgotten all their suffering. The swans were his delight and they joined him in his prayers and religious devotions, learning of the One True God who had come to save all men.

It was not long afterwards that Deoch, daughter of the King of Munster, came to marry Lairgnéan, King of Connacht, and hearing of Chaemóc's four wonderful swans, she announced her desire to have them as her wedding-present. Lairgnéan set off for Inis Gluare intent on seizing the swans from Chaemóc. Arriving at the church where they were resting, their heads bowed in silent prayer, he began to drag them from the altar. But he had not gone more than four paces when the plumage dropped from the birds and they were changed back into their human form. Three withered old men and a white-faced old woman now stood before Lairgnéan and he turned and fled in horror at the sight of them.

For the children of Lir had now been released from Aoife's curse, having lived through almost a thousand years, to the time when her prophecy came to be fulfilled. Knowing that they had little time left to them, they called for Chaemóc to baptize them and as he did so they died peacefully and happily. The saint carried their bodies to a large tomb and Fionnguala was buried at the centre, surrounded by her three beloved brothers. Chaemóc placed a large headstone on the mound and he inscribed it in oghram. It read, 'Lir's children, who rest here in peace at long last'.

The Wooing of Etain

MIDHIR THE PROUD WAS KING of the Daoine Sidhe, the fairy people of the Tuatha De Danann, and he dwelt at the grand palace in the Hollow Hills of Brí Leíth. He had a wife named Fuamnach with whom he had lived quite contentedly for a good many years. One day, however, while Midhir was out hunting with a group of his companions, he stumbled across the fairest maiden he had ever before laid eyes on, resting by a mountain stream. She had begun to loosen her hair to wash it and her chestnut tresses fell about her feet, shimmering magnificently in the sunlight. The King was enraptured by her perfect beauty and grace and he could not prevent himself from instantly falling in love with her. Nothing could persuade him to abandon the thought of returning to the palace with the maiden and making her his new wife. He boldly confessed to her this desire, hopeful that his noble bearing and royal apparel would not fail to win her approval. The maiden told him that her name was Etain. She was both honoured and delighted that the fairy king had requested her hand in marriage and agreed at once to return with him to Brí Leíth.

Within a short time, Etain's beauty had won her great fame throughout the land and the words 'as fair as Etain' became the highest compliment any man could bestow on a woman. Midhir had soon forgotten about his former wife and spent his days in the company of his new bride whom he doted on and could not bear to be parted from. Fuamnach was distressed and enraged to see them together, but her desire to be comforted and loved once more was entirely overlooked by her husband. When she could bear her cruel treatment no longer, she sought the help of the druid, Bressal, who was well known to the royal palace. Bressal heard Fuamnach's story and took great pity on her. That evening, as Etain lay in bed, they both entered her chamber. A great tempest began to rage around them as the druid waved his wand over the sleeping woman and delivered his curse in grave, commanding tones. As soon as he had uttered his final words, the beautiful Etain was changed into a butterfly and swiftly carried off by the howling winds through the open window far beyond the palace of Midhir the Proud.

For seven long years, Etain lived a life of intolerable misery. She could find no relief from her endless flight and her delicate wings were tattered and torn by the fiery gusts that tossed and buffeted her throughout the length and breadth of the country. One day, when she had almost abandoned hope of ever finding rest again, a chance flurry thrust her through a window of the fairy palace of Aèngus Óg, the Danann god of love. All deities of the Otherworld possessed the ability to recognize their own kind, and Etain was immediately revealed to Aengus, despite her winged appearance. He could not entirely undo the druid's sorcery, but he took Etain into his care and conjured up a spell to return her to her human form every day, from dusk until dawn. During the daytime, Aengus set aside the sunniest corner of the palace gardens for her private use and planted it with the most colourful, fragrant flowers and shrubs. In the evening, when Etain was transformed once again into a beautiful maiden, she gave Aengus her love and they grew to treasure each other's company, believing they would spend many happy years together.

It was not long, however, before Fuamnach came to discover Etain's place of refuge. Still bent on revenge, she appeared at the palace of Aengus Óg in the form of a raven and alighted on an apple tree in the centre of the garden. She soon caught sight of a dainty butterfly resting on some rose petals and with a sudden swoop she opened her beak and lifted the fragile creature into the air. Once they were outside of the palace walls, a magic tempest began to blow around Etain. She found herself being carried away from the fairy mounds during the fierce storm, to the unfamiliar plains of Erin above ground where very few of the fairy people had ever dared to emerge.

As soon as he discovered that Etain had been outwitted by Fuamnach, Aengus sprinkled a magic potion into the air and called upon the gods to end the beautiful maiden's torturous wanderings above the earth's surface. A short time afterwards, Etain became trapped in a terrible gale and was hurled through the castle windows of an Ulster Chieftain named Etar. A great feast was in progress and all the noblemen of the province were gathered together for an evening of merry-making and dancing. Etar's wife sat at his right hand and she held a goblet of wine to her lips. Weary and thirsty from her flight, Etain came to rest on the rim of the vessel intending to sip some of the refreshing liquid. But as she leaned forward, she fell into the drinking-cup and was passed down the throat of the noblewoman as soon as she swallowed her next draught.

Several weeks after the great feast, Etar's wife was overjoyed to discover that she was carrying a child. The gods had fulfilled their promise and had caused Etain to nestle in her womb until the time when she could be reborn as a mortal child. After nine months, the Chieftain and his wife were blessed with a daughter and they gave her the name of Etain. She grew to become one of the most beautiful maidens in Ulster and although she bore the same name as before, she could remember nothing of her former life with the Daoine Sidhe.

It was at about this time that a distinguished warrior known as Eochaid Airem was crowned High King of Erin. One of the first tasks he set himself was to organize a splendid annual feast, gathering together all of the kingdom's noblemen to the royal palace for a month of glorious festivity. But the king was soon disappointed to discover that a great number of his noblemen would not accept his generous invitation. Deeply puzzled by this turn of events, he ordered several of them to appear before him and demanded an explanation.

'We cannot attend such a feast,' they told him, 'since the absence of a queen by your side would make it unwholesome. The people of Erin have never before served a king who does not possess a queen. There are many among us with daughters young and fair who would be more than willing to help restore your honour.'

The King was now made to realize that his integrity rested on securing a wife, and he immediately sent out horsemen to the four corners of Erin in search of a maiden who would make for him a suitable queen. Within a few days, a group of his messengers returned with the news that they had found the fairest creature in the land. Eochaid set forth at once to view with his own eyes the maiden his men had found for him.

He rode for some distance until at last he happened upon four nymph-like figures laughing and dancing in the sunshine at the edge of a small, meandering brook. One of them was indeed far more beautiful than the others. She was clothed in a mantel of bright purple which was clasped over her bosom with a brooch of bright, glittering gold. Underneath, she wore a tunic of the finest emerald silk, intricately decorated with silver fringes and sparkling jewels. Her skin was as white and smooth as snow, her eyes were as blue as hyacinths and her lips as red as the finest rubies. Two tresses of chestnut hair rested on her head. Each one was plaited into four strands and fastened at the ends with tiny spheres of gold. Eochaid shyly approached the maiden and began to question her softly:

'Who are you,' he inquired, 'and who was it created so rare and beautiful a vision as you?'

'I am Etain, daughter of Etar,' said the maiden. 'Your messengers warned me of your visit Eochaid and I have heard noble tales of you since I was a little child.'

'Will you allow me to woo you then, fair Etain,' asked the King, 'for I cannot conceive of any greater pleasure left to me.'

'It is you I have waited for,' replied Etain, 'and I will only be truly fulfilled if you take me with you to Tara where I will serve you well as queen.'

Overwhelmed with joy at these words, Eochaid grasped Etain's hand and lifted her onto the saddle next to him. They rode speedily towards the palace at Tara where news of the king's betrothal had already reached the ears of his subjects. A hearty welcome awaited the couple as they approached the great gates and they were married that same afternoon to the jubilant sounds of chiming bells and shouts of approval from the large crowd that had gathered to wish them well.

The Royal Assembly of Tara was now the grand occasion everybody looked forward to and preparations began in earnest for the series of lavish banquets and pageants that were to take place in the grounds of the palace. On the morning of first day of the Assembly, Etain made ready to welcome Eochaid's guests and she rode to the top of the hill beyond the gates to catch a glimpse of the first to arrive. After a time, a young warrior on horseback appeared in the distance making his way steadily towards her. He wore a robe of royal purple and his hair, which tumbled below his shoulders, was golden yellow in colour. His face was proud and radiant and his eyes lustrous and gentle. In his left hand, he held a five-pointed spear and in his right, a circular shield, laden with white gold and precious gems. The warrior came forward and Etain welcomed him zealously:

'We are honoured by your presence, young warrior,' said Etain. 'A warm reception awaits you at the palace where I shall be pleased to lead you.'

But the warrior hesitated to accompany her and began to speak in a pained, anxious voice.

'Do you not know me, Etain?' he asked. 'For years I have been searching every corner of the land for you. I am your husband, Midhir the Proud, from the fairy kingdom of the Ever Young.'

'My husband is Eochaid Airem, High King of Erin,' replied Etain. 'Are you not deceived by your own eyes? You are a stranger to me and I have never before heard of your kingdom.'

'Fuamnach is dead and it is now safe for you to return to your home,' Midhir told her. 'It was the sorcery of Fuamnach and Bressal that drove us apart, Etain. Will you come with me now to a land full of music, where men and women remain eternally fair and without blemish. There, in the land of your birth, we may again live happily as man and wife.'

'I will not readily abandon the King of Erin for a man unknown to me,' answered Etain. 'I would never seek to depart with you without the King's consent and I know he will not give it, since his love for me deepens with every passing day.'

Hearing these words, Midhir bowed his head in defeat. It was not in his nature to take Etain by force and he sadly bade her farewell, galloping furiously across the plains of Erin, his purple cloak billowing around him in the breeze.

Throughout the winter months that followed, Etain remained haunted by the image of the stranger who had visited her on the hill. She began to dream of a land filled with sunshine and laughter where she frequently appeared seated on a throne, smiling happily. She could not explain these dreams and did not dare to confide in her husband. Often, however, she would ride to the place where she had met with

Midhir the Proud and gaze outwards towards the flat, green carpet of land, secretly entertaining the hope that a rider on a white horse might suddenly appear on the horizon.

One fair summer's morning as Eochaid Airem peered out of the palace window, he noticed a young warrior in a purple cloak riding towards the Hill of Tara. The King was intrigued by the sight and ordered his horse to be saddled so that he might personally greet the stranger and establish the purpose of his visit to the palace.

'I am known to all as Midhir,' said the warrior. 'I have journeyed here to meet with Eochaid Airem, for I am told he is the finest chess-player in the land. I have with me a chessboard with which to test his skill if he is willing to meet my challenge.'

The warrior then produced from beneath his mantel a solid gold chessboard with thirty-two silver pieces, each one encrusted with the finest sapphires and diamonds.

'I would be more than delighted to play a game of chess with you,' replied the King, and he led the way to a brightly-lit chamber where they placed the board on a sturdy round table and sat down to play the first game. The King was not long in proving his reputation as a champion player and, as the young warrior seemed disappointed with his own performance, it was decided that they should play a second game. Again, the King was victorious and the warrior appeared to become more and more agitated. But it was Midhir's intention all along to win Eochaid's sympathy and to lure him into a false sense of security.

'Perhaps it would be best,' suggested the King, 'if we decided on a wager for our third and final game. Name your stake, choose any treasure you desire, and it will be forfeited to you if you are triumphant over me.'

'That is very generous of you,' replied Midhir, 'but I have more than enough wealth and possessions to satisfy me. Perhaps you have a wife, however, who would not protest too loudly if I stole from her a single kiss as my prize?'

'I am sure she would not object,' answered Eochaid cheerfully, for he felt certain that Etain would never have to deliver such a trophy.

The two played on, but this time the King struggled to keep control of the game and at length he was beaten by the younger man. Eochaid now fell silent and began to regret that he had so carelessly offered his wife as prize. In desperation and despair, he begged his opponent to surrender his claim to the pledged kiss. But Midhir insisted firmly on the forfeit and the King was forced to honour his part of the bargain.

'Perhaps you will find it in your heart to show me a little kindness,' Eochaid pleaded, 'and allow me time to reconcile myself to the dispatch of such a precious reward. Return to this palace one month from today and what you have asked for will not be denied you.'

'Your request is not unreasonable,' replied Midhir, 'and it leads me to believe that a kiss from your wife must be worth the long wait.'

Then Eochaid Airem appointed a day at the end of the month when Midhir would return to collect his prize and the young warrior departed the palace, his heart lighter than it had been for a very long time.

As the days passed by and the time approached for Etain to deliver her kiss, the King became more and more protective of his beautiful wife. Fearing that his handsome rival would appear at any moment, he gave the order for the palace to be surrounded by a great host of armed men and instructed them not to allow any stranger to enter the grounds. Once he had made certain that the outer courtyards were protected and that the doors to the inner chambers were properly guarded, Eochaid began to feel more at ease and decided to invite his closest friends to dine with him later that evening in the banqueting hall. Etain appeared next to him in a gown of shimmering silver and a row of servants carried trays of the most exotic food and flagons of the finest wine through to the long table. While the queen poured the wine for her hosts, the hall began to fill with laughter and conversation and it was not long before Eochaid called for his musicians to begin playing.

In the midst of this happy atmosphere, nobody noticed the tall, elegant figure enter the room and make his way towards the King, his face noble and determined, his spear held proudly in his left hand. Etain suddenly raised her eyes and saw before her the young rider whose image had filled her sleeping hours since their meeting on the Hill of Tara. He appeared more beautiful and resplendent than ever, more eloquent and powerful than her memory had allowed for. A wonderful feeling of warmth and affection stirred within Etain's breast as Midhir gazed tenderly upon her and she felt that somehow she had always known and loved the man who stood before her. Then Midhir addressed the King and his words were purposeful and resolute:

'Let me collect what has been promised me,' he said to Eochaid, 'It is a debt that is due and the time is ripe for payment.'

The King and his party looked on helplessly as Midhir encircled the fair Etain in his arms. As their lips met, a thick veil of mist appeared around them, and they were lifted gracefully into the air and out into the night. Eochaid and his noblemen rushed from the banqueting hall in pursuit of the couple, but all they could see were two white swans circling the star-filled sky above the royal palace. Eochaid wept bitterly for his loss and swore solemnly that he would not rest a single moment until every fairy mound in the land had been dug up and destroyed in his search for Midhir the Proud.

The Ulster Cycle:
Stories of Cuchulainn of the Red Guard

THE ULSTER CYCLE, also known as the Red Branch Cycle, is compiled of tales of Ulster's traditional heroes, chief among whom is Cuchulainn [*Pronounced Koo khul-in*], arguably the most important war-champion in ancient Irish literature. An account of his birth dating from the ninth century is retold here, although a great many variations exist.

From the age of six, Cuchulainn displays his supernatural ancestry and astounding strength. While still a child, he slays the terrifying hound of Culann. As a mere youth he is sent to train with the Knights of the Red Guard under Scathach and he alone is entrusted with the diabolical weapon known as the Gae Bolg. Later, he single-handedly defends Ulster against Queen Medb [*Pronounced Maev*] while the rest of the province sleeps under the charm of Macha. His most notable exploits spanning his hectic warrior's life up until his early death are recounted here.

Cuchulainn is said to have fallen at the battle of Muirthemne, circa 12 BC. He was finally overcome by his old enemy Lugaid, aided by the monstrous daughters of Calatin. As death approaches, Cuchulainn insists that he be allowed to bind himself upright to a pillar-stone. With his dying breath, he gives a loud, victorious laugh and when Lugaid attempts to behead his corpse, the enemy's right hand is severed as the sword of Cuchulainn falls heavily upon it. The hero's death is avenged by Conall the Victorious, but with the defeat of Cuchulainn, the end is sealed to the valiant reign of the Red Guard Knights in ancient Irish legend.

The Birth of Cuchulainn

❧

KING CONCHOBAR MAC NESSA was ruler of Ulster at the time when Cuchulainn, the mightiest hero of the Red Guard, came to be born. It happened that one day, the King's sister Dechtire, whom he cherished above all others, disappeared from the palace without warning, taking fifty of her maidens and her most valuable possessions with her. Although Conchobar summoned every known person in the court before him for questioning, no explanation could be discovered for his sister's departure. For three long years, the King's messengers scoured the country in search of Dechtire, but not one among them ever brought him news of her whereabouts.

At last, one summer's morning, a strange flock of birds descended on the palace gardens of Emain Macha and began to gorge themselves on every fruit tree and vegetable patch in sight. Greatly disturbed by the greed and destruction he witnessed, the King immediately gathered together a party of his hunters, and they set off in pursuit of the birds, armed with powerful slings and the sharpest of arrows. Fergus mac Roig, Conchobar's chief huntsman and guide, was among the group, as were his trusted warriors Amergin and Bricriu. As the day wore on, they found themselves being lured a great distance southward by the birds, across Sliab Fuait, towards the Plain of Gossa, and with every step taken they grew more angry and frustrated that not one arrow had yet managed to ruffle a single feather.

Nightfall had overtaken them before they had even noticed the light begin to fade, and the King, realizing that they would never make it safely back to the palace, gave the order for Fergus and some of the others to go out in search of a place of lodging for the party. Before long, Fergus came upon a small hut whose firelight was extremely inviting, and he approached and knocked politely on the door. He received a warm and hearty welcome from the old married couple within, and they at once offered him food and a comfortable bed for the evening.

But Fergus would not accept their kind hospitality, knowing that his companions were still abroad without shelter.

'Then they are all invited to join us,' said the old woman, and as she bustled about, preparing food and wine for her visitors, Fergus went off to deliver his good news to Conchobar and the rest of the group.

Bricriu had also set off in search of accommodation, and as he had walked to the opposite side of the woodlands, he was certain that he heard the gentle sound of harp music. Instinctively drawn towards the sweet melody, he followed the winding path through the trees until he came upon a regal mansion standing proudly on the banks of the river Boyne. He timidly approached the noble structure, but there was no need for him to knock, since the door was already ajar and a young maiden, dressed in a flowing gown of shimmering gold, stood in the entrance hall ready to greet him. She was accompanied by a young man of great stature and splendid appearance who smiled warmly at Bricriu and extended his hand in friendship:

'You are indeed welcome,' said the handsome warrior, 'we have been waiting patiently for your visit to our home this day.'

'Come inside, Bricriu,' said the beautiful maiden, 'why is it that you linger out of doors?'

'Can it be that you do not recognize the woman who appears before you?' asked the warrior.

'Her great beauty stirs a memory from the past,' replied Bricriu, 'but I cannot recall anything more at present.'

'You see before you Dechtire, sister of Conchobar mac Nessa,' said the warrior, 'and the fifty maidens you have been seeking these three years are also in this house. They have today visited Emain Macha in the form of birds in order to lure you here.'

'Then I must go at once to the King and inform him of what I have discovered,' answered Bricriu, 'for he will be overjoyed to know that Dechtire has been found and will be eager for her to accompany him back to the palace where there will be great feasting and celebration.'

He hurried back through the woods to rejoin the King and his companions. And when Conchobar heard the news of Bricriu's discovery, he could scarcely contain his delight and was immediately anxious to be reunited with his sister. A messenger was sent forth to invite Dechtire and the warrior to share in their evening meal, and a place was hurriedly prepared for the couple at the table inside the welcoming little hut. But Dechtire was already suffering the first pangs of childbirth by the time Conchobar's messenger arrived with his invitation. She excused herself by saying that she was tired and agreed instead to meet up with her brother at dawn on the following morning.

When the first rays of sunshine had brightened the heavens, Conchobar arose from his bed and began to prepare himself for Dechtire's arrival. He had passed a very peaceful night and went in search of Fergus and the others in the happiest of moods. Approaching the place where his men were sleeping, he became convinced that he had heard the stifled cries of an infant. Again, as he drew nearer, the sound was repeated. He stooped down and began to examine a small, strange bundle lying on the ground next to Bricriu. As he unwrapped it, the bundle began to wriggle in his arms and a tiny pink hand revealed itself from beneath the cloth covering.

Dechtire did not appear before her brother that morning, or on any morning to follow. But she had left the King a great gift – a newborn male child fathered by the noble warrior, Lugh of the Long Arm, a child destined to achieve great things for Ulster. Conchobar took the infant back to the palace with him and gave him to his sister Finnchoem to look after. Finnchoem reared the child alongside her own son Conall and grew to love him as if he had been born of her own womb. He was given the name of Setanta, a name he kept until the age of six, and the druid Morann made the following prophecy over him:

His praise will be sung by the most valorous knights,
And he will win the love of all
His deeds will be known throughout the land
For he will answer Ulster's call.

How Setanta Won the Name of Cuchulainn

❧

WITHIN THE COURT OF EMAIN MACHA, there existed an élite group of boy athletes whose outstanding talents filled the King with an overwhelming sense of pride and joy. It had become a regular part of Conchobar's daily routine to watch these boys at their various games and exercises, for nothing brought him greater pleasure than to witness their development into some of the finest sportsmen in Erin. He had named the group the Boy-Corps, and the sons of the most powerful chieftains and princes of the land were among its members, having proven their skill and dexterity in a wide and highly challenging range of sporting events.

Before Setanta had grown to the age of six, he had already expressed his desire before the King to be enrolled in the Boy-Corps. At first, Conchobar refused to treat the request seriously, since his nephew was a great deal younger than any other member, but the boy persisted, and the King at last agreed to allow him to try his hand. It was decided that he should join in a game of hurling one morning, and when he had dressed himself in the martial uniform of the Boy-Corps, he was presented with a brass hurley almost his own height off the ground.

A team of twelve boys was assembled to play against him and they sneered mockingly at the young lad before them, imagining they would have little difficulty keeping the ball out of his reach. But as soon as the game started up, Setanta dived in among the boys and took hold of the ball, striking it with his hurley and driving it a powerful distance to the other end of the field where it sailed effortlessly through the goal-posts. And after this first onslaught, he made it impossible for his opponents to retrieve the ball from him, so that within a matter of minutes he had scored fifty goals against the twelve of them. The whole corps looked on in utter amazement and the King, who had been eagerly following the game, was flushed with excitement. His nephew's show of prowess was truly astonishing and he began to reproach himself for having originally set out to humour the boy.

'Have Setanta brought before me,' he said to his steward, 'for such an impressive display of heroic strength and impertinent courage deserves a very special reward.'

Now on that particular day, Conchobar had been invited to attend a great feast at the house of Culann, the most esteemed craftsman and smith in the kingdom. A thought had suddenly entered Conchobar's head that it would be a very fitting reward for Setanta to share in such a banquet, for no small boy had ever before accompanied the King and the Knights of the Red Guard on such a prestigious outing. It was indeed a great honour and one Setanta readily acknowledged. He desperately wanted to accept the invitation, but only one thing held him back. He could not suppress the desire of a true sportsman to conclude the game he had begun and pleaded with the King to allow him to do so:

'I have so thoroughly enjoyed the first half of my game with the Boy-Corps,' he told the King, 'that I am loathe to cut it short. I promise to follow when the game is over if you will allow me this great liberty.'

And seeing the excitement and keenness shining in the boy's eyes, Conchobar was more than happy to agree to this request. He instructed Setanta to follow on before nightfall and gave him directions to the house of Culann. Then he set off for the banquet, eager to relate the morning's stirring events to the rest of Culann's house guests.

It was early evening by the time the royal party arrived at the dwelling place of Culann. A hundred blazing torches guided them towards the walls of the fort and a carpet of fresh green rushes formed a mile-long path leading to the stately entrance. The great hall was already lavishly prepared for the banquet and the sumptuous aroma of fifty suckling pigs turning on the spit filled every room of the house. Culann himself came forward to greet each one of his guests and he bowed respectfully before the King and led him to his place of honour at the centre of the largest table. Once his royal guest had taken his seat, the order was given for the wine to be poured and the laughter and music followed soon afterwards. And when it was almost time for the food to be served, Culann glanced around him one last time to make certain that all his visitors had arrived.

'I think we need wait no longer,' he said to the King. 'My guests are all present and it will now be safe to untie the hound who keeps watch over my home each night. There is not a hound in Erin who could equal mine for fierceness and strength, and even if a hundred men should attempt to do battle with him, every last one would be torn to pieces in his powerful jaws.'

'Release him then, and let him guard this place,' said Conchobar, quite forgetting that his young nephew had not yet joined the party. 'My men are all present and our appetites have been whetted by our long journey here. Let us delay no longer and begin the feasting at once.'

And after the gong had been sounded, a procession of elegantly-clad attendants entered the room carrying gilded trays of roasted viands and freshly harvested fruit and vegetables, which they set down on the table before the King and the hungry warriors of the Red Guard.

It was just at this moment that the young Setanta came to the green of Culann's fort carrying with him the hurley and the ball that had brought him victory against the Boy-Corps. As the boy drew nearer to the entrance of the fort, the hound's ears pricked up warily and it began to growl and bark in such a way as to be heard throughout the entire countryside. The whole company within the great hall heard the animal snarling ferociously and raced outdoors to discover what exactly it was that had disturbed the creature. They saw before them a young boy, who showed little sign of fear as he stood facing the fierce dog with gaping jaws. The child was without any obvious weapon of defence against the animal, but as it charged at him, he thrust his playing ball forcefully down its throat causing it to choke for breath. Then he seized the hound by the hind legs and dashed its head against a rock until blood spewed from its mouth and the life had gone out of it.

Those who witnessed this extraordinary confrontation hoisted the lad triumphantly into the air and bore him on their shoulders to where Conchobar and Culann stood waiting. The King, although more than gratified by the boy's demonstration of courage, was also much relieved to know that Setanta was safe. Turning to his host, he began to express his joy, but it was immediately apparent that Culann could share none of Conchobar's happiness. He walked instead towards the body of his dead hound and fell into a mournful silence as he stroked the lifeless form, remembering the loyal and obedient animal who had given its life to protect its master's property. Seeing Culann bent over the body of his faithful dog, Setanta came forward without hesitation and spoke the following words of comfort to him:

'If in all of Erin there is a hound to replace the one you have lost, I will find it, nurture it and place it in your service when it is fit for action. But, in the meantime, I myself will perform the duty of that hound and will guard your land and your possessions with the utmost pride.'

There was not one among the gathering who remained unmoved by this gesture of contrition and friendship. Culann, for his part, was overcome with gratitude and appreciation and declared that Setanta should bear the name of Cuchulainn, 'Culann's Hound', in remembrance of his first great act of valour. And so, at the age of six, the boy Setanta was named Cuchulainn, a name by which he was known and feared until the end of his days.

The Tragedy of Cuchulainn and Connla

❧

A S SOON AS CUCHULAINN had reached the appropriate age to begin his formal training as a Knight of the Red Guard, it was decided at the court of Conchobar mac Nessa that he should depart for the Land of Shadows, where Scathach, the wisest, strongest, most celebrated woman-warrior, had prepared the path of his instruction in the feats of war. The stronghold of Scathach lay in a mysterious land overseas, beyond the bounds of the Plain of Ill-luck. It could only be reached by crossing the Perilous Glen, a journey very few had survived, for the Glen teemed with the fiercest of goblins lying in wait to devour hopeful young pilgrims. But even if a youth managed to come through the Perilous Glen unharmed, he had then to cross the Bridge of Leaps, underneath which the sea boiled and hissed furiously. This bridge was the highest and narrowest ever built and it spanned the steepest gorge in the western world. Only a handful of people had ever crossed it, but those who did were privileged to become the highest ranking scholars of Scathach and the very finest of Erin's warriors.

Within a week of leaving the court of Emain Macha, Cuchulainn had arrived at the Plain of Ill-luck and although he had already suffered many trials along the way, he knew in his heart that the worst still lay ahead. As he gazed out over the vast stretch of barren land he was obliged to traverse, he grew despondent, for he could see that one half was covered in a porous clay which would certainly cause his feet to stick fast, while the other was overgrown with long, coarse, straw-coloured grass, whose pointed blades were designed to slash a man's limbs to pieces. And as he stood crestfallen, attempting to decide which of the two routes would prove less hazardous, he noticed a young man approaching on horseback from the east. The very appearance of the rider lifted Cuchulainn's spirits, but when he observed that the youth's countenance shone as splendidly as the golden orb of the sun (though he does not reveal himself, this is, of course, Cuchulainn's father, Lugh of the Long Arm), he immediately felt hopeful and reassured once more. The two began to converse together and Cuchulainn enquired of the young man which track he considered the best to follow across the Plain of Ill-luck. The youth pondered the question awhile and then, reaching beneath his mantel, he handed Cuchulainn a leather pouch containing a small golden wheel.

'Roll this before you as you cross the quagmire,' he told Cuchulainn, 'and it will scorch a path in the earth which you may follow safely to the stronghold of Scathach.'

Cuchulainn gratefully received the gift and bid farewell to the youth. And after he had set the wheel in motion, it led him safely, just as the young rider had promised, across the Plain of Ill-luck and through the Perilous Glen until he reached the outskirts of the Land of Shadows.

It was not long before he happened upon a small camp in the heart of the woodlands where the scholars of Scathach, the sons of the noblest princes and warriors of Erin, were busy at their training. He recognized at once his friend Ferdia, son of the Firbolg, Daman, and the two men embraced each other warmly. After Cuchulainn had told Ferdia all of the latest news from Ulster, he began to question his friend about the great woman-warrior who was set to educate him in arms.

'She dwells on the island beyond the Bridge of Leaps,' Ferdia told him, 'which no man, not even myself, has ever managed to cross. It is said that when we have achieved a certain level of valour, Scathach herself will teach us to cross the bridge, and she will also teach us to thrust the Gae Bolg, a weapon reserved for only the bravest of champions.'

'Then I must prove to her that I am already valorous,' replied Cuchulainn, 'by crossing that bridge without any assistance from her.'

'You are unlikely to succeed,' warned Ferdia, 'for if a man steps on one end of the bridge, the middle rises up and flings him into the waters below where the mouths of sea-monsters lie open, ready to swallow him whole.'

But these words of caution merely fired Cuchulainn's ambition to succeed in his quest. Retiring to a quiet place, he sat down to recover his strength from his long journey and waited anxiously for evening to fall.

The scholars of Scathach had all gathered to watch Cuchulainn attempt to cross the Bridge of Leaps and they began to jeer him loudly when after the third attempt he had failed to reach the far side. The mocking chorus that greeted his failure greatly infuriated the young warrior but prompted him at the same time to put all his strength and ability into one final, desperate leap. And at the fourth leap, which came to be known as 'the hero's salmon-leap', Cuchulainn landed on the ground of the island at the far side of the bridge. Lifting himself off the ground, he strode triumphantly to the fortress of Scathach and beat loudly on the entrance door with the shaft of his spear. Scathach appeared before him, wonder-struck that a boy so young and fresh of face had demonstrated such courage and vigour. She agreed at once to accept him as her pupil, promising to teach him all the feats of war if he would pledge himself to remain under her tuition and guidance for a period not less than a full year and a day.

During the time that Cuchulainn dwelt with Scathach, he grew to become her favourite pupil, for he acquired each new skill with the greatest of ease and approached every additional challenge set him with the utmost enthusiasm. Scathach had never before deemed any of her students good enough to be trained in the use of the Gae Bolg, but she now considered Cuchulainn a champion worthy of this special honour and presented him one morning with the terrible weapon. Then she instructed him on how to use it and explained that it should be hurled with the foot, and upon entering the enemy it would fill every inch of his body with deadly barbs, killing him almost instantly.

It was while Cuchulainn remained under Scathach's supervision that the Land of Shadows came under attack from the fiercest of tribal warriors, led by the Princess Aife. After several weeks of bloody battle, during which no solution to the conflict could be reached, it was agreed that Scathach and Aife should face each other in single combat. On hearing this news, Cuchulainn expressed the gravest concern and was adamant that he would accompany Scathach to the place where the contest was due to take place. Yet Scathach feared that something untoward might befall her young protégé, and she placed a sleeping-potion in Cuchulainn's drink with the power to prevent him waking until she was safely reached her meeting place with Aife. But the potion, which would have lasted twenty-four hours in any other man, held Cuchulainn in a slumber for less than one hour and when he awoke he seized his weapon and went forth to join the war against Aife.

And not only did he slay three of Aife's finest warriors in the blink of an eyelid, he insisted on trading places with Scathach and facing the tribal-leader by himself. But before going into battle against her, he asked Scathach what it was that Aife prized above all other things.

'What she most loves are her two horses, her chariot, and her charioteer,' she informed Cuchulainn. So he set off to meet Aife, forearmed with this knowledge.

The two opponents met on the Path of Feats and entered into a vicious combat there. They had only clashed swords three or four times however, before Aife delivered Cuchulainn a mighty blow, shattering his powerful sword to the hilt and leaving him defenceless. Seeing the damage to his weapon, Cuchulainn at once cried out:

'What a terrible fate that charioteer beyond has met with. Look, his chariot and his two beautiful horses have fallen down the glen.'

And as Aife glanced around, Cuchulainn managed to seize her by the waist, squeezing firmly with his hands until she could hardly breathe and had dropped her sword at his feet. Then he carried her over his shoulder back to the camp of Scathach and flung her on the ground where he placed his knife at her throat.

'Do not take my life from me, Cuchulainn,' Aife begged, 'and I will agree to whatever you demand.'

It was soon settled between Scathach and Cuchulainn that Aife should agree to a lasting peace and, as proof of her commitment, they pronounced that she should bind herself over to remain a full year as Cuchulainn's hostage in the Land of Shadows. And after nine months, Aife gave birth to a son whom she named Connla, for she and Cuchulainn had grown to become the best of friends and the closest of lovers with the passing of time.

Now sadly, the day arrived for Cuchulainn to depart the Land of Shadows, and knowing that Aife would not accompany him, he spoke the following wish for his son's future:

'I give you this golden ring for our child,' he told Aife. 'And when he has grown so that the ring fits his finger, send him away from here to seek out his father in Erin.

'Counsel him on my behalf to keep his identity secret,' he added, 'so that he may stand proud on his own merit and never refuse a combat, or turn out of his way for any man.'

Then after he had uttered these words, Cuchulainn took his leave of Aife and made his way back to his own land and his people.

Seven years had passed, during which time Cuchulainn had chosen Emer, daughter of Forgall, one of the finest maidens in Ulster, to become his wife, and the two lived a very happy life together. He rarely thought of Aife and the son he had left behind in the Land of Shadows, for he had also risen to become captain of the House of the Red Branch of Conchobar mac Nessa and was by far the busiest and most respected warrior in the kingdom.

It was at this time, however, that Connla, son of Cuchulainn, set out on his journey to be reunited with his father in Erin, approaching her shores on the precise day that all the great warriors and noble lords of Ulster were assembled for an annual ceremony on the Strand of Footprints. They were very much surprised to see a little boat of bronze appear on the crest of the waves, and in it a small boy clutching a pair of gilded oars, steering his way steadily towards them. The boy seemed not to notice them and every so often he stopped rowing and bent down to pick up a stone from the heap he had collected at the bottom of the boat. Then, putting one of these stones into a sling, he launched a splendid shot at the sea-birds above, bringing the creatures down, stunned, but unharmed, one after another, in a manner far too quick for the naked eye to perceive. The whole party looked on in amazement as the lad performed these wonderful feats, but the King soon grew uncomfortable at the spectacle he witnessed and called Condere, son of Eochaid, to him:

'This boy's arrival here does not bode well for us,' said the King. 'For if grown-up men of his kind were to follow in his wake, they would grind us all to dust. Let someone go to meet him and inform him that he is not welcome on Erin's soil.'

And as the boy came to moor his boat, Condere approached him and delivered Conchobar's message.

'Go and tell your King,' said the boy, 'that even if everyone among you here had the strength of a hundred men, and you all came forward to challenge me, you would not be able to persuade me to turn back from this place.'

Hearing these words, the King grew even more concerned and he called Conall the Victorious to him:

'This lad mocks us,' Conchobar told him, 'and it is now time for a show of force against him.'

So Conall was sent against the boy, but as he approached the lad put a stone in his sling and sent it whizzing with a noise like thunder through the air. It struck Conall on the forehead, knocking him backwards to the ground and before he could even think about rising to his feet, the boy had bound his arms and legs with the strap from his shield. And in this manner, the youth made a mockery of the host of Ulster, challenging man after man to confront him, and succeeding on every occasion to defeat his opponents with little or no effort.

At last, when King Conchobar could suffer this humiliation no longer, he sent a messenger to Dundalk to the house of Cuchulainn requesting that he come and do battle against the young boy whom Conall the Victorious could not even manage to overcome. And hearing that her husband was prepared to meet this challenge, Emer, his wife, went and pleaded with him not to go forward to the Strand of Footprints:

'Do not go against the boy,' she begged Cuchulainn, 'since the great courage he possesses has convinced me that he is Connla, son of Aife. Hear my voice, Cuchulainn, and do not go forward to murder your only child.'

'Even if he were my son,' replied Cuchulainn, 'I would slay him for the honour of Ulster.'

And he ordered his chariot to be yoked without further delay and set off in the direction of the strand.

Soon afterwards, he came upon the young boy sitting in his boat polishing stones and calmly awaiting his next opponent. Cuchulainn strode towards him, demanding to know his name and lineage. But the boy would not reveal his identity or the slightest detail of the land of his birth. Then Cuchulainn lost patience with him and they began to exchange blows. With one daring stroke, the boy cut off a lock of Cuchulainn's hair, and as he watched it fall to the ground, the older warrior became greatly enraged.

'Enough of this child's play,' he shouted and, dragging the boy from the boat, he began to wrestle with him in the water. But the boy's strength was astonishing and he managed twice to push Cuchulainn's head beneath the waves, almost causing him to drown. And it was on the third occasion that this occurred, when Cuchulainn gasped helplessly for air, that he remembered the Gae Bolg which Scathach had entrusted him with, and he flung it at the boy through the water. At once, the boy loosened his powerful hold and reached agonizingly towards his stomach, where the blood flowed freely from the vast gaping wound the weapon had made there.

'That is a weapon Scathach has not yet taught me to use,' said the boy. 'Carry me now from the water, for I am gravely injured.'

And as Cuchulainn bore the boy in his arms towards the shore he noticed a golden ring on his middle finger.

'It is true then,' he murmured sadly to himself, and set the boy down on the ground before the King and the men of Ulster.

'You see here before you my son,' Cuchulainn announced solemnly, 'the child I have mortally wounded for the good of Ulster.'

'Alas, it is so,' spoke Connla in a feeble voice, 'and I wish with all my heart that I could remain with you to the end of five years. For in that time, I would grow among you and conquer the world before you on every side, so that soon you would rule as far as Rome. But since this cannot be, let me now take my leave of the most famous among you before I die.'

So, one after another, the most courageous knights of the Red Guard were brought before Connla and he placed his arms around the neck of each of them and embraced them affectionately. Then Cuchulainn came forward and his son kissed his father tenderly before drawing his last breath. And as he closed his eyes, a great lament was raised among them and they dug a grave for the boy and set a splendid pillar-stone at its head. Connla, son of Aife, was the only son Cuchulainn ever had and he lived to regret for the rest of his days that he had destroyed so precious a gift.

The Combat of Ferdia and Cuchulainn

❧

BEYOND THE BORDERS OF ULSTER in the province of Connacht, there ruled a spirited and domineering queen named Medb, daughter of Eochaid Fedlech, whose husband, King Ailill, was the meekest and gentlest of creatures. Medb's nature was such that whatever she desired she took for her own, and whatever law displeased her, she refused to obey, so that her husband gave her whatever she demanded and nothing was ever too great a task for him to complete on her behalf. Medb was also the strongest and mightiest of warriors and she had gathered together a powerful army, convinced that one day she would conquer the whole land of Erin.

One evening as Medb and her husband lay together, they began to count up and compare their numerous possessions, for it was one of Medb's favourite entertainments to ridicule Ailill by proving that she had acquired far more treasures and wealth than he had over the years. Weapons, rings and jewellery were counted out, as well as chariots, horses, mansions and plots of land, but each of them was found to possess precisely the same amount as the other. So they began to count the herds of cattle and sheep that roamed the pastures beyond the walls of the castle and it was then that Ailill remembered the Bull of Finnbennach and began to tease his wife about the animal, reminding her of how the bull had deserted her herd in favour of his because it refused to remain in the hands of a woman. As soon as Medb heard these words, all of her property lost its value for her, and she grew adamant that she would soon find a bull to equal the Bull of Finnbennach even if she had to scour the entire countryside for it and bring it back to Connacht by force.

Mac Roth, the King's steward, was summoned to appear before Medb and when she questioned him on the whereabouts of such a bull, he was able to tell her without any hesitation exactly where the best specimen in the country might be found:

'It belongs to Daire mac Fiachna in the province of Ulster,' he told the Queen. 'It is known as the Brown Bull of Cooley and is regarded as the finest beast in the whole of Erin.'

'Then you must go to the son of Fiachna and ask him for the loan of the bull for a year,' replied Medb, 'informing him that at the end of this time, the beast will be safely returned to him, together with fifty of the finest heifers my kingdom has to offer. And if Daire chooses to bring the bull here himself, he may add to his reward a measure of land equalling the size of his present domain in Ulster and a splendid war chariot worthy of the bravest of Connacht's warriors.'

On the following morning, a group of nine foot-messengers led by mac Roth set off in the direction of Ulster, carrying with them a number of gifts from Queen Medb to the owner of the bull, including an oak chest loaded with gold and silver ornaments and several decorated bronze flagons filled with the finest mead in the land. The mere sight of such a treasure-laden party approaching the fort of Daire mac Fiachna raised the spirits of all who set eyes on them and a very warm welcome was lavished on the men. Then Daire himself came forward to greet the party and enquired of them the purpose of their journey to his home. Mac Roth began to tell him of the squabble between Medb and Ailill and of how the Queen had decided that she must quickly find a bull to match the impressive Bull of Finnbennach. Flattered that his own beast had achieved such fame in Connacht, Daire was immediately disposed to help Queen Medb as best he could, but when he heard of the generous reward he would receive in return for the loan of his property, he was well pleased with himself and gave the order at once for the Bull of Cooley to be prepared for its journey to Connacht the next day.

The evening was spent feasting and drinking and a happy atmosphere prevailed for a time as the men of the two provinces exchanged friendly conversation. But as the wine flowed, the tongues of Queen Medb's messengers began to loosen and in the company of their hosts they began to brag of their army's great strength:

'It is just as well for Daire,' boasted one of Medb's envoys, 'that he has surrendered the beast willingly to us. For if he had refused to do so, the

Queen's mighty army would have marched on Ulster and taken the bull from him without any trouble at all.'

When Daire's men heard these offensive remarks, they went straightaway to their master's quarters and demanded that he avenge such a dreadful insult. Mac Roth was immediately summoned to appear before Daire who angrily informed him of the conversation that had been overheard.

'Go back to your Queen,' said Daire, 'and tell her that she shall never take from me by foul means what she cannot win by fair. Let Medb and Ailill invade Ulster if they dare, for we are well equipped to meet the challenge.'

Before the break of day, Medb's messengers had set off for Connacht to deliver the unhappy tidings to their Queen. But when Medb saw that they had not returned with the Brown Bull of Cooley, she did not fly into the rage they had expected. Instead, she spoke calmly to mac Roth:

'I have foreseen this result,' she told him. 'Your dispute with the son of Fiachna is of little consequence, for I have always known that if the Brown Bull of Cooley was not given willingly, he would be taken by force. That time is now arrived, and taken he shall be!'

So began the Queen of Connacht's great war on Ulster, one of the bloodiest wars the country had ever before endured. From every corner of Erin came the allies of Medb and Ailill, including Fraech, son of Fidach, and Calatin, accompanied by his twenty-seven sons. Warriors of great renown from the provinces of Leinster and Munster swelled the numbers of Medb's armed legions, and they were joined by many heroic Ulstermen, among them Fergus mac Roy and Cormac, son of Conchobar, who had defected from their own army, unhappy with their King's leadership.

Not a day or a night passed without a fierce and fiery combat between the armies of Connacht and Ulster. Rivers and streams ran crimson with blood and the bodies of the slain littered the emerald hills and plains. Medb was not slow to display her true worth as a warrior in her own right and Fergus, her chief scout, proved himself a most loyal and courageous comrade in arms. Yet there was none among Medb's great army who could emulate the feats of one particular Ulster warrior, a youthful figure who seemed utterly invincible and who drove himself against them time and time again, bursting with renewed vitality and strength on each occasion.

Cuchulainn, leader of Ulster's Red Guard, was well known to both Fergus and Cormac, but he had grown stronger and more powerful than they had ever imagined possible during their brief time of exile. And as they observed his powers of command and his exceptional skill on the battlefield, they became increasingly alarmed and went before the Queen to warn her that she was faced with no ordinary opponent. Medb grew worried at this news and took counsel with the most prominent figures of her army. After some deliberation, it was decided that her most valiant warrior should be sent to do battle against Cuchulainn. The son of Daman, known as Ferdia, was nominated for this task, for he had been trained alongside Cuchulainn under the great woman-warrior Scathach in the Land of Shadows and had risen to become Connacht's champion warrior, a man feared and respected by all who encountered him.

Nothing had ever yet challenged the deep bond of friendship formed between Ferdia and Cuchulainn during their time together in the Land of Shadows. The love and respect the two men felt for each other had remained constant over the years, and whenever they found occasion to be together, it was not unusual for people to mistake them for brothers. When Ferdia discovered what Medb demanded of him, he was greatly disturbed, and though he was loathe to oppose the wishes of his sovereign, he immediately refused the Queen's request and dismissed her messengers. Then Medb sent her druids and men of poetry to Ferdia's tent, instructing them to recite the most savage and mocking verses in the loudest of voices for everybody to hear.

It was for the sake of his own honour that Ferdia agreed to meet with Medb and Ailill without any further delay. The King and Queen were more than delighted to receive him and Medb wasted no time reeling off the numerous rewards Ferdia could hope to receive if he would only obey her simple wish. But Ferdia showed no interest in the riches that were intended for him, so that Medb grew more and more angry and frustrated. She had little or nothing to lose by playing her one last card and with a tone of false resignation she addressed Ferdia once more:

'It must be true what Cuchulainn has said of you,' said Medb slyly. 'He said that you feared death by his hands and that you would be wise not to go against him. Perhaps it is just as well that the two of you do not meet.'

On hearing this, Ferdia could scarcely contain his anger:

'It was unjust of Cuchulainn to say such a thing,' he roared. 'He well knows that it is not cowardice, but love, that prevents me facing him. So it is settled then. Tomorrow I will go forth to his camp and raise my weapon against him.'

But even as he spoke these words, a mood of gloom and despair descended upon Ferdia and he walked out into the black night, his head bowed in sadness. His closest companions and servants were also overcome with grief to discover what it was that Ferdia was compelled to do, for each was troubled by the knowledge that one of the two great champion warriors of Erin would fail to return home alive.

Word had soon reached Cuchulainn that Medb had chosen his dearest friend to face him in combat and, as he watched Ferdia's war chariot approach, he was forced to acknowledge in his own mind that he would much rather fall by his friend's weapon than slay Ferdia with his own. Yet, at the same time, he could not fully understand why his fosterbrother had so easily given into the wishes of Queen Medb. The betrayal he felt could not be ignored and he prepared himself to greet Ferdia with a degree of caution and reserve. As Ferdia stood down from his chariot, Cuchulainn did not rush forward to embrace him as he would have done in the past, but remained at a distance, waiting for his friend to make the first gesture of friendship.

'I wish that we could have met again in more favourable circumstances,' said Ferdia. 'With all my heart I long to embrace you, old friend.'

'I once would have trusted such words,' answered Cuchulainn, 'but I no longer place any trust in what you say when I know that you have abandoned our friendship for the sake of a treacherous queen and the rewards she no doubt promised you.'

'I see that treason has overcome our love,' replied Ferdia sadly, 'but it is just as well that you think this way. It is best not to remember our friendship, but to meet each other as true enemies of war.'

And so they began to choose the weapons they would use against each other and it was agreed that they would begin the day's fighting with small javelins. They hurled these at each other, backwards and forwards through the air with great energy and speed, but by the close of day, not one spear had pierced the shield of either champion. As nightfall approached, they called a truce, and agreed to resume combat with different weapons at dawn on the following morning.

On the second day, Cuchulainn and Ferdia took up the fight once more, remaining seated in their chariots as they cast heavy, broad-bladed spears at each other across the ford from noon until sundown. But on this day, they both suffered many wounds that stained their flesh red with blood. When they had grown weary of the battle, they again agreed to stop fighting until morning and, placing their weapons in the hands of their servants, they moved towards each other and kissed and embraced warmly in remembrance of their friendship. Their horses shared the same paddock that evening and their charioteers gathered round the same fire. Healing herbs were laid on their wounds and they both rested until daybreak.

As the third day of combat was about to commence and the two men stood opposite each other once more, Cuchulainn was suddenly struck by the change which seemed to have occurred overnight in his friend. Ferdia's brow was now deeply furrowed and his eyes reflected a deep, dark sadness. He no longer held himself upright and he lurched forward wearily to meet his opponent. Filled with pity and sorrow, Cuchulainn pleaded with Ferdia to abandon the fighting, but his friend merely shook his head, insisting that he must fulfil his contract with Queen Medb and King Ailill. They proceeded to choose their weapons and armed themselves with full-length shields and hard-smiting swords. Then they began to strike each other savagely and viciously until they had each carved great wedges of flesh from the other's shoulder-blades and thighs. Still the combat could not be resolved and they decided to part once more for the evening, their bodies torn to shreds and their friendship shattered irreparably. And on this occasion, no kiss was exchanged between them, no curing herbs were exchanged, and their horses and charioteers slept in separate quarters.

As the sun was about to rise on the fourth morning, Ferdia arose and walked out alone to the ford of combat. He wore the jaded, sorrowful expression of a man who senses death close at hand and he began to arm himself with particular care and attention. He knew instinctively that the decisive day of the battle had arrived and that one of them would certainly fall before the evening had drawn to a close. Next to his skin he wore a tunic of silk, speckled with gold and over this he placed a thick leather smock. He then laid a huge, flat stone, which he had carried all the way from Africa, across his torso and covered it with a solid iron apron. On his head he placed a crested war-helmet, adorned with crystals and rubies. He carried in his left hand a massive shield with fifty bosses of bronze and in his right, he clutched his mighty battle-sword. And when at last he was satisfied that he had protected himself against injury as best he could, he remained by the ford, performing many impressive feats with his sword while he awaited the arrival of Cuchulainn.

It was decided between the two warriors on this fourth day that they should use whatever weapons they had to hand and once they had gathered these together the fighting began in earnest. So wild was their rage on that morning, so bitter and violent the clashing of their swords, even the goblins and demons of the air fled in fear. Every creature of the forest shrieked in terror and ran for cover, while the waters themselves changed course, recoiling from the horror and ruthlessness of the combat. And as the afternoon came and went, the wounds inflicted were now deeper and more savage. Each man, although staggering with exhaustion, sought to outdo the other and remained watchful of just such an opportunity. Then, at last, in a moment of acute weariness, Cuchulainn lowered his heavy shield and as soon as he had done so, Ferdia thrust at him with his blade, driving it cleanly through his breast, causing the blood to flow freely down the battle-warrior's tunic. Again, Ferdia struck with his sword and this time it entered Cuchulainn's stomach so that he curled over in agony and began writhing on the earth. And knowing that he must save himself before it was too late, Cuchulainn reached for the Gae Bolg, a weapon he was resolved to use only as a last resort. Taking careful aim, he let fly the instrument with his right foot so that it passed through Ferdia's protective iron apron, through to the flat stone which it broke in three pieces and into the body of his friend filling every joint and every limb with its deadly barbs.

Cuchulainn hastened towards where his friend lay and pulled him gently to his bosom.

'Death is almost upon me,' sighed Ferdia, 'and it is a sad day for us that our friendship should come to such an end. Do not forget the love we once had, Cuchulainn.'

And as Ferdia perished in his arms, Cuchulainn wept piteously, clasping his friend's cold hand lovingly in his own. Then he lifted the body from the damp earth and carried it northwards across the ford to a place where they would not be disturbed by the approaching armies of Ulster. Daylight faded and as Cuchulainn lay down next to Ferdia he fell into a death-like swoon from which he could not be roused for a full seven days.

The Fenian Cycle:
Tales of Finn Mac Cumaill and the Fianna

THE **CENTRAL CHARACTER OF THE FENIAN, or Ossianic Cycle is Finn mac Cumaill [*Pronounced Finn mac Cool.*], thought to be a real historical person** who lived in Ireland some time in the third century AD. A myriad of stories now exists detailing the adventures of this distinguished warrior who rose to leadership of the Fianna and whose stronghold was situated on the Hill of Allen near Co. Kildare. The tales in this cycle generally take place in the Midlands of Ireland and describe a much later epoch when life was less turbulent and the climate of war had been replaced by a more harmonious and romantic atmosphere. The men of the Fianna were not merely military soldiers therefore, but highly accomplished hunter-fighters, often trained in the wilderness, and forced to submit to a number of rigourous tests before they were accepted into the Fianna. Alongside warrior attributes, members of the Fianna were also expected to know by heart the full poet's repertoire, numbering twelve books, and to possess the gift of poetic composition. Oisín [*Pronounced Usheen.*], son of Finn mac Cumaill, is traditionally regarded as the greatest poet of all ancient Irish tales.

The parentage of Finn and the cause of the feud between himself and the Clan of Morna are recounted in this chapter, followed by the story of The Pursuit of Diarmuid and Gráinne which is considered to be one of the most striking and inventive tales of the cycle. The visit of Oisín to Tír na N-Óg is a much later addition to the Fenian tales, and only made a first appearance in literary form in the mid-eighteenth century.

Finn also appears in mythology from the Isle of Man and Scotland where he is known as Finn MacCool, and Fingal, depending on the part of the country, and there are many variations of the spelling of his surname. His son Ossian, from the Irish Oisin of the Fenian Cycle, has a different number of brothers in different legends, as well as variations in the spelling of his name. The feats of the great Féinn, of the wise warrior Fionn, and vhis sons, Osgar and Ossian, form the basis of some of the most dazzling Scottish legends, for Scotland is a country of many great heroes, and storytellers like nothing better than to remember their deeds.

The Coming of Finn mac Cumaill

❧

MANY HUNDREDS OF YEARS after the death of Cuchulainn and the Knights of the Red Guard, the Fianna of Erin reached the height of their fame under the leadership of Finn mac Cumaill. The great warriors of the Fianna were every bit as courageous as their forerunners and each was carefully chosen for his strength and fearlessness on the battlefield. They were also powerful hunters who loved the outdoor life, and many among them possessed the gift of poetry which led to the writing of beautiful tributes to the land of their birth, with its breathtaking mountain valleys and swift-flowing, silver streams. These noble Fenian fighters were above all champion protectors of Erin and during their reign no foreign invader ever dared to set foot on her illustrious shores.

Cumall, son of Trenmor of Clan Brascna, was the father of Finn mac Cumaill and he served as one of the bravest leaders of the Fianna until the day he was slain by his rival, Goll mac Morna, at the battle of Cnucha. Following his death, the Clan of Morna took control of the Fianna and the relatives and friends of Cumall were forced into hiding in the dense forests of the midlands where they built for themselves makeshift homes and yearned for the day when their household would again be restored to power. The Clan of Morna stole from the dead leader the Treasure Bag of the Fianna, filled with strange magical instruments from the Eastern World that had the power to heal all wounds and illnesses. It was placed in the charge of Lia, a chieftain of Connacht, for it was he who had dealt Cumall the first significant wound in the battle of Cnucha.

After the defeat of her husband, Muirne, wife of Cumall, hurriedly abandoned her home and fled to the west to the woodlands of Kerry, accompanied by two of her most trusted handmaidens. For she was carrying the child of the deceased warrior and wished to bring it safely into the world, out of the reach of the bloodthirsty sons of Morna. Within the month, Muirne had given birth to a son and she gave him the name of Demna. And as she gazed upon the infant's face, she was struck by its likeness to the face of Cumall, not yet cold in his grave. Tears of sorrow and anguish flooded down her cheeks and she grasped the child fiercely to her bosom, making a solemn promise to protect him from all harm and evil until he should grow to manhood.

But it was not long before Goll mac Morna received news of the birth of Cumall's heir and he rode forth in great haste through the forests of Erin towards Kerry, intent on destroying the infant. That evening, as she lay sleeping, Muirne had a disturbing vision of a war chariot with wheels of fire approaching her home and she arose at once and summoned her handmaidens to her.

'The sons of Morna have knowledge of our whereabouts,' she told them, 'and the child is unsafe while he remains here with me. Take him under cover of darkness to a safe retreat and do not rest until you are certain you have discovered the remotest dwelling in Erin where he may grow to adulthood unharmed and untroubled.'

The two handmaidens took the tiny bundle from Muirne's arms and set off in the piercingly cold night air towards the protection of the woods. They journeyed for fourteen days by secret paths until they reached the mountains of Slieve Bloom and here, under the shelter of the sprawling oak trees, they finally came to rest, satisfied at last that they had found a true place of sanctuary.

In the fullness of time, the boy Demna grew fair and strong and the two women who cared for him taught him how to hunt and how to spear fish and they marvelled at the speed and zealousness with which he learned to do these things. Before he had reached the age of ten, he could outrun the fastest wild deer of the forests and was so accomplished in the use of his various weapons that he could bring down a hawk with a single shot from his sling, or pin down a charging wild boar with one simple thrust of his spear. It was obvious too that he had the makings of a fine poet, for he was at one with nature and grew to love her fruits, whether listening for hours to the sound of a running brook, or gazing in awe and wonder at the delicate petals of mountain snowdrops. And his nursemaids were overjoyed with their charge and knew that Muirne would be proud of the son they had reared on her behalf, though she may never again lay eyes on the child.

One day, when Demna was in his fourteenth year and had grown more adventurous in spirit, he went out alone and journeyed deep into the mountains until he had reached the place known as Mag Life on the shores of the Liffey. Here, he came upon a chieftain's stronghold and, as he peered beyond the walls of the castle, he observed a group of young boys his own age engaged in a game of hurling. He boldly approached them and expressed his desire to join them in their sport, so they presented him with a hurley and invited him to play along. Though he was outnumbered by the rest of them and was unfamiliar with the rules of the game, Demna quickly proved that he could play as well as any of them and managed, on every occasion, to take the ball from the best players in the field. He was invited to join the group for another game on the following day and, this time, they put one half of their number against him. But again, he had little difficulty beating them off. On the third day, the group decided to test his ability even further and all twelve of them went against him. Demna was triumphant once more and his athletic skill was much admired and applauded. After this, the boys went before their chieftain and told him the story of the youth who had bravely defeated them. The chieftain asked for the young man to be brought before him and when he laid eyes on Demna's beautiful golden hair and saw the milky whiteness of his skin, he pronounced that he should be given the name of Finn, meaning 'fair one', and it was by this name that he was always known thereafter.

At the end of three months, there was not a living person in the land who had not heard rumours of the daring feats of Finn, the golden-haired youth. And it was not long before Goll mac Morna had dispatched his horsemen throughout the countryside to track down the son of Cumall, ordering them to bring him back dead or alive. Finn's two foster-mothers grew anxious that he would be found and they called Finn back home to them and advised him to leave his home in the mountains of Slieve Bloom:

'The champion warriors of the sons of Morna will arrive soon,' they told him, 'and they have been instructed to kill you if they find you here. It was Goll, son of Morna, who murdered your father Cumall. Go from us now, Finn, and keep your identity secret until you are strong enough to protect yourself, for the sons of Morna know that you are the rightful leader of the Fianna and they will stop at nothing until you are dead.'

And so Finn gathered together his belongings and set off in the direction of Loch Lein in the west where he lived for a time in the outdoors, safe from the attention of everyone. At length, however, he began to yearn for the company of other warriors and could not suppress his desire to volunteer himself in military service to the King of Bantry. Even though he did not make himself known to any of his companions, it was not long before their suspicions were aroused, for there was not a soldier more intrepid, nor a hunter more accomplished in the whole of the kingdom. The King himself was curious to learn more about the young warrior and invited him to visit the palace. The two men sat down to a game of chess and the King was greatly surprised to witness the ease with which the youth managed to defeat him. They decided to play on, and Finn won seven games, one after another. Then the King gave up the contest and began to question his opponent warily:

'Who are you,' he asked, 'and who are your people?'

'I am the son of a peasant of the Luagni of Tara,' replied Finn.

'I do not believe this to be the truth,' said the King, 'I am convinced that you are the son that Muirne bore to Cumall. You need not fear me if this is so and I advise you, as proof, to depart here without delay, since I do not wish you to be slain by the sons of Morna while under my poor protection.'

Then Finn realized that he had little choice but to continue his wanderings over the lonely plains of Erin. And it was always the case that whenever he came into contact with other people, his beauty and noble bearing betrayed him, so that the eyes of all were fixed upon him, and the news of his presence promptly spread throughout the region.

He journeyed onwards into Connacht, restricting himself to those areas of the wilderness where he felt certain he would not encounter another living soul. But as he was on his way one morning, he heard the unmistakable sound of a woman wailing and soon came upon her in a clearing of the woods, kneeling over the body of a dead youth.

'I have good cause to mourn in such a fashion,' said the woman looking up at Finn, 'for my only son has been struck down without mercy by the tall warrior who has just passed by here.'

'And what was your son's name who suffered this cruel, unwarranted fate?' enquired Finn.

'Glonda was his name,' replied the woman, 'and I ask you, under bond as a warrior, to avenge his death, since I know of no other who can help me.'

Without hesitating a moment longer, Finn set off in pursuit of the warrior, following the tracks through the woods until he came to the dwelling place of Lia Luachair on the outskirts of Connacht. Taking up the old woman's challenge, he drew his sword and began attacking Lia, striking him down with little effort. It was then that Finn noticed a strange bag on the floor at the older man's feet, and as he looked inside, the treasures of Cumall and the Fianna were revealed to him, and he was overcome with pride that he had unwittingly slain the man who had dealt his father the first wound at Cnucha.

It was at this time that Finn grew weary of his solitary life and began to gather around him all the young warriors of the country who had come to admire his courage and determination. And one of the first tasks he set himself was to go in search of his uncle Crimall and the rest of the Clan Brascna who were still in hiding from the sons of Morna. Accompanied by his followers, he crossed the River Shannon and marched into Connacht where he found his uncle and a number of the old Fianna lying low in the heart of the forest. Crimall stepped forwards and lovingly embraced his nephew, for it was apparent at once that the young stranger before him was the son of Cumall. Then Finn presented the old man with the Bag of Treasures and told him the story from beginning to end of how he had come upon it and slain its custodian. And as he spoke, Crimall laid out the treasures on the ground before them and all who gazed upon them grew fresh of face and strong in body and the burden of age and sorrow was instantly lifted from their brows.

'Our time of deliverance is close at hand,' shouted Crimall joyfully, 'for it has been foretold that he who recovers the Treasure Bag of the Fianna from the hands of the enemy is the one who will lead the Clan of Brascna to victory once more. Go now Finn,' he added, 'and seek out the ancient bard known as Finnegas, since he is the one destined to prepare you for the day when you will rise to your rightful position as head of the Fianna.'

Hearing these words, Finn bade the company farewell and set off alone towards the shores of the River Boyne in the east, eager to meet with the wise old druid who had schooled his father in the ways of poetry and story-telling, whose masterful instruction was deemed essential for any man aspiring to leadership of the Fianna.

For seven long years, Finnegas had lived on the banks of the Boyne, seeking to catch the Salmon of Fec. The salmon, which swam in a deep pool overhung by hazel boughs, was famous throughout the land, for it was prophesied that the first person to eat of its flesh would enjoy all the wisdom of the world. And it happened one day that while Finn was sitting by the river with Finnegas at his side, the salmon swam boldly towards them, almost daring them to cast their rods into the water. Finnegas lost no time in doing so and was astounded when the fish got caught on his hook, struggling only very weakly to release itself. He hauled the salmon onto the shore and watched its silver body wriggle in the sand until all life had gone out of it. When it finally lay still, he gave the salmon over to Finn and ordered him to build a fire on which to cook it.

'But do not eat even the smallest morsel,' Finnegas told him, 'for it is my reward alone, having waited patiently for seven years.'

Finn placed a spit over the fire and began turning it as requested until the fish was cooked through. He then placed it on a plate and took it to Finnegas.

'And have you eaten any of the salmon?' asked the poet.

'No,' answered Finn, 'but I burned my thumb while cooking it and put it in my mouth to relieve the pain.'

'Then you are indeed Finn mac Cumaill,' said Finnegas, 'and I bear you no ill-will for having tasted the salmon, for in you the prophecy is come true.'

Then Finnegas gave Finn the rest of the salmon to eat and it brought him instant knowledge of all he desired to know. And that evening he composed the finest of verses, proving that he possessed a talent equal to the most gifted poets in Erin:

May-day! delightful day!
Bright colours play the vale along.
Now wakes at morning's slender ray
Wild and gay the Blackbird's song.

Now comes the bird of dusty hue,
The loud cuckoo, the summer-lover;
Branchy trees are thick with leaves;
The bitter, evil time is over.

Loaded bees with puny power
Goodly flower-harvest win;
Cattle roam with muddy flanks;
Busy ants go out and in.

Through the wild harp of the wood
Making music roars the gale–
Now it settles without motion,
On the ocean sleeps the sail.

Men grow mighty in the May,
Proud and gay the maidens grow;
Fair is every wooded height;
Fair and bright the plain below.

A bright shaft has smit the streams,
With gold gleams the water-flag;
Leaps the fish and on the hills
Ardour thrills the leaping stag.

Loudly carols the lark on high,
Small and shy his tireless lay,
Singing in wildest, merriest mood,
Delicate-hued, delightful May.
T.W. Rolleston, May-Day

The Rise of Finn to Leadership of the Fianna

❧

AFTER FINN HAD EATEN of the Salmon of Fec which gave him all the gifts of wisdom, he had only to put his thumb in his mouth and whatever he wished to discover was immediately revealed to him. He knew beyond all doubt that he had been brought into the world to take the place of Cumall as head of the Fianna, and was confident at last that he had learned from Finnegas all that he would ever need to know. Turning his back on the valley of the Boyne, he set off to join Crimall and his followers in the forests of Connacht once more in order to plan in earnest for his future. He had by now become the most courageous of warriors, yet this quality was tempered by a remarkable generosity and gentleness of spirit that no man throughout the length and breath of the country could ever hope to rival. Finn was loved and admired by every last one of his comrades and they devoted their lives to him, never once slackening in their efforts to prove themselves worthy of his noble patronage.

It was decided among this loyal group that the time had come for Finn to assert his claim to the leadership of the Fianna and they went and pledged him their support and friendship in this bravest of quests. For it was well known that the Clan of Morna, who continued to rule the Fenian warriors, would not surrender their position without a bitter struggle. Finn now believed himself ready for such a confrontation and the day was chosen when he and his army would march to the Hill of Tara and plead their case before Conn Céadchathach, the High King of Erin.

As it was now the month of November and the Great Assembly of Tara was once more in progress, a period of festivity and good-will, when every man was under oath to lay aside his weapon. Chieftains, noblemen, kings and warriors all journeyed to Tara for the splendid event and old feuds were forgotten as the wine and mead flowed freely and the merry-making and dancing lasted well into the small hours. It was not long before Finn and his band of followers had arrived at Tara and they proceeded at once to the main banqueting hall where they were welcomed by the King's attendants and seated among the other Fenian warriors. As soon as he had walked into the hall, however, all eyes had been turned towards Finn, and a flurry of hushed enquiries circulated around the room as to the identity of the golden-haired youth. The King too, was quick to acknowledge that a stranger had entered his court, and he picked up a goblet of wine and instructed one of his servants to present it to the young warrior. At this gesture of friendship, Finn felt reassured in approaching the King, and he walked forward to the royal table and introduced himself to one and all.

'I am Finn, son of Cumall,' he declared, 'and I have come to take service with you, High King of Erin, just as my father did before me as head of the Fianna.'

And when he heard these words, Goll mac Morna, who sat at the King's right hand, grew pale in anger, and shuddered to hear the King respond favourably to the young warrior:

'I would be honoured to have you serve in my ranks,' replied Conn Céadchathach. 'If you are the son of Cumall, son of Trenmor, then you are also a friend of mine.'

After this, Finn bound himself in loyalty to the King, and his own band of men followed his example, and each was presented with a sword of the Fianna which they accepted with great pride and humility.

Everybody in the kingdom had either heard of Aillen the goblin or seen the creature with their own eyes. Every year during the Great Assembly, Conn Céadchathach increased the number of men guarding the royal city, but still the goblin managed to pass undetected through the outer gates, moving swiftly towards the palace and setting it alight with its flaming breath. Not even the bravest of warriors could prevent Aillen from reeking havoc on Tara, for he carried with him a magic harp and all who heard its fairy music were gently lulled to sleep. The King lived in hope however, that one day the goblin would be defeated and he adamantly refused to be held to ransom by the creature, insisting that the annual festivities take place as normal. A handsome reward awaited that warrior who could capture or destroy Aillen, but none had yet succeeded in doing so. It was at this time that Goll mac Morna conceived of his wicked plan to belittle his young rival before the King, for he could see that Conn Céadchathach secretly entertained the hope that Finn would rescue Tara from further destruction. He called the young warrior to him and told him of the one true way to win the King's favour, being careful not to mention the enchanting harp or the difficulty of the task that lay ahead:

'Go and bind yourself before the King to rid this city of the terrible goblin who every year burns it to the ground,' said Goll. 'You alone possess the courage to do this Finn, and you may name your price if you are successful.'

So Finn went before the King and swore that he would not rest in peace until he had slain Aillen the goblin.

'And what would you have as your reward?' asked the King.

'If I manage to rid you of the goblin,' Finn replied, 'I should like to take up my rightful position as captain of the Fianna. Will you agree, under oath, to such a reward?'

'If this is what you desire,' answered the King, 'then I bind myself to deliver such a prize.'

Satisfied with these words, Finn took up his weapon and ventured out into the darkness to begin his lonely vigil over the palace.

As night fell and the November mists began to thicken round the hill of Tara, Finn waited anxiously for the goblin to appear. After some time, he saw an older warrior enter the courtyard and make his way towards him. He noticed that the warrior held in his hand a long, pointed spear, protected by a case of the soft, shining leather.

'I am Fiacha,' said the warrior gently, 'and I was proud to serve under your father, Cumall, when he was leader of the Fianna. The spear I carry is the spear of enchantment which Cumall placed in my charge upon his death.

'Take this weapon,' he added, 'and as soon as you hear the fairy music, lay its blade against your forehead and you will not fall under the melody's spell.'

Finn thanked the warrior for his gift and turned it over to inspect it, admiring its shining handle of Arabian gold and the sharp steel body of the blade that glinted challengingly in the moonlight. Then he began to roam the ramparts once more, straining his ear to catch the first notes of the magic harp. He gazed out over the wide, frosty plains of Meath but still there was no sign of the evil goblin. He had almost given up hope that Aillen would appear and had sat down wearily on the hard, frozen earth, when he caught sight of a shadowy, phantom-like figure in the distance, floating eerily over the plain towards the royal palace. At first the strange music that wafted through the air was scarcely audible, but as the goblin drew nearer, the sweet sound of the harp strings filled the air like a potent fragrance, intoxicating the senses and inducing a warm, drowsy feeling. Finn was immediately enraptured by the sound and his eyelids slowly began to droop as the music weaved its magic spell over him. But something within him struggled against the opiate of the melody and his fingers searched for the spear of enchantment. Releasing the weapon from its leather shroud, he lay the cold steel blade against his forehead and drew a long, deep breath as he allowed its rejuvenating strength to flow through his tired limbs.

As soon as Aillen had reached the crest of the Hill of Tara he began to spit blazing fire-balls through the palace gates, unaware that Finn had escaped the enchantment of the harp. Now Aillen had never before come face to face with an alert and animate mortal, and the sudden appearance of the young warrior quenching the flames with the cloak off his back prompted a shriek of terror and alarm. Turning swiftly around in the direction he had come from, Aillen fled for his safety, hoping to reach the fairy mound at Sliabh Fuaid before Finn could overtake him. But the young warrior was far too fleet of foot and before the goblin had managed to glide through the entrance of the mound, Finn had cast his spear, striking down the goblin with a single fatal blow through the chest. Then Finn bent over the corpse and removed Aillen's head and carried it back to the palace so that all were made aware that he had put an end to the reign of destruction.

When the sun had risen on the following morning, the King was overjoyed to discover that his kingdom remained untouched by the goblin's flame. He knew at once that Finn must have fulfilled his promise and was eager to express his gratitude. He called together all the men of the Fianna and sent his messenger to Finn's chamber requesting him to appear before him. Then the King stood Finn at his right hand and addressed his audience slowly and solemnly with the following words:

'Men of Erin,' said the King, 'I have pledged my word to this young warrior that if he should ever destroy the goblin Aillen, he would be granted leadership of the Fianna. I urge you to embrace him as your new leader and to honour him with your loyalty and service. If any among you cannot agree to do this, let him now resign his membership of the Fianna.'

And turning to face Goll mac Morna, the King asked him:

'Do you swear service to Finn mac Cumaill, or is it your decision to quit the Fianna?'

'The young warrior has risen nobly to his position,' replied Goll, 'and I now bow to his superiority and accept him as my captain.'

Then Goll mac Morna swore allegiance to Finn and each warrior came forward after him and did the same in his turn. And from this day onwards it was deemed the highest honour to serve under Finn mac Cumaill, for only the best and bravest of Erin's warriors were privileged to stand alongside the most glorious leader the Fianna had ever known.

The Pursuit of Diarmuid and Gráinne

❧

FOLLOWING THE DEATH OF HIS WIFE MAIGNES, Finn mac Cumaill had spent an unhappy year alone as a widower. The loss of his wife had come as a severe blow to the hero of the Fianna and even though he was surrounded by loved ones, including his beloved son Oisín and his grandson Oscar, who watched over and comforted him, he could not rid himself of thoughts of Maignes and was increasingly overwhelmed by deep feelings of loneliness and despair.

One morning, seeing his father in such a pitiful state of grief, Oisín called upon his most trusted friend, Diorruing O'Baoiscne, and together they agreed that something must be done to rescue Finn from his prolonged melancholy. It was Diorruing who suggested that perhaps the time had come for Finn to take a new wife and the two young men began to consider who best would fill this role. And as they pondered this question, Oisín suddenly remembered that the High King of Erin, Cormac mac Art, was said to possess one of the most beautiful daughters in the land. Her name was Gráinne, and although several suitors had sought her hand, it was known that she had not consented to marry any of them and was still in search of a husband.

Oisín and Diorruing went before Finn and expressed their concern that he had not yet recovered his good spirits. Finn listened attentively, and he could not deny that every word they spoke was the truth. But he had tried, he told them, to put aside all memory of his wife, and his attempts so far had been utterly futile.

'Will you let us help you then?' Oisín asked his father. 'For we feel certain that you would be better off with a strong woman by your side. The maiden you seek is named Gráinne, daughter of Cormac mac Art, and if you will allow it, we will journey to Tara on your behalf and request her hand in marriage.'

After they had persuaded Finn that he had little to lose by agreeing to such a venture, both Oisín and Doirruing set off for the royal residence at Tara. So impressive was their stature as warriors of the Fianna, that as soon as they arrived, they were respectfully escorted through the palace gates and permitted an immediate audience with the King. And when Cormac mac Art heard that Finn mac Cumaill desired to take his daughter for a wife, he was more than pleased at the prospect, yet at the same time, he felt it his duty to inform Oisín of the outcome of Gráinne's previous courtships:

'My daughter is a wilful and passionate woman,' the King told Oisín. 'She has refused the hand of some of the finest princes and battle-champions Erin has ever known. Let her be brought before us so that she may give you her own decision on the matter, for I would rather not incur your displeasure by saying yes, only to have her go against me.'

So Gráinne was brought before them and the question was put to her whether or not she would have Finn mac Cumaill for a husband. And it was without the slightest show of interest or enthusiasm that Gráinne made the following reply:

'If you consider this man a fitting son-in-law for you, father, then why shouldn't he be a suitable husband for me?'

But Oisín and Doirruing were satisfied with this answer and taking their leave of the King after having promised to visit as soon as possible in the company of Finn mac Cumaill, they hastened back to the Hill of Allen to deliver the good news.

Within a week, the royal household of Tara was busy preparing itself to welcome the leader of the Fianna and the captains of the seven battalions of his great army. An elaborate banquet was prepared in their honour and King Cormac mac Art received his visitors with great pride and excitement. Then he led the way to the vast dining hall and they all sat down to enjoy a merry evening of feasting and drinking. Seated at Cormac's left hand was his wife, Eitche, and next to her sat Gráinne, resplendent in a robe of emerald silk which perfectly enhanced her breathtaking beauty. Finn mac Cumaill took pride of place at the King's right hand and beside him were seated the most prominent warriors of the Fianna according to his rank and patrimony.

After a time, Gráinne struck up a conversation with her father's druid Daire who sat close by, demanding to know of him the cause of the great celebrations taking place.

'If you are not aware of the reason,' said the druid, 'then it will indeed be hard for me to explain it to you.'

But Gráinne continued to pester Daire with the same question until eventually he was forced to give her a more direct answer:

'That warrior next to your father is none other than Finn mac Cumaill,' said the druid, 'and he has come here tonight to ask you to be his wife.'

And so, for the first time, Gráinne scrutinized the figure she had so flippantly agreed to marry, and having studied his face at some length she fell silent for a time. Then she addressed the druid once more:

'It comes as a great surprise to me,' said Gráinne, 'that it is not for his own son Oisín, or even his grandson Oscar, that Finn seeks me as a wife, since it would be far more appropriate if I married one of these two than marry this man who must be three times my own age.'

'Do not say such things,' answered Daire worriedly, 'for if Finn were to hear you, he would certainly now refuse you and none among the Fianna would ever dare to look at you afterwards.'

But Gráinne merely laughed to hear these words and her eye began to wander in the direction of the young Fenian warriors at the banqueting table. As she surveyed each of them in turn, she questioned the druid as to their identity, desiring to know what exceptional qualities they each had to recommend them. And when her eyes came to rest upon one particularly handsome warrior with dusky-black hair, her interest was very keenly aroused.

'That is Diarmuid, son of Dubne,' the druid informed her, 'who is reputed to be the best lover of women and of maidens in all the world.'

As she continued to sip her wine, Gráinne stared even more closely at the black-haired youth until eventually she called her attendant to her and whispered in her ear:

'Bring me the jewelled goblet from my chamber closet that holds enough wine for nine times nine men.' she told her. 'Have it filled to the brim with wine, then set it down before me.'

When her servant returned with the heavy goblet Gráinne added to it the contents of a small phial she had secretly hidden in a fold of her gown.

'Take the goblet to Finn first of all,' she urged her handmaiden, 'and bid him swallow a draught of wine in honour of our courtship. After he has done so, pass the goblet to all of the company at the high table, but be careful not to allow any of the youthful warriors of the Fianna to drink from it.'

The servant did as she was requested and it was not long before all who swallowed the wine from Gráinne's cup had fallen into a deep and peaceful slumber. Then Gráinne rose quietly from her place at the table and made her way towards where Diarmuid was seated.

'Will you receive my love, Diarmuid,' Gráinne asked him, 'and escape with me tonight to a place far away from here?'

'It is Finn mac Cumaill you are set to wed,' answered the young warrior, stunned at her suggestion. 'I would not do such a thing for any woman who is betrothed to the leader of the Fianna.'

'Then I place you under bonds as a warrior of the King,' said Gráinne, 'to take me out of Tara tonight and to save me from an unhappy union with an old man.'

'These are evil bonds indeed,' said Diarmuid, 'and I beg you to withdraw them, for I cannot understand what it is I have done to deserve such unwarranted punishment.'

'You have done nothing except allow me to fall in love with you,' replied Gráinne, 'ever since the day, many years ago, when you visited the palace and joined in a game of hurling on the green of Tara. I turned the light of my eyes on you that day, and I never gave my love to any other man from that time until now, nor will I ever, Diarmuid.'

Torn between his loyalty to Finn, and an allegiance to the sacred bonds Gráinne had placed him under, Diarmuid turned to his Fenian friends for counsel and advice. But all of them, including Oisín, Oscar, Diorruing and Cailte, advised that he had little choice but to go with Gráinne:

'You have not invited Gráinne's love,' Oisín told him, 'and you are not responsible for the bonds she has laid upon you. But he is a miserable wretch who does not honour his warrior's oath. You must follow Gráinne therefore, and accept this destiny, though your own death may come of it.'

Filled with despair and sorrow at these words, Diarmuid gathered up his weapons and then moving towards his comrades, he embraced each of them sadly, knowing that his days with the Fianna had now come to an end, to be replaced by days of tortured exile, when Finn mac Cumaill would ruthlessly pursue the couple from one end of Erin to the next.

As soon as the flight of Diarmuid and Gráinne had been brought to his attention, the leader of the Fianna was consumed with violent jealousy and rage and swore the bitterest revenge on the pair. At once, Finn mac Cumaill called for his horses to be saddled and a great host of his men set off on the trail of the couple, journeying for days along the most secluded tracks through the densest forests of Erin until they had crossed the river Shannon and arrived near to the place known as Doire Da Both. On the outskirts of this forest, the Fenian trackers discovered a makeshift camp dusted with the ashes of a small fire, which although now cold, left them in little doubt that they were moving very closely behind their prey.

On the following evening, after they had travelled a lengthy distance deeper into the forest, Finn and his men came upon a form of wooden enclosure built of saplings, stones and mud, containing seven narrow doors. Climbing to one of the tallest trees, Finn's chief scout peered inside the structure and saw there Diarmuid and a woman lying next to him on a blanket of deer-skin. The men of the Fianna were ordered to stand guard at each of the seven exits and then Finn himself approached the hut and shouted loudly for Diarmuid to come forward and surrender himself to them. Diarmuid awoke abruptly from his sleep and taking Gráinne by the hand thrust his head through the smallest of the doors. But his eyes betrayed not the slightest glimmer of fear to see Finn and his great warriors surrounding the hut. Instead, he clasped Gráinne closer to him and planted three kisses on her lips for all the men of the Fianna to observe. Finn mac Cumaill was seized by a fury on seeing this, and proclaimed at once that the removal of Diarmuid's head by whatever method his men were forced to employ would alone prove fitting reprisal for so brazen a show of disrespect.

Now Aengus Óg, the god of love, was the foster-father of Diarmuid, son of Dubne, the deity who had protected and watched over the couple since the night they had fled the palace of Tara. And witnessing their plight at the hands of the Fianna, Aengus now took it upon himself to come to their aid, drifting invisibly towards them on the breeze.

'Come and take shelter under my cloak,' he appealed to them, 'and we will pass unseen by Finn and his people to a place of refuge and safety.'

But Diarmuid insisted that he would remain behind to face his former comrades as a true warrior, and requested that Aengus take only Gráinne with him. So Aengus drew Gráinne under his mantel for protection and they both rose up into the air, gliding towards the woodlands of the south where they felt certain Diarmuid would survive to meet up with them later.

After he had bid Aengus and Gráinne farewell, Diarmuid stood upright, tall and proud, and prepared himself for the task of fighting his way through the formidable band of Fenian warriors. Taking up his weapon, he approached the first of the seven doors and demanded to know which of his former comrades stood behind it waiting to do combat with him:

'I wish you no harm, Diarmuid,' replied the gentle voice of Oisín. 'Let me guide you out through this door, and I promise I will not raise a finger to hurt you.'

And on each of the other doors upon which he knocked, apart from the very last, Diarmuid met with the same response, for it appeared that not one among his old friends of the Fianna was prepared to meet him with hostility. Finally, however, Diarmuid arrived at the seventh door and this time when he knocked, the response was anything but warm and friendly:

'It is I, Finn mac Cumaill,' came the thundering reply, 'a man who bears you no love, as you well know. And if you should come out through this gate I would take great pleasure in striking you down and cleaving asunder every last bone in your body.'

'I will not go out by any other door in that case,' answered Diarmuid, 'for I would not wish such raw anger to be unleashed on any of my friends gathered here whose desire it is to let me go free.'

And then, having driven the shafts of his mighty spears firmly into the earth, Diarmuid used them to spring high into the air, leaping over the walls of the wooden hut, clean over the heads of Finn and his men. So swift was this manoeuvre, so light his descent on the grass beyond the warrior group, that none could trace the path of his escape and they stood looking on in amazement, deliberating a long time whether or not it was some goblin of the air who had helped carry Diarmuid so effortlessly to freedom.

It was not long before Diarmuid had arrived at the clearing in the woods where Aengus and Gráinne waited anxiously to see him. Great was their relief to know that he had escaped the Fianna unharmed and they both listened in admiration as he related to them the tale of his daring escape. When the excitement of the reunion had abated however, Aengus Óg grew more serious and spoke earnestly to his foster-son and Gráinne:

'I must now depart from you,' he said to them, 'but I leave you with these words of advice. Do not slacken in caution while Finn mac Cumaill remains in pursuit of you. Never enter a cave with only one opening; and never take refuge on an island with only one harbour. Always eat your meals in a place different to where you have cooked them; never rest your head where you eat your meal, and wherever you sleep tonight, make sure you choose a fresh bed on the following night.'

For many months afterwards, Diarmuid and Gráinne followed the advice of Aengus Óg and lived precisely as he had counselled them. But the time came when they grew weary once more of shifting from place to place and they longed for even two nights together when they might sleep under the same familiar oak tree or heather bush. They had by now reached the forests of the west and had entered a bower guarded by the fierce giant Searbhán.

'Surely we may rest awhile here, Diarmuid,' said Gráinne. 'Is it not the most unlikely thing in the world that Finn and his men would find us out in such a lonely and shaded part of the woods?'

And seeing the look of exhaustion on Gráinne's face, Diarmuid agreed to go in search of Searbhán to beg permission to shelter in the forest. The giant also took pity on Gráinne and it was soon settled that the couple were free to roam the forests and hunt for their food for up to three days provided neither of them touched the quicken tree of Dubros growing in its centre or ate any of its sweet-smelling berries. For this particular tree belonged to the people of the Fairymounds who did not wish that any mortal should eat of its fruit and share the gift of immortality. And so Diarmuid accepted responsibility for both himself and Gráinne and swore upon his sword that during their short stay the berries would remain the sacred property of the fairies.

As for Finn mac Cumaill and his loyal followers of the Fianna, they had not tired in their quest for revenge and were little more than half a day's journey away from the outskirts of Searbhán's forest. And it was while Finn awaited news from his scouts, sent forth to search for evidence of Diarmuid and Gráinne, that he observed a group of horsemen approaching the Fenian camp. He recognized these riders at once as the offspring of the sons of Morna who had murdered his father at the battle of Cnucha and with whom he still had a long-standing feud. But it soon became apparent that these young warriors had travelled a great distance to beg forgiveness for the sins of their fathers and to be reconciled to the Fianna.

Now when Finn's scouts returned to inform him that Diarmuid and Gráinne rested under the protection of Searbhán beneath the tree of Dubros, Finn made up his mind to test the commitment of the warriors of the Clan of Morna:

'If you truly seek forgiveness,' he told them, 'go forth into the woods and bring me one of two things, either the head of Diarmuid, son of Dubne, or a fistful of berries from the tree of Dubros.'

And when the offspring of Morna heard this request, they answered the leader of the Fianna innocently:

'We would be honoured to perform such a task. Point us in the direction of the woods and we shall soon return with one of these two prizes.'

When they were still quite a long way off however, Diarmuid spotted the warriors of Clan Morna approaching and he made ready his weapon for attack. And as they came closer he jumped to the earth from a tree above, blocking the path of their progress.

'Who are you,' Diarmuid asked them, 'and why have you come to the forest of Searbhán?'

'We are of the Clan of Morna,' they replied, 'and we have been sent here by Finn mac Cumaill to perform one of two tasks, either to recover the head of Diarmuid, son of Dubne, or to escape here with a fistful of berries from the tree of Dubros.'

'I am the man whose head you seek,' replied Diarmuid, 'and over there is the tree bearing the fruit you are required to remove. But it will be no easy task for you to accomplish either of these things. Choose now which of the two feats you would attempt to perform.'

'I would sooner fight for your head,' answered the eldest of the warriors, 'than go against the giant Searbhán.'

So the children of Morna began wrestling with Diarmuid who had little or no difficulty overcoming them and within minutes they had been bound hand and foot by him.

Then Gráinne, who had been watching the struggle with some amusement, came forward and began to question Diarmuid about the berries. And when she heard of their magic properties, and of how, in particular, they could make the old young and beautiful once more, she insisted that she must taste them before putting any other food in her mouth again. It was useless for Diarmuid to try and persuade her otherwise, and he began to sharpen his spear, resigned to the fact that he must soon confront the tree's ferocious guardian. Seeing that he was reluctant to break his bond of friendship with the giant, the children of Morna offered to go and get the berries for Gráinne. But although Diarmuid would not agree to this, he was nonetheless touched by their generosity and offered to loosen their bonds so that they might witness the combat.

And so Diarmuid, accompanied by the children of Morna, went forward and roused the giant from his sleep, demanding that he hand over some of the precious berries for Gráinne to eat. Furious at this request, the giant swung his mighty club over his shoulder and brought it down hard in Diarmuid's direction. But Diarmuid managed to leap aside, avoiding any injury, and then hurled himself at the giant forcing him to loosen his hold on the club so that it fell heavily to the ground. Seizing the weapon, Diarmuid delivered three strong blows to the giant's head, dashing his brains to pieces. And when he was certain that Searbhán was dead, he climbed the tree of Dubros and plucked the juiciest berries, handing one bunch to Gráinne and the other to the children of Morna.

'Take these berries to Finn,' he told the warriors, 'and do not pretend to him that you have seen me. Tell him instead that you have earned his forgiveness by slaying the giant with your own bare hands.'

The children of Morna were more than happy to do this, and they expressed their gratitude to Diarmuid that he had finally brought peace between the two clans. And having placed the berries carefully in their saddlebags, they made their way back towards Finn and the men of the Fianna.

As soon as he laid eyes on the berries, Finn mac Cumaill placed them under his nose and announced at once that it was Diarmuid, not the offspring of Morna, who had gathered them:

'For I can smell his skin on them,' roared Finn, 'and I will now go myself in search of him and remove his head with my own sword.'

And he tore through the forest as fast as his horse could carry him until he reached the tree of Dubros where he suspected Diarmuid and Gráinne must be hiding. Here he sat down and called for Oisín to bring his chess-board to him. The two began to play a long and complicated game, for they were each as skilled as the other, until eventually they reached a point where the victor of the game would be decided by Oisín's next move. And Diarmuid, who had been closely following the game from above, could not prevent himself from helping his friend. Impulsively, he threw a berry down from one of the branches where it landed on the board indicating to Oisín how the game should be won. At this, Finn rose rapidly to his feet and calling all the warriors of the Fianna together he ordered them to surround the tree. Then Garb of Sliab Cua announced that Diarmuid had slain his father and that nothing would make him happier than to avenge this death. So Finn agreed to this and Garb climbed the tree in pursuit of Diarmuid.

Again, however, Aengus Óg was watchful of his foster-son and rushed to his aid without the Fianna's knowledge. And as Diarmuid flung Garb backwards from the branches with one swift movement of his foot, Aengus put the form of his foster-son upon him so that his own warriors took off his head believing him to be Diarmuid, son of Dubne. After they had done this, Garb was again changed back into his own shape causing great distress to all who witnessed the transformation. And of the nine Fenian warriors Finn mac Cumaill ordered to ascend the tree in search of Diarmuid, the same fate befell each of them so that Finn fell into a heavy mood of anguish and grief. And when Diarmuid announced that he would descend the tree and slaughter every living person under Finn's protection, Finn at last could tolerate the killing no longer and begged for it to come to an end.

So Diarmuid and Aengus Óg appeared before Finn and it was agreed among the three of them that peace should be restored between Finn and Diarmuid. Then the leader of the Fianna and five of his captains went to the stronghold of the High King of Erin to secure a pardon for Diarmuid and Gráinne. Once this had been done, the couple were allowed to return to their native country of west Kerry where they built for themselves a fine home and lived in peace and harmony together for a great many years to follow.

Oisín in Tír na N-Óg (The Land of Youth)

F INN MAC CUMAILL, the mightiest warrior of the Fianna, had no equal among mortal men and his reputation as one of the fiercest fighters in Ireland spread with each glorious victory on the battlefield. His young son, Oisín, was a particular favourite with him, for the boy showed signs of remarkable courage at an early age and had clearly inherited his father's voracious thirst for adventure. Each time Finn gazed at his golden-haired son a memory of Blaí, the boy's mother, stirred within his breast, filling him with both joy and sorrow. Blaí was now lost to him, but the child she had borne him possessed her great beauty and gift of poetry. Oisín was a true warrior and the greatest of Fenian poets. Many women had fallen in love with him, but none had yet succeeded in winning his heart. The son of Finn mac Cumaill was happiest fighting alongside his father, or roaming the dense forests that chimed with birdsong in the company of his trusty hounds.

While hunting in the middle of the woods one summer's morning, just as the silver veil of mist was rising from the shores of Loch Lein, Oisín was struck by the most enchanting vision. A young maiden appeared before him, seated majestically on a milk-white steed. Oisín had never seen her kind before, but felt certain she must have come from the fairy world. Her luxuriant golden hair, adorned by an elaborate jewelled crown, cascaded over her shoulders and she was clothed in a mantle of the finest red silk. Her saddle was made of purple and gold and her horse's hooves were placed in four shoes of gold, studded with the most precious gems. She moved gracefully towards Oisín, who was immediately entranced by her radiance and perfection. The maiden's cheeks were as delicate as the satin petals of a rose; her eyes were as bright and pure as two drops of dew on a violet; her skin was as white and delicate as the first snows of winter.

'I am Niamh [*Pronounced Niav.*] daughter of the great King who rules the Land of Youth,' she spoke softly. 'Your name is well known to me, brave Oisín, son of the noble Finn mac Cumaill. I have hastened here for love's sake, to woo you.'

Oisín stood bewitched before the maiden as she began to sing to him of Tír na N-Óg, the Land of Youth. Her music drifted lightly towards him like a perfumed summer breeze, and it was the sweetest sound the young warrior had ever heard.

Delightful land of honey and wine
Beyond what seems to thee most fair –
Rich fruits abound the bright year round
And flowers are found of hues most rare.

Unfailing there the honey and wine
And draughts divine of mead there be,
No ache nor ailing night or day –
Death or decay thou ne'er shalt see!

A hundred swords of steel refined,
A hundred cloaks of kind full rare,
A hundred steeds of proudest breed,
A hundred hounds – thy meed when there!

The royal crown of the King of Youth
Shall shine in sooth on thy brow most fair,
All brilliant with gems of luster bright
Whose worth aright none might declare.

All things I've named thou shalt enjoy
And none shall cloy – to endless life –
Beauty and strength and power thou'lt see
And I'll e'er be thy own true wife!
Michael Comyn, Niamh sings to Oisin

'Niamh of the Golden Hair,' Oisín spoke to her. 'I have never before met a maiden so pleasing to the eye and I long to visit the kingdom of which you sing. I would be honoured to take you as my bride and will depart this land of mortals without delay to be with you.'

Before reaching up to grasp her hand, he looked around him only once, catching a final glimpse of his father's great palace and the beautiful woodlands he had now chosen to leave behind. Bidding a valiant farewell in his heart to the men of the Fianna, he mounted the powerful horse which carried them both away towards the cliffs of the west, and further on into the crashing waves.

For five days and five nights they rode, crossing the great plains of Erin and journeying on through various kingdoms of the Otherworld. The deep sea opened up to greet them and they passed underneath the bed of the ocean into a land of golden light. Regal citadels, surrounded by luscious green lawns and exotic, vibrantly coloured blooms, gleamed in the rays of sparkling sunshine. A youthful knight, clad in a magnificent raiment of purple and silver, suddenly appeared alongside them, riding a white mare. A fair young maiden sat next to him on the saddle holding a golden apple in the palm of her hand. Niamh again told Oisín of the beauty of Tír na N-Óg, a land even more beautiful than the splendid images now before them. They journeyed onwards, passing from this luminous world through a raging, violent tempest, moving as swiftly as the howling winds and driving rains would carry them across mountains, valleys and bottomless dark lakes until the bright orb of the sun emerged in all its splendour once more.

The kingdom now before them was far more breathtaking than Oisín had ever imagined possible. A silver-pebbled stream wound its way towards a gently undulating hill dotted with purple and yellow orchids which breathed a rich, opulent fragrance into the air. A magnificent castle stood on the hilltop, shaded by giant leafy trees laden with ripe golden pears. The sound of honey-bees buzzing from flower to flower united melodiously with the singing of birds, languidly pruning their feathers in the amber glow of early twilight. A large crowd moved forward to welcome the couple. Minstrels played soothing, magical airs and delicate blossoms were strewn at their feet creating a soft carpet for them to tread on. The happy pair were escorted to the palace where the King and Queen had prepared a large wedding banquet. The King warmly embraced his new son-in-law and ordered the seven days of feasting and celebrations to commence.

As each new day dawned in the Land of Youth it brought with it an abundance of joy for Oisín and Niamh. Time stood absolutely still in this perfect world and they had only to wish for something and it would instantly appear. Before long, the couple were blessed with three healthy children: two handsome sons, and a beautiful daughter. The son of Finn mac Cumaill had won the admiration and respect of every person in the kingdom and he enthralled each and every subject with tales of his Fenian friends and the splendid adventures they had survived together. Only one thing now threatened to destroy his happiness. At night, Oisín was tormented by dreams of Erin and of his people, the Fianna. These dreams became more and more powerful with the passing of time and he ached with the desire to visit his homeland once again. Such a dreadful anxiety could not be hidden from Niamh, for she knew what troubled her husband and could not bear to see him suffer this deep sadness and unrest.

'Go, Oisín,' she told him, 'though it breaks my heart, I will not hinder you. But you must promise me, in the name of our love for each other and for our children, that you will not dismount on Erin's soil, for time has autonomy in the land of Erin. Hear my warning that if you touch the earth, you will never again return to the Land of Youth.'

Having listened carefully to these words of caution, Oisín rode away, guided by his magical steed across the plains leading back to his beloved country. After five long days, he arrived in his native land and made his way to the home of his father. Cheered by memories of his youth and the joyous welcome home he knew he would soon receive, he rode to the far side of the forest and waited anxiously for the thick mist to clear so that the great house would be revealed in all its regal splendour. Yet when the drizzling clouds finally dispersed, Oisín was shocked to discover only a pile of crumbling stones where the stronghold of Finn mac Cumaill had once stood firm. Utterly distressed and bewildered, he turned his horse swiftly around and galloped away in search of any mortal creature who might bring him news of the Fianna.

After what seemed an eternity, he spotted on the horizon a strange band of men toiling and sweating in their efforts to lift a slab of granite from the ground. Oisín marvelled at their small frames and their lack of strength in lifting such a trifling load.

'I am searching for the dwelling place of Finn mac Cumaill and the Fianna,' he shouted to the men.

'We have often heard of Finn,' replied a stooped, wizened figure, the eldest of the group. 'But it has been many hundreds of years since the great battle of Gabra where he and the last of the Fianna lost their lives.'

'I can see you possess the blood of such mighty ancestors,' added another of the band. 'Can you lend us your strength to shift this stone?'

Niamh's words of counsel to Oisín had not been forgotten, but he was angered by these men of Erin who stood before him so weak and feeble. Filled with a great pride in his own strength and ability, he bent forward from his horse to assist in the lifting of the slab. But the angle at which he had leaned towards the men, added to the weight of the stone, caused the animal's saddle-girth to snap and Oisín could not save himself from falling to the ground. In an instant, his steed had disappeared into thin air, his royal garments had turned to grimy sackcloth and his youthful warrior's face had become creased and lined as the burden of three hundred years of mortal life fell on him. Withered and blind, he reached out with his bony arms, grasping in the dark for some form of comfort. A wretched, pitiful cry escaped his lips and he heard again Niamh's parting words to him. As he lay helpless on the cold, damp earth, he began to weep inconsolably for the wife and children to whom he could never now return in the Land of Eternal Youth.

Legends of Witchcraft

WITCHCRAFT CONSPIRED to manipulate the lives of men and women, across the lands, and across the ages. The old woman in the village might have powers that not everyone could understand, and when something went wrong, when illness fell, someone had to be given blame for the misfortune. The witchlore of Scotland was spawned and accentuated under the reign of James VI and I, who had an overwhelming superstition of and belief in them. Ultimately, however, the belief in witches reflects a pagan fear of spirits and creatures of the unknown. Witches could cast spells that enchanted, calmed, killed and controlled, and for that they were dreaded and continually plotted against. All witches were eventually defeated, but until that time, it was only safe to keep charms against unusual knots, or black cats, or strange happenings on the sea, for who really knew their origin?

The Brownie

❦

IN SCOTLAND THERE'S A CREATURE that's not a witch, or a warlock, or even really a fairy. He's a brownie, and he's ugly so he's not often seen by mortal eyes. For brownies are small creatures, with great bulging eyes, and faces that are furred like the backside of a donkey. Their teeth are like battered stones, and when they smile they set fear in the hearts of all men. But a brownie is a helpful soul, and although they are not often wanted round about a house or a farm, they work a kind of magic, and help to clean and to tend the farm or run the mill, for just the price of a bowl of cream, and the odd bit of oatmeal.

There once was a brownie who lived round about a house on a farm in Wester Ross in Kintail. The house on the farm was empty, so the brownie had made himself a happy home there. In this same village, near the house on the farm, lived a young miller, who shared a house with his mother. Now his mother was a greedy woman, and she dabbled in magic of all sorts, not all of it white to be sure, and she had set her sights on the young lassie at the big house on the hill, to be the wife of her young miller son.

The lassie was pretty, and her nature was kind, but the young miller was already in love with another, a servant girl who went by the name of Katie. Now Katie was as fair as the morning sky, and her cheeks were flushed with roses. She was a bonnie lass, and she would work hard with her husband to tend a mill and to make him into something grand.

Now the young miller's mother would have nothing of it: 'Look, ye must marry this farmer's daughter, with a big farm and everything, and it would be yours because her father's getting on.'

But the miller was stubborn, and he cared only for Katie.

'I can't help it mother, I love Katie, and I am gonna marry her,' he said firmly, to which his mother replied, 'You're not gonna marry Katie, because Katie is gonna die.'

But the miller's will was stronger than his love for his mother, and he married Katie in secret and took her to live in a deserted house on a farm. Now there were stories told in those parts about the brownie who had made his home there, but the miller was a friendly sort, and not easily scared, and so he convinced young Katie that it would be safe and together they went to meet with the brownie. Katie was a fair lass, and she could see that an appearance did not make a man, and although the brownie frightened her, she could sense his good nature and agreed to live there.

They settled in happily, in the house on the farm, and the brownie was made a fine bed of straw and bracken, and fed all the best bit of oatmeal and cream. For that he tended their mill, and each day new sacks of grain were laid neatly against the mill walls. He interfered not at all in their lives, but they came to love his quiet presence, his charming ways. For he would slip down the chimney as they slept and lay things just right, so that when they woke, the wee house gleamed from every corner.

As is wont to happen, especially with those who are young and in love, the young lady of the house became heavy with child, and as she grew more and more tired, the brownie would work harder, until he spent many a day in the house of the miller and Katie. He became a friend to Katie, and she became accustomed to his horrible face, warmed by his quiet presence, his charming ways. And when the baby was due to come, it was the brownie who she called to fetch her husband the miller, and he scampered with glee down the path to the mill.

Now the miller too had grown fond of the brownie, but he was more traditional than wee Katie, and he felt that the presence of his mother was necessary for that bairn to be born. And so he left Katie with the brownie, who mopped her brow as she called out with pain, and who stroked her face with his own furred hand. But as soon as the footfall of the miller's mother was heard on the path, he leapt up the chimney and disappeared from the room. For brownies are magic beings themselves and they know the dangers of a witch, especially those who dabble in magic that is not all white.

The miller's mother was friendly and calm, and in her pain and distress, Katie could not help but trust her. She allowed her mother-in-law to braid her hair, and to set her back against pillows that were freshly stuffed. A tiny black kitten was set by her side to keep company with her and the new baby. Then, turning the lassie's bed towards the door, she bid her farewell and left.

Now Katie was soothed by the presence of the witch, but when she left the pains began again in earnest and she moaned and writhed for two whole days before the miller was forced to go for help. He went first to his mother, but she feigned an illness and said she could not come back with him. And so he returned to the farm where he found poor Katie sick with exhaustion and great pain.

'I'll go for the howdie woman,' he said, for the howdie woman delivered most of the babies in the village, having the gift for midwifery. But Katie would not hear of it, so frightened she had become.

'Don't leave me here,' she sobbed. 'Send the brownie.' And that thought stopped them short, for many folk were frightened to visit them at their home because of that same brownie, and they wondered now if the howdie woman would fear to come as well.

But Katie's pain was dragging her deeper into a dreadful state, and the roses had disappeared from her cheeks. There was no sight of the bairn and there was nothing for it but to call the brownie to help.

The brownie was only too glad to help, and in the cover of darkness, with a great cloak wrapped across his hideous face, he rode off across the hills to fetch the howdie woman. And she came at once, for her calling was stronger than her fear, and she sat herself behind the brownie and wrapped her arms about him for warmth and for safety. And she whispered in his ear as they rode, 'Katie will be well again, no doubt, but I hope I don't see that brownie. I am terrified of that brownie!'

But the brownie said, 'No, don't worry, I can assure you for certain that you'll not see anything worse than what you're cuddling now.' And he drove the howdie woman to the door of the house and made off with the horse, into the darkness.

The howdie woman had seen no birth like this, and for four more days she sat with Katie, who was expiring quickly now, torn by pains that wracked her thin frame, and struggling to keep sane as they plunged her into a burning hell with every contraction.

The miller sat brooding in a chair, helpless against this pain he could not understand, and suddenly he sat up and snapped his fingers. 'I'll bet a shilling,' he said then, 'that this is the work of my mother.'

So he rode straight to the house of his mother and shouted at her, 'Take that spell off my Katie. I know you've done something.'

And his mother shook her head, and said, 'I will not. I told you she is gonna die, and you are gonna marry the farmer's daughter.' She stood firm then and would not help his poor Katie.

So poor Katie seemed destined to die in agony, and he ran away then into the night, straight to the wee brownie, for he had no one else to whom he could turn. And the brownie thought for a while, and said, 'I'll tell you what you can do. Take me down to your mother.'

'Oh, no,' said the miller, 'that wouldn't help us at all. God himself couldn't help me against my mother.'

'Ah,' said the brownie, 'but you take me down because I can become invisible, and if you were to rush in and tell your mother, "Oh, mother, mother, you've got a beautiful grandson!" and then run off again, I will stay behind to see what happens. And I'll be invisible.'

And so it was decided that the brownie would come along, and when they reached the house of his mother, the miller ran in and cried, 'Mother, you have got a beautiful grandson.'

And she said, 'What?' her face a mask of alarm and fury.

'Oh yes,' shouted the miller, 'But I can't stop, I must see Katie.' And with that he ran back over the hills to wait for the brownie.

And as he went out the door, the woman stamped her feet and pulled at her hair, cursing all the time, 'Who told him about the witches' knots in Katie's hair? How did he know about the black cat? Who told him about the raven's feathers in those great white pillows? And who told them that I'd turned her feet to the door?'

And then the brownie skipped away, as fast as his legs would carry him, over the hills to greet the miller, and together they ran back to the house on the farm where Katie lay with the howdie woman.

Now the howdie woman had only to set eyes on the grinning brownie when she was up and out the door in a flash, but the brownie set himself to work, stroking the poor lass's cheek and mopping her brow, warming her with his quiet presence and his charming ways. He untied her head, and brushed it down around her shoulders, crooning softly in her ears. Then he took those great new pillows and set them aflame in the hearth until only dust remained of those evil black feathers. And then, with one angry twist, he took the head from the kitten and burnt her too, out of sight, of course, of poor Katie. And so it was, when the brownie moved the bed round, so that her feet faced the door no longer, that the cry of an infant was heard in that house on the farm. Katie slept then, and when she woke, her baby was cleaned and swaddled, and the roses returned to her cheeks once more.

But the brownie had gone, for brownies often do that, just disappear, never to be seen again. They missed the wee man's quiet presence and his charming ways, but he had milled enough grain for twenty odd years, and they lived on that house on the farm with their new baby in comfort and in good fortune.

The Three Knots

❧

THERE ONCE WAS A FAMILY on the island of Heisker in Ulst. They were farm people and worked hard all the year, but when the harvest was over, and the grain tucked safely away for the frosty months ahead, they took it upon themselves to plan a little trip to Lewis, to visit some friends there.

It was the same every year, they crossed the sea and got to Lewis where they had a grand time of it, and then they went home again, to cosy themselves away for the long frosty months. And so it was this time, that they gathered an able crew and set off.

At Lewis things seemed much the same as they ever had. The man of the family went to greet the woman of the house they were visiting, and they talked for many hours, of days of old, and of good friends and family. And just as he made preparations to get off to bed, a tall lithe woman entered the room, with hair as black as a raven's back. Her eyes were cool and dark, and she whispered something to the woman of the house, and then she left, stopping only to stroke the woman's hair.

'Who's that ugly black thing,' asked the man, curious about the familiarity between the two women.

And the woman sighed and replied, 'Is that what you say? Ugly, is she? Woe betide you, man, but you'll be lost in love with her before you leave Lewis; if you can, of course.' And with that she rose and went off to bed.

Now the man scowled with the thought of it, for he had three great strong bairns and a lovely wife, as fair and pink and white as this thing was black. 'Indeed,' he muttered to himself, 'I won't fall in love with her.' He spat a bit of the old tobacco into the iron sink and prepared to retire himself.

Now he rose in the morning and the first thing that ate at his mind was the thought of that tall lithe girl, with hair as black as a raven's back, and he went downstairs, stormy as the North Sea waters. That night the girl came again to the house, though she'd not been out of his mind since her last visit, and he hated her even more, all tall and lithe and black, with those cool dark eyes. But when she left he longed for her like he'd longed for no other, and he grew black himself with rage and with desire.

Now this went on every day for a week, with the man from Heisker growing silent and cold, so his wife felt afraid and begged him to take leave of that house.

'We've had a good visit now, and it's time for us to be making for home,' she said firmly to her husband, and with the last tiny shred of rational thought left in his mind, which longed for the tall, lithe girl, with hair as black as a raven's back, he agreed.

And so it was that their belongings were packed, and their big strong boat made good, and they arrived at the sea to leave. But as the first foot was set inside that big boat, a great black gale was brewed and flung at them, and they could go no further. There was nothing for it but to return to the house from which they'd come, and to that tall, lithe woman.

And again the next morning they set out, but the mists drew around them then, cool and dark, and they could go no further. There was nothing for it but to return to the house from which they'd come, and to the cool dark eyes of that woman.

But as they walked away from the coast, they met a wee old witch, with hair that was whiter than the down of a thistle, and a small wrinkled face that spoke of great wisdom. And she stopped them there, and beckoned them aside.

'Well, my good folks,' she said, 'you've a bit of trouble leaving this dark place.'

They nodded, and listened intently.

'It's no wonder,' said the wee old witch, 'seeing the kind of place you've been staying. What will you give to me for fine weather to go tomorrow?'

'Anything, anything we'll give to you,' said the wife earnestly, and looked to her husband, but his eyes were trained on the hill, on the house with the tall, lithe woman, with the cool dark eyes, and his face was rent by a longing such as she'd never seen before. 'We'll do anything,' she said again firmly.

'A pound of snuff,' said the old witch. 'And I'll need to have a word with the skipper. Send him by this evening.' And with that she showed them to the door.

So later that night the skipper of the big strong boat was sent to see the old witch, and there she handed him a rope with three big knots.

'Here you are,' she said. 'You take this aboard and you'll have a good day for sailing tomorrow. It'll not be long before you're at Lewis harbour. Now if you haven't enough wind, just open one of these knots. And then if that is not enough still, untie the second. But whatever you do, by God, don't untie the third.'

And so it happened that on that next morning, the day dawned clear and bright, with a fresh puff of wind to set them on their course. They loaded the boat, and without a backward glance, they headed to sea. And the man of the family let out a sigh of relief so long and frenzied that the others averted their eyes. His thoughts were once again pure, and the magic of that old witch had set him free. He called to the skipper.

'Untie a knot,' he said grandly, 'let's get us home at once.' And so a knot was untied, and a swift breeze blew up that sent them cutting through the waves.

'And again,' he cried, the wind cold on his body, his soul cleansed and clear. And another knot was untied, so that a great wind was let loose on the tiny ship, and they flew across the water now, the sails stretched to the limit.

And the man of the family settled himself on deck, and with the sea air licking his face, he felt safe from all danger, and perhaps a little too confident. For he called out then, 'Let's test that old woman's magic. What means that third knot?'

And his crew cowered away from him, and his wife shook her head, but he insisted, and being the man of the family, and in charge of his boat and his own fate, he had his way and the knot was untied.

What happened then is a story for the ears of the fearless only, for from the sea rose a sight that clamped shut the mouths of the men, and the wife and their children until their dying day. It was a shape, tall and lithe, with a face of sorts, from which shone cold dark eyes. And a hand was reached down, and the man of the family plucked from amongst them, and into the sea. And then the boat itself was lifted high above the waves, placed on the sands of Heisker from where she'd never move again.

She's still there, a warning to all who think that magic can be tested, and the land there has come to be called Port Eilein na Culaigh, or Port of the Island of the Boat.

The Daughter of Duart

❦

T HERE ONCE WAS A MAN, MacLean of Duart, who sent his daughter to become a scholar. Now in those days, an education was a novelty for a lassie, but so highly did he think of his daughter that he found the money, and sent her away. And a long time she was away, too, for it was three or four years before her feet touched the MacLean soil once more.

While she was gone, the man, MacLean of Duart, would sit himself in her room, and look around him. It was a fine room, it was, for so highly did he think of his daughter that he found the money to buy her everything she ever wanted. There were books a plenty, but since MacLean of Duart could not read, they meant nothing to them, with their drawings of cats, and circles, and great long poems. There were pictures, too, on the walls of that room, and a soft cover on the bed, that made it look just so. For she was a clever girl, and she knew how to make a room feel warm.

MacLean of Duart was lonely without his daughter, but he carried on working his land, and the day came again when she returned home to him there. And so it was that he took his daughter on his arm, and led her up into the hills, where the clouds quivered around them, and the air shone bright and blue. Then they looked around them, at all the beauty of the land, and he turned to her, his eyes alight with pride and joy, and he said to his daughter, 'How much have you learned?'

And his daughter stopped, and she looked about, across the mossy hills to the sea beyond, and there she pointed to a tall ship, which fought a course away from them against the waves.

'There,' she said, 'that ship. I have learned enough to bring it to shore.'

And her father laughed warmly, and taking her arm again, he said, 'Well, then, lass, bring her in.'

The ship turned then, and made its way across the waters towards them. And it kept on coming, as the water grew shallow and the sands rose up to meet it, and then the rocks were there, thrusting their way through the waves as the prow of the ship drew nigh. And that ship kept on coming until it was about to be wrecked on the rocks.

MacLean of Duart looked at his daughter then, and he said with a soft voice, 'Save them now, lass. Why don't you save them now.'

And his daughter shrugged her shoulders, and she smiled an easy smile, then said, 'But I can't. I don't know how to do that.'

There was silence then, filled by the crash of the ship upon the rocks. He turned to her then, did MacLean of Duart, and he laid down her arm. He looked at his daughter with new eyes, and he said to her, 'Well, then. If that is the education I have bought you, if that is what you have learned, then I would rather your room than your company.'

He strode home, and built a great fire. And when his daughter came in after him, he cut her to bits and burnt her there, saying, as he poked the flames, 'I will never have your sort in the same place as myself.'

And he went to her room, and gathered together her books, and her pictures, and threw them on the fire. Then he took her soft cover from her bed and put that on, too, till there was no trace of the girl who was his daughter. For MacLean of Duart thought so highly of his daughter that he could not allow her to practise the education she'd gathered, for he would have nothing to do with black magic, and she had mastered the art.

The Cauldron

❧

THE LITTLE ISLAND OF SANDRAY juts firmly through the waves of the Atlantic Ocean, which spits and surges around it. No human lives there, although sheep graze calmly on the succulent green grass, freshened by the moist salt air, and kept company by the fairy folk who live in a verdant knoll. But once upon a time there were men and women on the island of Sandray, and one was a herder's wife, called Mairearad, who kept a tiny cottage on the northernmost tip.

She had in her possession a large copper cauldron, blackened with age and with use. One day, as she wiped it clean of the evening meal, she was visited by a Woman of Peace, a fairy woman who tiptoed quietly into the cottage and asked to take away the cauldron for a short time. Now this was an older fairy, with a nature that was gentle and kind, and she presented little danger to Mairearad. She had a wizened fairy face, and features as tiny as the markings of a butterfly, and she moved swiftly and silently, advising no one of her coming or going. Mairearad passed her the cauldron, and as the Woman of Peace retreated down the cottage path, towards the twin hills that marked the fairy's Land of Light, she said to the fairy,

A smith is able to make
Cold iron hot with a coal;
The due of the kettle is bones,
And to bring it back again whole.

And so it was that the cauldron was returned that evening, left quietly on the cottage doorstop, filled with juicy bones.

The Woman of Peace came again, later that day, and without saying a word, indicated the cauldron. And as days turned into years, an unspoken relationship developed between the two women, fairy and mortal. Mairearad would loan her cauldron, and in exchange she would have it filled with delicious bones. She never forgot to whisper, as the fairy drew out of sight,

A smith is able to make
Cold iron hot with a coal;
The due of the kettle is bones,
And to bring it back again whole.

Then one day, Mairearad had to leave her cottage for a day, to travel to Castlebay, across the sea on Barra.

She said to her husband before she left, 'When the Woman of Peace comes to the doorstep, you must let her take the cauldron, but do not forget to say to her what I always say.'

And so her husband worked his field, as he always did, and as he returned for his midday meal he met with a curious sight, for scurrying along the path in front of him was a wee woman, her face gnarled with age, her eyes bright and shrewd. Suddenly he felt an inexplicable fear, for most men have had fed to them as bairns the tales of fairies and the cruel tricks they play, their enchantments and their evil spells. He remembered them all now in a rush of tortuous thought, and pushed past the fairy woman to slam the cottage door. She knocked firmly, but he refused to answer, panting with terror on the other side of the door.

At last there was silence, and then, a weird howl echoed around the cottage walls and there was a scrambling on the roof. Through the chimney was thrust the long brown arm of the fairy woman, and she reached straight down to the fire upon which the cauldron sat, and pulled it with a rush of air, through the cottage roof.

Mairearad's husband was still pressed against the door when she returned that evening, and she looked curiously at the empty hearth, remarking, 'The Woman of Peace always returns the cauldron before darkness falls.'

Then her husband hung his head in shame and told her how he'd barred the door, and when the fairy had taken the cauldron, he'd forgotten to ask for its return. Well Mairearad scolded her husband, and putting on her overcoat and boots, she left the cottage, lantern in hand.

Darkness can play tricks as devilish as those of the fairies themselves, and it was not long before the dancing shadows, and whispering trees sent a shiver along the spine of the fierce wife Mairearad, but still she pressed on, safe in the knowledge that the Woman of Peace was her friend. She reached the threshold of the Land of Light and saw on a fire, just inside the door, her cauldron, filled as usual with tender bones. And so she grabbed it, and half-fearing where she was, began to ran, exciting the attention of the black fairy dogs that slept beside an old man who guarded the entrance.

Up they jumped, and woke the old man, who cried out,

Silent woman, dumb woman,
Who has come to us from the Land of the Dead
Since you have not blessed the brugh –
Unleash Black and let go Fierce.

And he let the dogs free to chase the terrified woman right back to the door of her cottage, baying and howling, spitting with determination and hunger. As she ran she dropped the tasty bones, buying herself a moment or two's respite from the snarling dogs. For fairy dogs are faster than any dogs on earth, and will devour all human flesh that comes across their paths. Mairearad fled down the path, finally reaching her door and slamming it shut behind her. There she told her breathless story to her husband, and they held one another's ears against the painful wailing of the hounds. Finally there was silence.

Never again did the fairy Woman of Peace come to Mairearad's cottage, nor did she borrow the cauldron. Mairearad and her husband missed the succulent bones, but never again did they trouble the fairy folk. They are long dead now, buried on the grassy verge on the island of Sandray, where the sheep graze calmly on the succulent green grass, freshened by the moist salt air, kept company by the fairy folk who live in a verdant knoll.

The Horned Women

A RICH WOMAN SAT UP LATE ONE NIGHT carding and preparing wool, while all the family and servants were asleep. Suddenly a knock was given at the door, and a voice called, "Open! open!"

"Who is there?" said the woman of the house.
"I am the Witch of one Horn," was answered.

The mistress, supposing that one of her neighbours had called and required assistance, opened the door, and a woman entered, having in her hand a pair of wool-carders, and bearing a horn on her forehead, as if growing there. She sat down by the fire in silence, and began to card the wool with violent haste. Suddenly she paused, and said aloud: "Where are the women? they delay too long."

Then a second knock came to the door, and a voice called as before, "Open! open!"

The mistress felt herself obliged to rise and open to the call, and immediately a second witch entered, having two horns on her forehead, and in her hand a wheel for spinning wool.

"Give me place," she said; "I am the Witch of the two Horns," and she began to spin as quick as lightning.

And so the knocks went on, and the call was heard, and the witches entered, until at last twelve women sat round the fire—the first with one horn, the last with twelve horns.

And they carded the thread, and turned their spinning-wheels, and wound and wove, all singing together an ancient rhyme, but no word did they speak to the mistress of the house. Strange to hear, and frightful to look upon, were these twelve women, with their horns and their wheels; and the mistress felt near to death, and she tried to rise that she might call for help, but she could not move, nor could she utter a word or a cry, for the spell of the witches was upon her.

Then one of them called to her in Irish, and said, "Rise, woman, and make us a cake."

Then the mistress searched for a vessel to bring water from the well that she might mix the meal and make the cake, but she could find none.

And they said to her, "Take a sieve and bring water in it."

And she took the sieve and went to the well; but the water poured from it, and she could fetch none for the cake, and she sat down by the well and wept.

Then a voice came by her and said, "Take yellow clay and moss, and bind them together, and plaster the sieve so that it will hold."

This she did, and the sieve held the water for the cake; and the voice said again:

"Return, and when thou comest to the north angle of the house, cry aloud three times and say, 'The mountain of the Fenian women and the sky over it is all on fire.'"

And she did so.

When the witches inside heard the call, a great and terrible cry broke from their lips, and they rushed forth with wild lamentations and shrieks, and fled away to Slievenamon, where was their chief abode. But the Spirit of the Well bade the mistress of the house to enter and prepare her home against the enchantments of the witches if they returned again.

And first, to break their spells, she sprinkled the water in which she had washed her child's feet, the feet-water, outside the door on the threshold; secondly, she took the cake which in her absence the witches had made of meal mixed with the blood drawn from the sleeping family, and she broke the cake in bits, and placed a bit in the mouth of each sleeper, and they were restored; and she took the cloth they had woven, and placed it half in and half out of the chest with the padlock; and lastly, she secured the door with a great crossbeam fastened in the jambs, so that the witches could not enter, and having done these things she waited.

Not long were the witches in coming back, and they raged and called for vengeance.

"Open! open!" they screamed; "open, feet-water!"

"I cannot," said the feet-water; "I am scattered on the ground, and my path is down to the Lough."

"Open, open, wood and trees and beam!" they cried to the door.

"I cannot," said the door, "for the beam is fixed in the jambs and I have no power to move."

"Open, open, cake that we have made and mingled with blood!" they cried again.

"I cannot," said the cake, "for I am broken and bruised, and my blood is on the lips of the sleeping children."

Then the witches rushed through the air with great cries, and fled back to Slievenamon, uttering strange curses on the Spirit of the Well, who had wished their ruin; but the woman and the house were left in peace, and a mantle dropped by one of the witches in her flight was kept hung up by the mistress in memory of that night; and this mantle was kept by the same family from generation to generation for five hundred years after.

Legends of Giants

GIANTS ARE commonly-appearing creatures in Celtic tales. They are usually a force to be reckoned with, standing as monstrously large obstacles between the heroes and their goals or the women they love. Influences from other cultures can clearly be seen, for example the episode in 'Conall Yellowclaw' featuring a one-eyed giant which resembles the story of Polyphemus from the Greek epic *The Odyssey*. Of course, not all giants are malevolent, for example the Celtic hero Finn mac Cumaill is often portrayed as a giant and the Giant's Causeway in Ireland is attributed to his making. The following stories however tend to focus on the more hostile kind. Though the giant first encountered in the story 'The Lad with the Goat-skin' is not the main antagonist, he plays an integral part in the tale by giving Tom his special club.

Conall Yellowclaw

❦

ONALL YELLOWCLAW WAS A STURDY TENANT in Erin: he had three sons. There was at that time a king over every fifth of Erin. It fell out for the children of the king that was near Conall, that they themselves and the children of Conall came to blows. The children of Conall got the upper hand, and they killed the king's big son. The king sent a message for Conall, and he said to him—"Oh, Conall! what made your sons go to spring on my sons till my big son was killed by your children? but I see that though I follow you revengefully, I shall not be much better for it, and I will now set a thing before you, and if you will do it, I will not follow you with revenge. If you and your sons will get me the brown horse of the king of Lochlann, you shall get the souls of your sons."

"Why," said Conall, "should not I do the pleasure of the king, though there should be no souls of my sons in dread at all. Hard is the matter you require of me, but I will lose my own life, and the life of my sons, or else I will do the pleasure of the king."

After these words Conall left the king, and he went home: when he got home he was under much trouble and perplexity. When he went to lie down he told his wife the thing the king had set before him. His wife took much sorrow that he was obliged to part from herself, while she knew not if she should see him more.

"Oh, Conall," said she, "why didst not thou let the king do his own pleasure to thy sons, rather than be going now, while I know not if ever I shall see thee more?"

When he rose on the morrow, he set himself and his three sons in order, and they took their journey towards Lochlann, and they made no stop but tore through ocean till they reached it. When they reached Lochlann they did not know what they should do. Said the old man to his sons, "Stop ye, and we will seek out the house of the king's miller."

When they went into the house of the king's miller, the man asked them to stop there for the night. Conall told the miller that his own children and the children of his king had fallen out, and that his children had killed the king's son, and there was nothing that would please the king but that he should get the brown horse of the king of Lochlann.

"If you will do me a kindness, and will put me in a way to get him, for certain I will pay ye for it."

"The thing is silly that you are come to seek," said the miller; "for the king has laid his mind on him so greatly that you will not get him in any way unless you steal him; but if you can make out a way, I will keep it secret."

"This is what I am thinking," said Conall, "since you are working every day for the king, you and your gillies could put myself and my sons into five sacks of bran."

"The plan that has come into your head is not bad," said the miller.

The miller spoke to his gillies, and he said to them to do this, and they put them in five sacks. The king's gillies came to seek the bran, and they took the five sacks with them, and they emptied them before the horses. The servants locked the door, and they went away.

When they rose to lay hand on the brown horse, said Conall, "You shall not do that. It is hard to get out of this; let us make for ourselves five hiding holes, so that if they hear us we may go and hide." They made the holes, then they laid hands on the horse. The horse was pretty well unbroken, and he set to making a terrible noise through the stable. The king heard the noise. "It must be my brown horse," said he to his gillies; "find out what is wrong with him."

The servants went out, and when Conall and his sons saw them coming they went into the hiding holes. The servants looked amongst the horses, and they did not find anything wrong; and they returned and they told this to the king, and the king said to them that if nothing was wrong they should go to their places of rest. When the gillies had time to be gone, Conall and his sons laid their hands again on the horse. If the noise was great that he made before, the noise he made now was seven times greater. The king sent a message for his gillies again, and said for certain there was something troubling the brown horse. "Go and look well about him." The servants went out, and they went to their hiding holes. The servants rummaged well, and did not find a thing. They returned and they told this.

"That is marvellous for me," said the king: "go you to lie down again, and if I notice it again I will go out myself."

When Conall and his sons perceived that the gillies were gone, they laid hands again on the horse, and one of them caught him, and if the noise that the horse made on the two former times was great, he made more this time.

"Be this from me," said the king; "it must be that some one is troubling my brown horse." He sounded the bell hastily, and when his waiting-man came to him, he said to him to let the stable gillies know that something was wrong with the horse. The gillies came, and the king went with them. When Conall and his sons perceived the company coming they went to the hiding holes.

The king was a wary man, and he saw where the horses were making a noise.

"Be wary," said the king, "there are men within the stable, let us get at them somehow."

The king followed the tracks of the men, and he found them. Every one knew Conall, for he was a valued tenant of the king of Erin, and when the king brought them up out of the holes he said, "Oh, Conall, is it you that are here?"

"I am, O king, without question, and necessity made me come. I am under thy pardon, and under thine honour, and under thy grace." He told how it happened to him, and that he had to get the brown horse for the king of Erin, or that his sons were to be put to death. "I knew that I should not get him by asking, and I was going to steal him."

"Yes, Conall, it is well enough, but come in," said the king. He desired his look-out men to set a watch on the sons of Conall, and to give them meat. And a double watch was set that night on the sons of Conall.

"Now, O Conall," said the king, "were you ever in a harder place than to be seeing your lot of sons hanged tomorrow? But you set it to my goodness and to my grace, and say that it was necessity brought it on you, so I must not hang you. Tell me any case in which you were as hard as this, and if you tell that, you shall get the soul of your youngest son."

"I will tell a case as hard in which I was," said Conall. "I was once a young lad, and my father had much land, and he had parks of year-old cows, and one of them had just calved, and my father told me to bring her home. I found the cow, and took her with us. There fell a shower of snow. We went into the herd's bothy, and we took the cow and the calf in with us, and we were letting the shower pass from us. Who should come in but one cat and ten, and one great one-eyed fox-coloured cat as head bard over them. When they came in, in very deed I myself had no liking for their company. 'Strike up with you,' said the head bard, 'why should we be still? and sing a cronan to Conall Yellowclaw.' I was amazed that my name was known to the cats themselves. When they had sung the cronan, said the head bard, 'Now, O Conall, pay the reward of the cronan that the cats have sung to thee.' 'Well then,' said I myself, 'I have no reward whatsoever for you, unless you should go down and take that calf.' No sooner said I the word than the two cats and ten went down to attack the calf, and in very deed, he did not last them long. 'Play up with you, why should you be silent? Make a cronan to Conall Yellowclaw,' said the head bard. Certainly I had no liking at all for the cronan, but up came the one cat and ten, and if they did not sing me a cronan then and there! 'Pay them now their reward,' said the great fox-coloured cat. 'I am tired myself of yourselves and your rewards,' said I. 'I have no reward for you unless you take that cow down there.' They betook themselves to the cow, and indeed she did not last them long.

"'Why will you be silent? Go up and sing a cronan to Conall Yellowclaw,' said the head bard. And surely, oh king, I had no care for them or for their cronan, for I began to see that they were not good comrades. When they had sung me the cronan they betook themselves down where the head bard was. 'Pay now their reward, said the head bard; and for sure, oh king, I had no reward for them; and I said to them, 'I have no reward for you.' And surely, oh king, there was catterwauling between them. So I leapt out at a turf window that was at the back of the house. I took myself off as hard as I might into the wood. I was swift enough and strong at that time; and when I felt the rustling toirm of the cats after me I climbed into as high a tree as I saw in the place, and one that was close in the top; and I hid myself as well as I might. The cats began to search for me through the wood, and they could not find me; and when they were tired, each one said to the other that they would turn back. 'But,' said the one-eyed fox-coloured cat that was commander-in-chief over them, 'you saw him not with your two eyes, and though I have but one eye, there's the rascal up in the tree.' When he had said that, one of them went up in the tree, and as he was coming where I was, I drew a weapon that I had and I killed him. 'Be this from me!' said the one-eyed one—'I must not be losing my company thus; gather round the root of the tree and dig about it, and let down that villain to earth.' On this they gathered about the tree, and they dug about the root, and the first branching root that they cut, she gave a shiver to fall, and I myself gave a shout, and it was not to be wondered at.

"There was in the neighbourhood of the wood a priest, and he had ten men with him delving, and he said, 'There is a shout of a man in extremity and I must not be without replying to it.' And the wisest of the men said, 'Let it alone till we hear it again.' The cats began again digging wildly, and they broke the next root; and I myself gave the next shout, and in very deed it was not a weak one. 'Certainly,' said the priest, 'it is a man in extremity—let us move.' They set themselves in order for moving. And the cats arose on the tree, and they broke the third root, and the tree fell on her elbow. Then I gave the third shout. The stalwart men hastened, and when they saw how the cats served the tree, they began at them with the spades; and they themselves and the cats began at each other, till the cats ran away. And surely, oh king, I did not move till I saw the last one of them off. And then I came home. And there's the hardest case in which I ever was; and it seems to me that tearing by the cats were harder than hanging tomorrow by the king of Lochlann."

"Och! Conall," said the king, "you are full of words. You have freed the soul of your son with your tale; and if you tell me a harder case than that you will get your second youngest son, and then you will have two sons."

"Well then," said Conall, "on condition that thou dost that, I will tell thee how I was once in a harder case than to be in thy power in prison tonight."

"Let's hear," said the king.

"I was then," said Conall, "quite a young lad, and I went out hunting, and my father's land was beside the sea, and it was rough with rocks, caves, and rifts. When I was going on the top of the shore, I saw as if there were a smoke coming up between two rocks, and I began to look what might be the meaning of the smoke coming up there. When I was looking, what should I do but fall; and the place was so full of heather, that neither bone nor skin was broken. I knew not how I should get out of this. I was not looking before me, but I kept looking overhead the way I came—and thinking that the day would never come that I could get up there. It was terrible for me to be there till I should die. I heard a great clattering coming, and what was there but a great giant and two dozen of goats with him, and a buck at their head. And when the giant had tied the goats, he came up and he said to me, 'Hao O! Conall, it's long since my knife has been rusting in my pouch waiting for thy tender flesh.' 'Och!' said I, 'it's not much you will be bettered by me, though you should tear me asunder; I will make but one meal for you. But I see that you are one-eyed. I am a good leech, and I will give you the sight of the other eye.' The giant went and he drew the great caldron on the site of the fire. I myself was telling him how he should heat the water, so that I should give its sight to the other eye. I got heather and I made a rubber of it, and I set him upright in the caldron. I began at the eye that was well, pretending to him that I would give its sight to the other one, till I left them as bad as each other; and surely it was easier to spoil the one that was well than to give sight to the other.

"When he saw that he could not see a glimpse, and when I myself said to him that I would get out in spite of him, he gave a spring out of the water, and he stood in the mouth of the cave, and he said that he would have revenge for the sight of his eye. I had but to stay there crouched the length of the night, holding in my breath in such a way that he might not find out where I was.

"When he felt the birds calling in the morning, and knew that the day was, he said—'Art thou sleeping? Awake and let out my lot of goats.' I killed the buck. He cried, 'I do believe that thou art killing my buck.'

"'I am not,' said I, 'but the ropes are so tight that I take long to loose them.' I let out one of the goats, and there he was caressing her, and he said to her, 'There thou art thou shaggy, hairy white goat; and thou seest me, but I see thee not.' I kept letting them out by the way of one and one, as I flayed the buck, and before the last one was out I had him flayed bag-wise. Then I went and I put my legs in place of his legs, and my hands in place of his forelegs, and my head in place of his head, and the horns on top of my head, so that the brute might think that it was the buck. I went out. When I was going out the giant laid his hand on me, and he said, 'There thou art, thou pretty buck; thou seest me, but I see thee not.' When I myself got out, and I saw the world about me, surely, oh, king! joy was on me. When I was out and had shaken the skin off me, I said to the brute, 'I am out now in spite of you.'

"'Aha!' said he, 'hast thou done this to me. Since thou wert so stalwart that thou hast got out, I will give thee a ring that I have here; keep the ring, and it will do thee good.'

"'I will not take the ring from you,' said I, 'but throw it, and I will take it with me.' He threw the ring on the flat ground, I went myself and I lifted the ring, and I put it on my finger. When he said me then, 'Is the ring fitting thee?' I said to him, 'It is.' Then he said, 'Where art thou, ring?' And the ring said, 'I am here.' The brute went and went towards where the ring was speaking, and now I saw that I was in a harder case than ever I was. I drew a dirk. I cut the finger from off me, and I threw it from me as far as I could out on the loch, and there was a great depth in the place. He shouted, 'Where art thou, ring?' And the ring said, 'I am here,' though it was on the bed of ocean. He gave a spring after the ring, and out he went in the sea. And I was as pleased then when I saw him drowning, as though you should grant my own life and the life of my two sons with me, and not lay any more trouble on me.

"When the giant was drowned I went in, and I took with me all he had of gold and silver, and I went home, and surely great joy was on my people when I arrived. And as a sign now look, the finger is off me."

"Yes, indeed, Conall, you are wordy and wise," said the king. "I see the finger is off you. You have freed your two sons, but tell me a case in which you ever were that is harder than to be looking on your son being hanged tomorrow, and you shall get the soul of your eldest son."

"Then went my father," said Conall, "and he got me a wife, and I was married. I went to hunt. I was going beside the sea, and I saw an island over in the midst of the loch, and I came there where a boat was with a rope before her, and a rope behind her, and many precious things within her. I looked myself on the boat to see how I might get part of them. I put in the one foot, and the other foot was on the ground, and when I raised my head what was it but the boat over in the middle of the loch, and she never stopped till she reached the island. When I went out of the boat the boat returned where she was before. I did not know now what I should do. The place was without meat or clothing, without the appearance of a house on it. I came out on the top of a hill. Then I came to a glen; I saw in it, at the bottom of a hollow, a woman with a child, and the child was naked on her knee, and she had a knife in her hand. She tried to put the knife to the throat of the babe, and the babe began to laugh in her face, and she began to cry, and she threw the knife behind her. I thought to myself that I was near my foe and far from my friends, and I called to the woman, 'What are you doing here?' And she said to me, 'What brought you here?' I told her myself word upon word how I came. 'Well then,' said she, 'it was so I came also.' She showed me to the place where I should come in where she was. I went in, and I said to her, 'What was the matter that you were putting the knife on the neck of the child?' 'It is that he must be cooked for the giant who is here, or else no more of my world will be before me.' Just then we could be hearing the footsteps of the giant, 'What shall I do? what shall I do?' cried the woman. I went to the caldron, and by luck it was not hot, so in it I got just as the brute came in. 'Hast thou boiled that youngster for me?' he cried. 'He's not done yet,' said she, and I cried out from the caldron, 'Mammy, mammy, it's boiling I am.' Then the giant laughed out HAI, HAW, HOGARAICH, and heaped on wood under the caldron.

"And now I was sure I would scald before I could get out of that. As fortune favoured me, the brute slept beside the caldron. There I was scalded by the bottom of the caldron. When she perceived that he was asleep, she set her mouth quietly to the hole that was in the lid, and she said to me 'was I alive?' I said I was. I put up my head, and the hole in the lid was so large, that my head went through easily. Everything was coming easily with me till I began to bring up my hips. I left the skin of my hips behind me, but I came out. When I got out of the caldron I knew not what to do; and she said to me that there was no weapon that would kill him but his own weapon. I began to draw his spear and every breath that he drew I thought I would be down his throat, and when his breath came out I was back again just as far. But with every ill that befell me I got the spear loosed from him. Then I was as one under a bundle of straw in a great wind for I could not manage the spear. And it was fearful to look on the brute, who had but one eye in the midst of his face; and it was not agreeable for the like of me to attack him. I drew the dart as best I could, and I set it in his eye. When he felt this he gave his head a lift, and he struck the other end of the dart on the top of the cave, and it went through to the back of his head. And he fell cold dead where he was; and you may be sure, oh king, that joy was on me. I myself and the woman went out on clear ground, and we passed the night there. I went and got the boat with which I came, and she was no way lightened, and took the woman and the child over on dry land; and I returned home."

The king of Lochlann's mother was putting on a fire at this time, and listening to Conall telling the tale about the child.

"Is it you," said she, "that were there?"

"Well then," said he, "'twas I."

"Och! och!" said she, "'twas I that was there, and the king is the child whose life you saved; and it is to you that life thanks should be given." Then they took great joy.

The king said, "Oh, Conall, you came through great hardships. And now the brown horse is yours, and his sack full of the most precious things that are in my treasury."

They lay down that night, and if it was early that Conall rose, it was earlier than that that the queen was on foot making ready. He got the brown horse and his sack full of gold and silver and stones of great price, and then Conall and his three sons went away, and they returned home to the Erin realm of gladness. He left the gold and silver in his house, and he went with the horse to the king. They were good friends evermore. He returned home to his wife, and they set in order a feast; and that was a feast if ever there was one, oh son and brother.

The Wooing of Olwen

SHORTLY AFTER THE BIRTH of Kilhuch, the son of King Kilyth, his mother died. Before her death she charged the king that he should not take a wife again until he saw a briar with two blossoms upon her grave, and the king sent every morning to see if anything were growing thereon. After many years the briar appeared, and he took to wife the widow of King Doged. She foretold to her stepson, Kilhuch, that it was his destiny to marry a maiden named Olwen, or none other, and he, at his father's bidding, went to the court of his cousin, King Arthur, to ask as a boon the hand of the maiden. He rode upon a grey steed with shell-formed hoofs, having a bridle of linked gold, and a saddle also of gold. In his hand were two spears of silver, well-tempered, headed with steel, of an edge to wound the wind and cause blood to flow, and swifter than the fall of the dew-drop from the blade of reed grass upon the earth when the dew of June is at its heaviest. A gold-hilted sword was on his thigh, and the blade was of gold, having inlaid upon it a cross of the hue of the lightning of heaven. Two brindled, white-breasted greyhounds, with strong collars of rubies, sported round him, and his courser cast up four sods with its four hoofs like four swallows about his head. Upon the steed was a four-cornered cloth of purple, and an apple of gold was at each corner. Precious gold was upon the stirrups and shoes, and the blade of grass bent not beneath them, so light was the courser's tread as he went towards the gate of King Arthur's palace.

Arthur received him with great ceremony, and asked him to remain at the palace; but the youth replied that he came not to consume meat and drink, but to ask a boon of the king.

Then said Arthur, "Since thou wilt not remain here, chieftain, thou shalt receive the boon, whatsoever thy tongue may name, as far as the wind dries and the rain moistens, and the sun revolves, and the sea encircles, and the earth extends, save only my ships and my mantle, my sword, my lance, my shield, my dagger, and Guinevere my wife."

So Kilhuch craved of him the hand of Olwen, the daughter of Yspathaden

Penkawr, and also asked the favour and aid of all Arthur's court.

Then said Arthur, "O chieftain, I have never heard of the maiden of whom thou speakest, nor of her kindred, but I will gladly send messengers in search of her."

And the youth said, "I will willingly grant from this night to that at the end of the year to do so."

Then Arthur sent messengers to every land within his dominions to seek for the maiden; and at the end of the year Arthur's messengers returned without having gained any knowledge or information concerning Olwen more than on the first day.

Then said Kilhuch, "Every one has received his boon, and I yet lack mine. I will depart and bear away thy honour with me."

Then said Kay, "Rash chieftain! dost thou reproach Arthur? Go with us, and we will not part until thou dost either confess that the maiden exists not in the world, or until we obtain her."

Thereupon Kay rose up.

Kay had this peculiarity, that his breath lasted nine nights and nine days under water, and he could exist nine nights and nine days without sleep. A wound from Kay's sword no physician could heal. Very subtle was Kay. When it pleased him he could render himself as tall as the highest tree in the forest. And he had another peculiarity—so great was the heat of his nature, that, when it rained hardest, whatever he carried remained dry for a handbreadth above and a handbreadth below his hand; and when his companions were coldest, it was to them as fuel with which to light their fire.

And Arthur called Bedwyr, who never shrank from any enterprise upon which Kay was bound. None was equal to him in swiftness throughout this island except Arthur and Drych Ail Kibthar. And although he was one-handed, three warriors could not shed blood faster than he on the field of battle. Another property he had; his lance would produce a wound equal to those of nine opposing lances.

And Arthur called to Kynthelig the guide. "Go thou upon this expedition with the Chieftain." For as good a guide was he in a land which he had never seen as he was in his own.

He called Gwrhyr Gwalstawt Ieithoedd, because he knew all tongues.

He called Gwalchmai, the son of Gwyar, because he never returned home without achieving the adventure of which he went in quest. He was the best of footmen and the best of knights. He was nephew to Arthur, the son of his sister, and his cousin.

And Arthur called Menw, the son of Teirgwaeth, in order that if they went into a savage country, he might cast a charm and an illusion over them, so that none might see them whilst they could see every one.

They journeyed on till they came to a vast open plain, wherein they saw a great castle, which was the fairest in the world. But so far away was it that at night it seemed no nearer, and they scarcely reached it on the third day. When they came before the castle they beheld a vast flock of sheep, boundless and without end. They told their errand to the herdsman, who endeavoured to dissuade them, since none who had come thither on that quest had returned alive. They gave to him a gold ring, which he conveyed to his wife, telling her who the visitors were.

On the approach of the latter, she ran out with joy to greet them, and sought to throw her arms about their necks. But Kay, snatching a billet out of the pile, placed the log between her two hands, and she squeezed it so that it became a twisted coil.

"O woman," said Kay, "if thou hadst squeezed me thus, none could ever again have set their affections on me. Evil love were this."

They entered the house, and after meat she told them that the maiden Olwen came there every Saturday to wash. They pledged their faith that they would not harm her, and a message was sent to her. So Olwen came, clothed in a robe of flame-coloured silk, and with a collar of ruddy gold, in which were emeralds and rubies, about her neck. More golden was her hair than the flower of the broom, and her skin was whiter than the foam of the wave, and fairer were her hands and her fingers than the blossoms of the wood anemone amidst the spray of the meadow fountain. Brighter were her glances than those of a falcon; her bosom was more snowy than the breast of the white swan, her cheek redder than the reddest roses. Whoso beheld was filled with her love. Four white trefoils sprang up wherever she trod, and therefore was she called Olwen.

Then Kilhuch, sitting beside her on a bench, told her his love, and she said that he would win her as his bride if he granted whatever her father asked.

Accordingly they went up to the castle and laid their request before him.

"Raise up the forks beneath my two eyebrows which have fallen over my eyes," said Yspathaden Penkawr, "that I may see the fashion of my son-in-law."

They did so, and he promised, them an answer on the morrow. But as they were going forth, Yspathaden seized one of the three poisoned darts that lay beside him and threw it back after them.

And Bedwyr caught it and flung it back, wounding Yspathaden in the knee.

Then said he, "A cursed ungentle son-in-law, truly. I shall ever walk the worse for his rudeness. This poisoned iron pains me like the bite of a gad-fly. Cursed be the smith who forged it, and the anvil whereon it was wrought."

The knights rested in the house of Custennin the herdsman, but the next day at dawn they returned to the castle and renewed their request.

Yspathaden said it was necessary that he should consult Olwen's four great-grandmothers and her four great-grand-sires.

The knights again withdrew, and as they were going he took the second dart and cast it after them.

But Menw caught it and flung it back, piercing Yspathaden's breast with it, so that it came out at the small of his back.

"A cursed ungentle son-in-law, truly," says he, "the hard iron pains me like the bite of a horse-leech. Cursed be the hearth whereon it was heated! Henceforth whenever I go up a hill, I shall have a scant in my breath and a pain in my chest."

On the third day the knights returned once more to the palace, and Yspathaden took the third dart and cast it at them.

But Kilhuch caught it and threw it vigorously, and wounded him through the eyeball, so that the dart came out at the back of his head.

"A cursed ungentle son-in-law, truly. As long as I remain alive my eyesight will be the worse. Whenever I go against the wind my eyes will water, and peradventure my head will burn, and I shall have a giddiness every new moon. Cursed be the fire in which it was forged. Like the bite of a mad dog is the stroke of this poisoned iron."

And they went to meat.

Said Yspathaden Penkawr, "Is it thou that seekest my daughter?"

"It is I," answered Kilhuch.

"I must have thy pledge that thou wilt not do towards me otherwise than is just, and when I have gotten that which I shall name, my daughter thou shalt have."

"I promise thee that willingly," said Kilhuch, "name what thou wilt."

"I will do so," said he.

"Throughout the world there is not a comb or scissors with which I can arrange my hair, on, account of its rankness, except the comb and scissors that are between the two ears of Turch Truith, the son of Prince Tared. He will not give them of his own free will, and thou wilt not be able to compel him."

"It will be easy for me to compass this, although thou mayest think that it will not be easy."

"Though thou get this, there is yet that which thou wilt not get. It will not be possible to hunt Turch Truith without Drudwyn the whelp of Greid, the son of Eri, and know that throughout the world there is not a huntsman who can hunt with this dog, except Mabon the son of Modron. He was taken from his mother when three nights old, and it is not known where he now is, nor whether he is living or dead."

"It will be easy for me to compass this, although thou mayest think that it will not be easy."

"Though thou get this, there is yet that which thou wilt not get. Thou wilt not get Mabon, for it is not known where he is, unless thou find Eidoel, his kinsman in blood, the son of Aer. For it would be useless to seek for him. He is his cousin."

"It will be easy for me to compass this, although thou mayest think that it will not be easy. Horses shall I have, and chivalry; and my lord and kinsman Arthur will obtain for me all these things. And I shall gain thy daughter, and thou shalt lose thy life."

"Go forward. And thou shalt not be chargeable for food or raiment for my daughter while thou art seeking these things; and when thou hast compassed all these marvels, thou shalt have my daughter for wife."

Now, when they told Arthur how they had sped, Arthur said, "Which of these marvels will it be best for us to seek first?"

"It will be best," said they, "to seek Mabon the son of Modron; and he will not be found unless we first find Eidoel, the son of Aer, his kinsman."

Then Arthur rose up, and the warriors of the Islands of Britain with him, to seek for Eidoel; and they proceeded until they came before the castle of Glivi, where Eidoel was imprisoned.

Glivi stood on the summit of his castle, and said, "Arthur, what requirest thou of me, since nothing remains to me in this fortress, and I have neither joy nor pleasure in it; neither wheat nor oats?"

Said Arthur, "Not to injure thee came I hither, but to seek for the prisoner that is with thee."

"I will give thee my prisoner, though I had not thought to give him up to any one; and therewith shalt thou have my support and my aid."

His followers then said unto Arthur, "Lord, go thou home, thou canst not proceed with thy host in quest of such small adventures as these."

Then said Arthur, "It were well for thee, Gwrhyr Gwalstawt Ieithoedd, to go upon this quest, for thou knowest all languages, and art familiar with those of the birds and the beasts. Go, Eidoel, likewise with my men in search of thy cousin. And as for you, Kay and Bedwyr, I have hope of whatever adventure ye are in quest of, that ye will achieve it. Achieve ye this adventure for me."

These went forward until they came to the Ousel of Cilgwri, and Gwrhyr adjured her for the sake of Heaven, saying, "Tell me if thou knowest aught of Mabon, the son of Modron, who was taken when three nights old from between his mother and the wall."

And the Ousel answered, "When I first came here there was a smith's anvil in this place, and I was then a young bird, and from that time no work has been done upon it, save the pecking of my beak every evening, and now there is not so much as the size of a nut remaining thereof; yet the vengeance of Heaven be upon me if during all that time I have ever heard of the man for whom you inquire. Nevertheless, there is a race of animals who were formed before me, and I will be your guide to them."

So they proceeded to the place where was the Stag of Redynvre.

"Stag of Redynvre, behold we are come to thee, an embassy from Arthur, for we have not heard of any animal older than thou. Say, knowest thou aught of Mabon?"

The stag said, "When first I came hither there was a plain all around me, without any trees save one oak sapling, which grew up to be an oak with an hundred branches. And that oak has since perished, so that now nothing remains of it but the withered stump; and from that day to this I have been here, yet have I never heard of the man for whom you inquire. Nevertheless, I will be your guide to the place where there is an animal which was formed before I was."

So they proceeded to the place where was the Owl of Cwm Cawlwyd, to inquire of him concerning Mabon.

And the owl said, "If I knew I would tell you. When first I came hither, the wide valley you see was a wooded glen. And a race of men came and rooted it up. And there grew there a second wood, and this wood is the third. My wings, are they not withered stumps? Yet all this time, even until today, I have never heard of the man for whom you inquire. Nevertheless, I will be the guide of Arthur's embassy until you come to the place where is the oldest animal in this world, and the one who has travelled most, the eagle of Gwern Abwy."

When they came to the eagle, Gwrhyr asked it the same question; but it replied, "I have been here for a great space of time, and when I first came hither there was a rock here, from the top of which I pecked at the stars every evening, and now it is not so much as a span high. From that day to this I have been here, and I have never heard of the man for whom you inquire, except once when I went in search of food as far as Llyn Llyw. And when I came there, I struck my talons into a salmon, thinking he would serve me as food for a long time. But he drew me into the deep, and I was scarcely able to escape from him. After that I went with my whole kindred to attack him and to try to destroy him, but he sent messengers and made peace with me, and came and besought me to take fifty fish-spears out of his back. Unless he know something of him whom you seek, I cannot tell you who may. However, I will guide you to the place where he is."

So they went thither, and the eagle said, "Salmon of Llyn Llyw, I have come to thee with an embassy from Arthur to ask thee if thou knowest aught concerning Mabon, the son of Modron, who was taken away at three nights old from between his mother and the wall."

And the salmon answered, "As much as I know I will tell thee. With every tide I go along the river upwards, until I come near to the walls of Gloucester, and there have I found such wrong as I never found elsewhere; and to the end that ye may give credence thereto, let one of you go thither upon each of my two shoulders."

So Kay and Gwrhyr went upon his shoulders, and they proceeded till they came to the wall of the prison, and they heard a great wailing and lamenting from the dungeon. Said Gwrhyr, "Who is it that laments in this house of stone?"

And the voice replied, "Alas, it is Mabon, the son of Modron, who is here imprisoned!"

Then they returned and told Arthur, who, summoning his warriors, attacked the castle.

And whilst the fight was going on, Kay and Bedwyr, mounting on the shoulders of the fish, broke into the dungeon, and brought away with them Mabon, the son of Modron.

Then Arthur summoned unto him all the warriors that were in the three islands of Britain and in the three islands adjacent; and he went as far as Esgeir Ocrvel in Ireland where the Boar Truith was with his seven young pigs. And the dogs were let loose upon him from all sides. But he wasted the fifth part of Ireland, and then set forth through the sea to Wales. Arthur and his hosts, and his horses, and his dogs followed hard after him. But ever and awhile the boar made a stand, and many a champion of Arthur's did he slay. Throughout all Wales did Arthur follow him, and one by one the young pigs were killed. At length, when he would fain have crossed the Severn and escaped into Cornwall, Mabon the son of Modron came up with him, and Arthur fell upon him together with the champions of Britain. On the one side Mabon the son of Modron spurred his steed and snatched his razor from him, whilst Kay came up with him on the other side and took from him the scissors. But before they could obtain the comb he had regained the ground with his feet, and from the moment that he reached the shore, neither dog nor man nor horse could overtake him until he came to Cornwall. There Arthur and his hosts followed in his track until they overtook him in Cornwall. Hard had been their trouble before, but it was child's play to what they met in seeking the comb. Win it they did, and the Boar Truith they hunted into the deep sea, and it was never known whither he went.

Then Kilhuch set forward, and as many as wished ill to Yspathaden Penkawr. And they took the marvels with them to his court. And Kaw of North Britain came and shaved his beard, skin and flesh clean off to the very bone from ear to ear.

"Art thou shaved, man?" said Kilhuch.

"I am shaved," answered he.

"Is thy daughter mine now?"

"She is thine, but therefore needst thou not thank me, but Arthur who hath accomplished this for thee. By my free will thou shouldst never have had her, for with her I lose my life."

Then Goreu the son of Custennin seized him by the hair of his head and dragged him after him to the keep, and cut off his head and placed it on a stake on the citadel.

Thereafter the hosts of Arthur dispersed themselves each man to his own country.

Thus did Kilhuch son of Kelython win to wife Olwen, the daughter of
Yspathaden Penkawr.

The Battle of the Birds

I WILL TELL YOU A STORY about the wren. There was once a farmer
who was seeking a servant, and the wren met him and said: "What
are you seeking?"

"I am seeking a servant," said the farmer to the wren.

"Will you take me?" said the wren.

"You, you poor creature, what good would you do?"

"Try me," said the wren.

So he engaged him, and the first work he set him to do was threshing
in the barn. The wren threshed (what did he thresh with? Why a flail to be
sure), and he knocked off one grain. A mouse came out and she eats that.

"I'll trouble you not to do that again," said the wren.

He struck again, and he struck off two grains. Out came the mouse
and she eats them. So they arranged a contest to see who was strongest,
and the wren brings his twelve birds, and the mouse her tribe.

"You have your tribe with you," said the wren.

"As well as yourself," said the mouse, and she struck out her leg
proudly. But the wren broke it with his flail, and there was a pitched
battle on a set day.

When every creature and bird was gathering to battle, the son of the
king of Tethertown said that he would go to see the battle, and that
he would bring sure word home to his father the king, who would be
king of the creatures this year. The battle was over before he arrived all
but one fight, between a great black raven and a snake. The snake was
twined about the raven's neck, and the raven held the snake's throat in
his beak, and it seemed as if the snake would get the victory over the
raven. When the king's son saw this he helped the raven, and with one

blow takes the head off the snake. When the raven had taken breath, and saw that the snake was dead, he said, "For thy kindness to me this day, I will give thee a sight. Come up now on the root of my two wings." The king's son put his hands about the raven before his wings, and, before he stopped, he took him over nine Bens, and nine Glens, and nine Mountain Moors.

"Now," said the raven, "see you that house yonder? Go now to it. It is a sister of mine that makes her dwelling in it; and I will go bail that you are welcome. And if she asks you, Were you at the battle of the birds? say you were. And if she asks, 'Did you see any one like me,' say you did, but be sure that you meet me tomorrow morning here, in this place." The king's son got good and right good treatment that night. Meat of each meat, drink of each drink, warm water to his feet, and a soft bed for his limbs.

On the next day the raven gave him the same sight over six Bens, and six Glens, and six Mountain Moors. They saw a bothy far off, but, though far off, they were soon there. He got good treatment this night, as before—plenty of meat and drink, and warm water to his feet, and a soft bed to his limbs—and on the next day it was the same thing, over three Bens and three Glens, and three Mountain Moors.

On the third morning, instead of seeing the raven as at the other times, who should meet him but the handsomest lad he ever saw, with gold rings in his hair, with a bundle in his hand. The king's son asked this lad if he had seen a big black raven.

Said the lad to him, "You will never see the raven again, for I am that raven. I was put under spells by a bad druid; it was meeting you that loosed me, and for that you shall get this bundle. Now," said the lad, "you must turn back on the self-same steps, and lie a night in each house as before; but you must not loose the bundle which I gave ye, till in the place where you would most wish to dwell."

The king's son turned his back to the lad, and his face to his father's house; and he got lodging from the raven's sisters, just as he got it when going forward. When he was nearing his father's house he was going through a close wood. It seemed to him that the bundle was growing heavy, and he thought he would look what was in it.

When he loosed the bundle he was astonished. In a twinkling he sees the very grandest place he ever saw. A great castle, and an orchard about the castle, in which was every kind of fruit and herb. He stood full of wonder and regret for having loosed the bundle—for it was not in his power to put it back again—and he would have wished this pretty place to be in the pretty little green hollow that was opposite his father's house; but he looked up and saw a great giant coming towards him.

"Bad's the place where you have built the house, king's son," says the giant.

"Yes, but it is not here I would wish it to be, though it happens to be here by mishap," says the king's son.

"What's the reward for putting it back in the bundle as it was before?"

"What's the reward you would ask?" says the king's son.

"That you will give me the first son you have when he is seven years of age," says the giant.

"If I have a son you shall have him," said the king's son.

In a twinkling the giant put each garden, and orchard, and castle in the bundle as they were before.

"Now," says the giant, "take your own road, and I will take mine; but mind your promise, and if you forget I will remember."

The king's son took to the road, and at the end of a few days he reached the place he was fondest of. He loosed the bundle, and the castle was just as it was before. And when he opened the castle door he sees the handsomest maiden he ever cast eye upon.

"Advance, king's son," said the pretty maid; "everything is in order for you, if you will marry me this very day."

"It's I that am willing," said the king's son. And on the same day they married.

But at the end of a day and seven years, who should be seen coming to the castle but the giant. The king's son was reminded of his promise to the giant, and till now he had not told his promise to the queen.

"Leave the matter between me and the giant," says the queen.

"Turn out your son," says the giant; "mind your promise."

"You shall have him," says the king, "when his mother puts him in order for his journey."

The queen dressed up the cook's son, and she gave him to the giant by the hand. The giant went away with him; but he had not gone far when he put a rod in the hand of the little laddie. The giant asked him—

"If thy father had that rod what would he do with it?"

"If my father had that rod he would beat the dogs and the cats, so that they shouldn't be going near the king's meat," said the little laddie.

"Thou'rt the cook's son," said the giant. He catches him by the two small ankles and knocks him against the stone that was beside him. The giant turned back to the castle in rage and madness, and he said that if they did not send out the king's son to him, the highest stone of the castle would be the lowest.

Said the queen to the king, "We'll try it yet; the butler's son is of the same age as our son."

She dressed up the butler's son, and she gives him to the giant by the hand. The giant had not gone far when he put the rod in his hand.

"If thy father had that rod," says the giant, "what would he do with it?"

"He would beat the dogs and the cats when they would be coming near the king's bottles and glasses."

"Thou art the son of the butler," says the giant and dashed his brains out too. The giant returned in a very great rage and anger. The earth shook under the sole of his feet, and the castle shook and all that was in it.

"OUT HERE WITH THY SON," says the giant, "or in a twinkling the stone that is highest in the dwelling will be the lowest." So they had to give the king's son to the giant.

When they were gone a little bit from the earth, the giant showed him the rod that was in his hand and said: "What would thy father do with this rod if he had it?"

The king's son said: "My father has a braver rod than that."

And the giant asked him, "Where is thy father when he has that brave rod?"

And the king's son said: "He will be sitting in his kingly chair."

Then the giant understood that he had the right one.

The giant took him to his own house, and he reared him as his own son. On a day of days when the giant was from home, the lad heard the sweetest music he ever heard in a room at the top of the giant's house. At a glance he saw the finest face he had ever seen. She beckoned to him to come a bit nearer to her, and she said her name was Auburn Mary but she told him to go this time, but to be sure to be at the same place about that dead midnight.

And as he promised he did. The giant's daughter was at his side in a twinkling, and she said, "Tomorrow you will get the choice of my two sisters to marry; but say that you will not take either, but me. My father wants me to marry the son of the king of the Green City, but I don't like him." On the morrow the giant took out his three daughters, and he said:

"Now, son of the king of Tethertown, thou hast not lost by living with me so long. Thou wilt get to wife one of the two eldest of my daughters, and with her leave to go home with her the day after the wedding."

"If you will give me this pretty little one," says the king's son, "I will take you at your word."

The giant's wrath kindled, and he said: "Before thou gett'st her thou must do the three things that I ask thee to do."

"Say on," says the king's son.

The giant took him to the byre.

"Now," says the giant, "a hundred cattle are stabled here, and it has not been cleansed for seven years. I am going from home today, and if this byre is not cleaned before night comes, so clean that a golden apple will run from end to end of it, not only thou shalt not get my daughter, but 'tis only a drink of thy fresh, goodly, beautiful blood that will quench my thirst this night."

He begins cleaning the byre, but he might just as well to keep baling the great ocean. After midday when sweat was blinding him, the giant's youngest daughter came where he was, and she said to him:

"You are being punished, king's son."

"I am that," says the king's son.

"Come over," says Auburn Mary, "and lay down your weariness."

"I will do that," says he, "there is but death awaiting me, at any rate." He sat down near her. He was so tired that he fell asleep beside her. When he awoke, the giant's daughter was not to be seen, but the byre was so well cleaned that a golden apple would run from end to end of it and raise no stain. In comes the giant, and he said:

"Hast thou cleaned the byre, king's son?"

"I have cleaned it," says he.

"Somebody cleaned it," says the giant.

"You did not clean it, at all events," said the king's son.

"Well, well!" says the giant, "since thou wert so active today, thou wilt get to this time tomorrow to thatch this byre with birds' down, from birds with no two feathers of one colour."

The king's son was on foot before the sun; he caught up his bow and his quiver of arrows to kill the birds. He took to the moors, but if he did, the birds were not so easy to take. He was running after them till the sweat was blinding him. About mid-day who should come but Auburn Mary.

"You are exhausting yourself, king's son," says she.

"I am," said he.

"There fell but these two blackbirds, and both of one colour."

"Come over and lay down your weariness on this pretty hillock," says the giant's daughter.

"It's I am willing," said he.

He thought she would aid him this time, too, and he sat down near her, and he was not long there till he fell asleep.

When he awoke, Auburn Mary was gone. He thought he would go back to the house, and he sees the byre thatched with feathers. When the giant came home, he said:

"Hast thou thatched the byre, king's son?"

"I thatched it," says he.

"Somebody thatched it," says the giant.

"You did not thatch it," says the king's son.

"Yes, yes!" says the giant. "Now," says the giant, "there is a fir tree beside that loch down there, and there is a magpie's nest in its top. The eggs thou wilt find in the nest. I must have them for my first meal. Not one must be burst or broken, and there are five in the nest."

Early in the morning the king's son went where the tree was, and that tree was not hard to hit upon. Its match was not in the whole wood.

From the foot to the first branch was five hundred feet. The king's son was going all round the tree. She came who was always bringing help to him.

"You are losing the skin of your hands and feet."

"Ach! I am," says he. "I am no sooner up than down."

"This is no time for stopping," says the giant's daughter. "Now you must kill me, strip the flesh from my bones, take all those bones apart, and use them as steps for climbing the tree. When you are climbing the tree, they will stick to the glass as if they had grown out of it; but when you are coming down, and have put your foot on each one, they will drop into your hand when you touch them. Be sure and stand on each bone, leave none untouched; if you do, it will stay behind. Put all my flesh into this clean cloth by the side of the spring at the roots of the tree. When you come to the earth, arrange my bones together, put the flesh over them, sprinkle it with water from the spring, and I shall be alive before you. But don't forget a bone of me on the tree."

"How could I kill you," asked the king's son, "after what you have done for me?"

"If you won't obey, you and I are done for," said Auburn Mary. "You must climb the tree, or we are lost; and to climb the tree you must do as I say." The king's son obeyed. He killed Auburn Mary, cut the flesh from her body, and unjointed the bones, as she had told him.

As he went up, the king's son put the bones of Auburn Mary's body against the side of the tree, using them as steps, till he came under the nest and stood on the last bone.

Then he took the eggs, and coming down, put his foot on every bone, then took it with him, till he came to the last bone, which was so near the ground that he failed to touch it with his foot.

He now placed all the bones of Auburn Mary in order again at the side of the spring, put the flesh on them, sprinkled it with water from the spring. She rose up before him, and said: "Didn't I tell you not to leave a bone of my body without stepping on it? Now I am lame for life! You left my little finger on the tree without touching it, and I have but nine fingers."

"Now," says she, "go home with the eggs quickly, and you will get me to marry tonight if you can know me. I and my two sisters will be arrayed in the same garments, and made like each other, but look at me when my father says, 'Go to thy wife, king's son;' and you will see a hand without a little finger."

He gave the eggs to the giant.

"Yes, yes!" says the giant, "be making ready for your marriage."

Then, indeed, there was a wedding, and it was a wedding! Giants and gentlemen, and the son of the king of the Green City was in the midst of them. They were married, and the dancing began, that was a dance! The giant's house was shaking from top to bottom.

But bed time came, and the giant said, "It is time for thee to go to rest, son of the king of Tethertown; choose thy bride to take with thee from amidst those."

She put out the hand off which the little finger was, and he caught her by the hand.

"Thou hast aimed well this time too; but there is no knowing but we may meet thee another way," said the giant.

But to rest they went. "Now," says she, "sleep not, or else you are a dead man. We must fly quick, quick, or for certain my father will kill you."

Out they went, and on the blue grey filly in the stable they mounted. "Stop a while," says she, "and I will play a trick to the old hero." She jumped in, and cut an apple into nine shares, and she put two shares at the head of the bed, and two shares at the foot of the bed, and two shares at the door of the kitchen, and two shares at the big door, and one outside the house.

The giant awoke and called, "Are you asleep?"

"Not yet," said the apple that was at the head of the bed.

At the end of a while he called again.

"Not yet," said the apple that was at the foot of the bed.

A while after this he called again: "Are your asleep?"

"Not yet," said the apple at the kitchen door.

The giant called again.

The apple that was at the big door answered.

"You are now going far from me," says the giant.

"Not yet," says the apple that was outside the house.

"You are flying," says the giant. The giant jumped on his feet, and to the bed he went, but it was cold—empty.

"My own daughter's tricks are trying me," said the giant. "Here's after them," says he.

At the mouth of day, the giant's daughter said that her father's breath was burning her back.

"Put your hand, quick," said she, "in the ear of the grey filly, and whatever you find in it, throw it behind us."

"There is a twig of sloe tree," said he.

"Throw it behind us," said she.

No sooner did he that, than there were twenty miles of blackthorn wood, so thick that scarce a weasel could go through it.

The giant came headlong, and there he is fleecing his head and neck in the thorns.

"My own daughter's tricks are here as before," said the giant; "but if I had my own big axe and wood knife here, I would not be long making a way through this."

He went home for the big axe and the wood knife, and sure he was not long on his journey, and he was the boy behind the big axe. He was not long making a way through the blackthorn.

"I will leave the axe and the wood knife here till I return," says he.

"If you leave 'em, leave 'em," said a hoodie that was in a tree, "we'll steal 'em, steal 'em."

"If you will do that," says the giant, "I must take them home." He returned home and left them at the house.

At the heat of day the giant's daughter felt her father's breath burning her back.

"Put your finger in the filly's ear, and throw behind whatever you find in it."

He got a splinter of grey stone, and in a twinkling there were twenty miles, by breadth and height, of great grey rock behind them.

The giant came full pelt, but past the rock he could not go.

"The tricks of my own daughter are the hardest things that ever met me," says the giant; "but if I had my lever and my mighty mattock, I would not be long in making my way through this rock also."

There was no help for it, but to turn the chase for them; and he was the boy to split the stones. He was not long in making a road through the rock.

"I will leave the tools here, and I will return no more."

"If you leave 'em, leave 'em," says the hoodie, "we will steal 'em, steal 'em."

"Do that if you will; there is no time to go back."

At the time of breaking the watch, the giant's daughter said that she felt her father's breath burning her back.

"Look in the filly's ear, king's son, or else we are lost."

He did so, and it was a bladder of water that was in her ear this time. He threw it behind him and there was a fresh-water loch, twenty miles in length and breadth, behind them.

The giant came on, but with the speed he had on him, he was in the middle of the loch, and he went under, and he rose no more.

On the next day the young companions were come in sight of his father's house. "Now," says she, "my father is drowned, and he won't trouble us any more; but before we go further," says she, "go you to your father's house, and tell that you have the likes of me; but let neither man nor creature kiss you, for if you do, you will not remember that you have ever seen me."

Every one he met gave him welcome and luck, and he charged his father and mother not to kiss him; but as mishap was to be, an old greyhound was indoors, and she knew him, and jumped up to his mouth, and after that he did not remember the giant's daughter.

She was sitting at the well's side as he left her, but the king's son was not coming. In the mouth of night she climbed up into a tree of oak that was beside the well, and she lay in the fork of that tree all night. A shoemaker had a house near the well, and about mid-day on the morrow, the shoemaker asked his wife to go for a drink for him out of the well. When the shoemaker's wife reached the well, and when she saw the shadow of her that was in the tree, thinking it was her own shadow—and she never thought till now that she was so handsome—, she gave a cast to the dish that was in her hand, and it was broken on the ground, and she took herself to the house without vessel or water.

"Where is the water, wife?" said the shoemaker.

"You shambling, contemptible old carle, without grace, I have stayed too long your water and wood thrall."

"I think, wife, that you have turned crazy. Go you, daughter, quickly, and fetch a drink for your father."

His daughter went, and in the same way so it happened to her. She never thought till now that she was so lovable, and she took herself home.

"Up with the drink," said her father.

"You home-spun shoe carle, do you think I am fit to be your thrall?"

The poor shoemaker thought that they had taken a turn in their understandings, and he went himself to the well. He saw the shadow of the maiden in the well, and he looked up to the tree, and he sees the finest woman he ever saw.

"Your seat is wavering, but your face is fair," said the shoemaker.

"Come down, for there is need of you for a short while at my house."

The shoemaker understood that this was the shadow that had driven his people mad. The shoemaker took her to his house, and he said that he had but a poor bothy, but that she should get a share of all that was in it.

One day, the shoemaker had shoes ready, for on that very day the king's son was to be married. The shoemaker was going to the castle with the shoes of the young people, and the girl said to the shoemaker, "I would like to get a sight of the king's son before he marries."

"Come with me," says the shoemaker, "I am well acquainted with the servants at the castle, and you shall get a sight of the king's son and all the company."

And when the gentles saw the pretty woman that was here they took her to the wedding-room, and they filled for her a glass of wine. When she was going to drink what is in it, a flame went up out of the glass, and a golden pigeon and a silver pigeon sprang out of it. They were flying about when three grains of barley fell on the floor. The silver pigeon sprung, and ate that up.

Said the golden pigeon to him, "If you remembered when I cleared the byre, you would not eat that without giving me a share."

Again there fell three other grains of barley, and the silver pigeon sprung, and ate that up as before.

"If you remembered when I thatched the byre, you would not eat that without giving me my share," says the golden pigeon.

Three other grains fall, and the silver pigeon sprung, and ate that up.

"If you remembered when I harried the magpie's nest, you would not eat that without giving me my share," says the golden pigeon; "I lost my little finger bringing it down, and I want it still."

The king's son minded, and he knew who it was that was before him.

"Well," said the king's son to the guests at the feast, "when I was a little younger than I am now, I lost the key of a casket that I had. I had a new key made, but after it was brought to me I found the old one. Now, I'll leave it to any one here to tell me what I am to do. Which of the keys should I keep?"

"My advice to you," said one of the guests, "is to keep the old key, for it fits the lock better and you're more used to it."

Then the king's son stood up and said: "I thank you for a wise advice and an honest word. This is my bride the daughter of the giant who saved my life at the risk of her own. I'll have her and no other woman."

So the king's son married Auburn Mary and the wedding lasted long and all were happy. But all I got was butter on a live coal, porridge in a basket, and they sent me for water to the stream, and the paper shoes came to an end.

The Lad with the Goat-Skin

LONG AGO, a poor widow woman lived down near the iron forge, by Enniscorth, and she was so poor she had no clothes to put on her son; so she used to fix him in the ash-hole, near the fire, and pile the warm ashes about him; and according as he grew up, she sunk the pit deeper. At last, by hook or by crook, she got a goat-skin, and fastened it round his waist, and he felt quite grand, and took a walk down the street. So says she to him next morning, "Tom, you thief, you never done any good yet, and you six foot high, and past nineteen;—take that rope and bring me a faggot from the wood."

"Never say't twice, mother," says Tom—"here goes."

When he had it gathered and tied, what should come up but a big giant, nine foot high, and made a lick of a club at him. Well become Tom, he jumped a-one side, and picked up a ram-pike; and the first crack he gave the big fellow, he made him kiss the clod.

"If you have e'er a prayer," says Tom, "now's the time to say it, before I make fragments of you."

"I have no prayers," says the giant; "but if you spare my life I'll give you that club; and as long as you keep from sin, you'll win every battle you ever fight with it."

Tom made no bones about letting him off; and as soon as he got the club in his hands, he sat down on the bresna, and gave it a tap with the kippeen, and says, "Faggot, I had great trouble gathering you, and run the risk of my life for you, the least you can do is to carry me home." And sure enough, the wind o' the word was all it wanted. It went off through the wood, groaning and crackling, till it came to the widow's door.

Well, when the sticks were all burned, Tom was sent off again to pick more; and this time he had to fight with a giant that had two heads on him. Tom had a little more trouble with him—that's all; and the prayers he said, was to give Tom a fife; that nobody could help dancing when he was playing it. Begonies, he made the big faggot dance home, with himself sitting on it. The next giant was a beautiful boy with three heads on him. He had neither prayers nor catechism no more nor the others; and so he gave Tom a bottle of green ointment, that wouldn't let you be burned, nor scalded, nor wounded. "And now," says he, "there's no more of us. You may come and gather sticks here till little Lunacy Day in Harvest, without giant or fairy-man to disturb you."

Well, now, Tom was prouder nor ten paycocks, and used to take a walk down street in the heel of the evening; but some o' the little boys had no more manners than if they were Dublin jackeens, and put out their tongues at Tom's club and Tom's goat-skin. He didn't like that at all, and it would be mean to give one of them a clout. At last, what should come through the town but a kind of a bellman, only it's a big bugle he had, and a huntsman's cap on his head, and a kind of a painted shirt. So this—he wasn't a bellman, and I don't know what to call him—bugleman, maybe, proclaimed that the King of Dublin's daughter was so melancholy that she didn't give a laugh for seven years, and that her father would grant her in marriage to whoever could make her laugh three times.

"That's the very thing for me to try," says Tom; and so, without burning any more daylight, he kissed his mother, curled his club at the little boys, and off he set along the yalla highroad to the town of Dublin.

At last Tom came to one of the city gates, and the guards laughed and cursed at him instead of letting him in. Tom stood it all for a little time, but at last one of them—out of fun, as he said—drove his bayonet half an inch or so into his side. Tom done nothing but take the fellow by the scruff o' the neck and the waistband of his corduroys, and fling him into the canal. Some run to pull the fellow out, and others to let manners into the vulgarian with their swords and daggers; but a tap from his club sent them headlong into the moat or down on the stones, and they were soon begging him to stay his hands.

So at last one of them was glad enough to show Tom the way to the palace-yard; and there was the king, and the queen, and the princess, in a gallery, looking at all sorts of wrestling, and sword-playing, and long-dances, and mumming, all to please the princess; but not a smile came over her handsome face.

Well, they all stopped when they seen the young giant, with his boy's face, and long black hair, and his short curly beard—for his poor mother couldn't afford to buy razors—and his great strong arms, and bare legs, and no covering but the goat-skin that reached from his waist to his knees. But an envious wizened bit of a fellow, with a red head, that wished to be married to the princess, and didn't like how she opened her eyes at Tom, came forward, and asked his business very snappishly.

"My business," says Tom, says he, "is to make the beautiful princess, God bless her, laugh three times."

"Do you see all them merry fellows and skilful swordsmen," says the other, "that could eat you up with a grain of salt, and not a mother's soul of 'em ever got a laugh from her these seven years?"

So the fellows gathered round Tom, and the bad man aggravated him till he told them he didn't care a pinch o' snuff for the whole bilin' of 'em; let 'em come on, six at a time, and try what they could do.

The king, who was too far off to hear what they were saying, asked what did the stranger want.

"He wants," says the red-headed fellow, "to make hares of your best men."

"Oh!" says the king, "if that's the way, let one of 'em turn out and try his mettle."

So one stood forward, with sword and pot-lid, and made a cut at Tom. He struck the fellow's elbow with the club, and up over their heads flew the sword, and down went the owner of it on the gravel from a thump he got on the helmet. Another took his place, and another, and another, and then half a dozen at once, and Tom sent swords, helmets, shields, and bodies, rolling over and over, and themselves bawling out that they were kilt, and disabled, and damaged, and rubbing their poor elbows and hips, and limping away. Tom contrived not to kill any one; and the princess was so amused, that she let a great sweet laugh out of her that was heard over all the yard.

"King of Dublin," says Tom, "I've quarter your daughter."

And the king didn't know whether he was glad or sorry, and all the blood in the princess's heart run into her cheeks.

So there was no more fighting that day, and Tom was invited to dine with the royal family. Next day, Redhead told Tom of a wolf, the size of a yearling heifer, that used to be serenading about the walls, and eating people and cattle; and said what a pleasure it would give the king to have it killed.

"With all my heart," says Tom; "send a jackeen to show me where he lives, and we'll see how he behaves to a stranger."

The princess was not well pleased, for Tom looked a different person with fine clothes and a nice green birredh over his long curly hair; and besides, he'd got one laugh out of her. However, the king gave his consent; and in an hour and a half the horrible wolf was walking into the palace-yard, and Tom a step or two behind, with his club on his shoulder, just as a shepherd would be walking after a pet lamb.

The king and queen and princess were safe up in their gallery, but the officers and people of the court that wor padrowling about the great bawn, when they saw the big baste coming in, gave themselves up, and began to make for doors and gates; and the wolf licked his chops, as if he was saying, "Wouldn't I enjoy a breakfast off a couple of yez!"

The king shouted out, "O Tom with the Goat-skin, take away that terrible wolf, and you must have all my daughter."

But Tom didn't mind him a bit. He pulled out his flute and began to play like vengeance; and dickens a man or boy in the yard but began shovelling away heel and toe, and the wolf himself was obliged to get on his hind legs and dance "Tatther Jack Walsh," along with the rest. A good deal of the people got inside, and shut the doors, the way the hairy fellow wouldn't pin them; but Tom kept playing, and the outsiders kept dancing and shouting, and the wolf kept dancing and roaring with the pain his legs were giving him; and all the time he had his eyes on Redhead, who was shut out along with the rest. Wherever Redhead went, the wolf followed, and kept one eye on him and the other on Tom, to see if he would give him leave to eat him. But Tom shook his head, and never stopped the tune, and Redhead never stopped dancing and bawling, and the wolf dancing and roaring, one leg up and the other down, and he ready to drop out of his standing from fair tiresomeness.

When the princess seen that there was no fear of any one being kilt, she was so divarted by the stew that Redhead was in, that she gave another great laugh; and well become Tom, out he cried, "King of Dublin, I have two halves of your daughter."

"Oh, halves or alls," says the king, "put away that divel of a wolf, and we'll see about it."

So Tom put his flute in his pocket, and says he to the baste that was sittin' on his currabingo ready to faint, "Walk off to your mountain, my fine fellow, and live like a respectable baste; and if ever I find you come within seven miles of any town, I'll—"

He said no more, but spit in his fist, and gave a flourish of his club. It was all the poor divel of a wolf wanted: he put his tail between his legs, and took to his pumps without looking at man or mortal, and neither sun, moon, or stars ever saw him in sight of Dublin again.

At dinner every one laughed but the foxy fellow; and sure enough he was laying out how he'd settle poor Tom next day.

"Well, to be sure!" says he, "King of Dublin, you are in luck. There's the Danes moidhering us to no end. Deuce run to Lusk wid 'em! and if any one can save us from 'em, it is this gentleman with the goat-skin. There is a flail hangin' on the collar-beam, in hell, and neither Dane nor devil can stand before it."

"So," says Tom to the king, "will you let me have the other half of the princess if I bring you the flail?"

"No, no," says the princess; "I'd rather never be your wife than see you in that danger."

But Redhead whispered and nudged Tom about how shabby it would look to reneague the adventure. So he asked which way he was to go, and Redhead directed him.

Well, he travelled and travelled, till he came in sight of the walls of hell; and, bedad, before he knocked at the gates, he rubbed himself over with the greenish ointment. When he knocked, a hundred little imps popped their heads out through the bars, and axed him what he wanted.

"I want to speak to the big divel of all," says Tom: "open the gate."

It wasn't long till the gate was thrune open, and the Ould Boy received Tom with bows and scrapes, and axed his business.

"My business isn't much," says Tom. "I only came for the loan of that flail that I see hanging on the collar-beam, for the king of Dublin to give a thrashing to the Danes."

"Well," says the other, "the Danes is much better customers to me; but since you walked so far I won't refuse. Hand that flail," says he to a young imp; and he winked the far-off eye at the same time. So, while some were barring the gates, the young devil climbed up, and took down the flail that had the handstaff and booltheen both made out of red-hot iron. The little vagabond was grinning to think how it would burn the hands o' Tom, but the dickens a burn it made on him, no more nor if it was a good oak sapling.

"Thankee," says Tom. "Now would you open the gate for a body, and I'll give you no more trouble."

"Oh, tramp!" says Ould Nick; "is that the way? It is easier getting inside them gates than getting out again. Take that tool from him, and give him a dose of the oil of stirrup."

So one fellow put out his claws to seize on the flail, but Tom gave him such a welt of it on the side of the head that he broke off one of his horns, and made him roar like a devil as he was. Well, they rushed at Tom, but he gave them, little and big, such a thrashing as they didn't forget for a while. At last says the ould thief of all, rubbing his elbow, "Let the fool out; and woe to whoever lets him in again, great or small."

So out marched Tom, and away with him, without minding the shouting and cursing they kept up at him from the tops of the walls; and when he got home to the big bawn of the palace, there never was such running and racing as to see himself and the flail. When he had his story told, he laid down the flail on the stone steps, and bid no one for their lives to touch it. If the king, and queen, and princess, made much of him before, they made ten times more of him now; but Redhead, the mean scruff-hound, stole over, and thought to catch hold of the flail to make an end of him. His fingers hardly touched it, when he let a roar out of him as if heaven and earth were coming together, and kept flinging his arms about and dancing, that it was pitiful to look at him. Tom run at him as soon as he could rise, caught his hands in his own two, and rubbed them this way and that, and the burning pain left them before you could reckon one. Well the poor fellow, between the pain that was only just gone, and the comfort he was in, had the comicalest face that you ever see, it was such a mixtherum-gatherum of laughing and crying. Everybody burst out a laughing—the princess could not stop no more than the rest; and then says Tom, "Now, ma'am, if there were fifty halves of you, I hope you'll give me them all."

Well, the princess looked at her father, and by my word, she came over to Tom, and put her two delicate hands into his two rough ones, and I wish it was myself was in his shoes that day!

Tom would not bring the flail into the palace. You may be sure no other body went near it; and when the early risers were passing next morning, they found two long clefts in the stone, where it was after burning itself an opening downwards, nobody could tell how far. But a messenger came in at noon, and said that the Danes were so frightened when they heard of the flail coming into Dublin, that they got into their ships, and sailed away.

Well, I suppose, before they were married, Tom got some man, like Pat Mara of Tomenine, to learn him the "principles of politeness," fluxions, gunnery, and fortification, decimal fractions, practice, and the rule of three direct, the way he'd be able to keep up a conversation with the royal family. Whether he ever lost his time learning them sciences, I'm not sure, but it's as sure as fate that his mother never more saw any want till the end of her days.

Legends of Fairies and Sea-folk

WHEN DARKNESS FELL across the land, and the hush of evening brought sounds that belonged to no mortal man, the time was ripe for fairies and other wee folk to leave their realm and enter our own. Anything strange, complex or perhaps a little frightening must have a cause, and it was these creatures who were held responsible for acts for which no one else would take the blame. The mischievous deeds of the fairies and their compatriots were the cause of much illness and heartache, but by the same token, they could make a hero of a man, and bring roses to the face of a sickly baby. Fairies were dangerous, and folk from the sea could be fierce and unfamiliar, but the infinite battle to live with them provided a formula, a structure for daily existence, when life and death and nature held all the fear of the unknown, and a crying baby, that tapping on the window, the light that glinted over the treetops meant something altogether different.

MacCodrum's Seal Wife

❧

DEEP IN THE COLD SEA, long before men chanced the waves for the first time, there lived a king and his queen, and their lovely sea-children. The children were elegant, graceful creatures, with deep brown eyes and voices that filled the sea with laughter and song. They dwelt deep in that sea, in happiness and in comfort, and spent days chasing one another through the schools of fish, catching a ride on a tail, hiding in a murky cave, frolicking in the waves that caressed their young bodies and made them strong.

And so their days were spent, and they were fed and loved by the kindly queen and her husband, who brushed their hair, and stroked their heads, and gave them a home like none other. Until the sad day when the queen became ill and died, and left her children forlorn and lonely, but still with the sea as their home, and the fish, and the warm waves to comfort them. Their voices were softer now, and their music still sweet, but the king was concerned about their uncombed hair, and their unstroked heads, and he began to search for a mother for the sea-children.

The king found them a mother in a darker part of the sea, where the sun could not light the coral reefs, or dance upon the weeds and the shimmering scales of the fish. The mother was in fact a witch, and she charmed the king with a magic potion that put him under her spell. She came with him to the lighter part of the sea, where the sun kissed the elegant bodies of the sea-children, glowed in their soft brown eyes, and she made her home there, combing their hair, and stroking their heads, but never loving them, and so the friendly waters grew cold, and although the light continued to dance, and the waves lapped at their bodies, the children were sad and downcast.

And so it was that the witch decided to dispose of these sea-children, and from the depths of her wicked being she created a cruel spell that would rid the sea-children of their elegance and their beauty. She turned them to seals, who could live no longer in the marine palace of their father the king, their graceful limbs replaced by heavy bodies and sleek dark fur. They were to live in the sea for all but one day each year when they could find a secluded shore and transform, for just that day, into children once more.

But the witch could not rob the children of everything, and although their bodies were ungainly, and they were beautiful children no longer, they re-tained their soft brown eyes, and their music was as pure and mellifluous as the wind in the trees, as the birds who flew above the water.

Time went on, and the seals grew used to their shiny coats, and to the sea, where they played once again in the waves, and fished, and sang, but they loved too becoming children again, that one day each year, and it was when they had shed their coats, beautiful children once more, that they were seen for the first time by human eyes, those belonging to a fisherman who lived on an isolated rock, a man called Roderic MacCodrum, of the Clan Donald, in the Outer Hebrides.

On this fateful day he walked to the beach to rig his boat when he heard the sound of exquisite singing, and he hid himself behind some driftwood and watched the delightful dance of the sea-children, who waved arms that were no longer clumsy seal flippers, and who ran with legs that were long and lean. Their soft brown eyes were alight with happiness and never before had Roderic MacCodrum seen such a sight.

His eyes sparkled. He must have one. And so it was that Roderic MacCodrum stole one of the glistening pelts that lay cast to the side of the beach, and put it above the rafters in his barn, safe from the searching eyes of the young seal woman who came to call.

The seal woman was elegant and beautiful, her long hair hiding her comely nakedness. She implored him to return her coat to her, but he feigned concern and told her that he knew not where it was. In despair she sat down on his doorstep, her head in her hands, and it was then that he offered her a life on land, as his wife and lover. Because she had no seal skin like her brothers and sisters, and no place to go, she agreed, and so it was that the seal woman came to live with Roderic MacCodrum, where she lived happily, or so it was thought, and bore him many children.

But the seal woman, or Selkie as she came to be called, had a cold, lonely heart, and although she loved and nurtured her children, and grew to find a kind of peace with her husband, she longed for the waves, for the cold fresh waters of the sea. And she would sit on its shores and she would sing a song that was so haunting, so melancholy that the seals would come to her here and cease their frolicking to return her unhappy song, to sing with her of times gone by when the waves and the water comforted them and made them strong, when the sun in the lighter part of the sea kissed their elegant bodies and made them gleam with light.

And then at night she would return to her cottage, and light the peat in the hearth, and make a home for her family, all the while living her life in her dreams of the sea.

It was her unknowing child who found the beautiful fur coat, fallen from its hiding place in the rafters, where it had remained unseen for all those years, and she brought it to her mother whose eyes glowed with a warmth that none had seen before. Her mother kissed her then, and all her brothers and sisters, and whispered that they must look out for her, for she would be back.

Roderic MacCodrum of the Seals, as he had come to be known, returned to his cottage that night to find it empty and cold, like the heart of the seal woman he had married, and his children were lined on the beaches, bereft and alone, for their mother had left for the chill waters and she had not come back.

Their mother never came back, for she had gone with that lustrous fur coat, that gleamed in the light like her soft brown eyes when she saw it. They heard her, though, for from the sea came those same lilting melodies, happier now, to be sure. And they often saw a graceful seal, who came closer to shore than the others, and who seemed to beckon, and in whose presence they felt a strange comfort, a familiar warmth, especially when the sun caught those soft brown eyes they knew so well.

The Fairies and the Blacksmith

T HERE ONCE WAS A BLACKSMITH by the name of Alasdair MacEachern, and he lived in a cottage on the Isle of Islay with his son Neil. They lived alone for the blacksmith's poor wife had breathed no more than once or twice when Neil was born to them, but Alasdair MacEachern, or Alasdair of the Strong Arm, as he came to be known, found great comfort in his son and they lived contentedly, with familiar habits and routines that brought them much happiness.

Neil was a slim youth, with unruly hair and eyes that shone with dreams. He was quiet, but easy, and his slight, pale frame gave him the countenance of one weaker than he was. When Neil was but a child the neighbours of Alasdair MacEachern had warned the blacksmith of the fairies who lived just over the knoll, the fairies who would find one so slight and dreamy a perfect prize for their Land of Light. And so it was that each night Alasdair MacEachern hung above the door to his cottage a branch of rowan, a charm against the fairies who might come to steal away his son.

They lived many years this way, until the day came when Alasdair MacEachern had to travel some distance, sleeping the night away from his cottage and his son. Before he left, he warned his son about the rowan branch, and Neil agreed to put it in its place above the door that night. Neil loved the green grass of the hills, and to breathe in the crisp, sunlit air of the banks of the streams that trickled through their land, but he loved more his life with his father and his work on the forge. He had no wish for a life of dancing and eternal merriment in the Land of Light.

And so it was that Neil wished his father a fond farewell, swept the cottage, tended to the goats and to the chickens, and made himself a feast of corn-bread and oatcakes, and goat's cheese and milk, and took himself to the soft green grass of the hills, and walked there by the sunlit banks of the streams until dark fell upon him. And then Neil returned to his cottage next to the forge, and he swept the crumbs from his pockets, and tended to the goats and to the chickens, and laid himself in his tiny box-bed in the corner of the room, by the roaring hearth, and fell fast asleep. Not once had the thought of the branch of rowan crept across his sleepy mind.

It was late in the afternoon when Alasdair of the Strong Arm returned to his cottage, and he found the hearth quite cold, and the floor unswept, and the goats and the chickens untended. His son was there, for he answered his fa-ther's call, but there was no movement from his box-bed in the corner and Alasdair crossed the room with great concern.

'I am ill, Father,' said a small, weak voice, and there laid the body of Neil, yellowed and shrunk, hardly denting his meagre mattress.

'But how ... how could, in just one day ...' Alasdair stared with shock at his son, for he smelled old, of decay, and his skin was like charred paper, folded and crisp and creased. But it was his son, no doubt, for the shape and the face were the same. And Neil laid like this for days on end, changing little, but eating steadily, his appetite strange and fathomless. And it was because of this strange illness that Alasdair MacEachern paid a visit to a wiseman, who came at once to the bedside of Neil, for he was a boy well regarded by his neighbours.

The wiseman looked only once at Neil, and drew the unhappy blacksmith outside the cottage. He asked many questions and then he was quiet. When he finally spoke his words were measured, and his tone quite fearful. The blood of Alasdair MacEachern ran cold.

'This is not your son Neil,' said the man of knowledge. 'He has been carried off by the Little People and they have left a changeling in his place.'

'Alas, then, what can I do?' The great blacksmith was visibly trembling now, for Neil was as central to his life as the fiery heat of the forge itself. And then the wiseman spoke, and he told Alasdair MacEachern how to proceed.

'You must first be sure that is a changeling lying in the bed of Neil, and you must go back to the cottage and collect as many egg shells as you can, filling them with water and carrying them as if they weighed more than ten tons of iron and bricks. And then, arrange them round the side of the fire where the changeling can see you. His words will give him away.'

So Alasdair MacEachern gathered together the shells of twenty eggs and did as he was bidden, and soon a thin voice called out from his son's bed, 'In all of my eight hundred years I have never seen such a sight.' And with a hoot and a cackle, the changeling sank back into the bed.

Alasdair returned to the wiseman and confirmed what had taken place. The old man nodded his head.

'It is indeed a changeling and he must be disposed of, before you can bring back your son. You must follow these steps: light a large, hot fire in the centre of the cottage, where it can be easily seen by the changeling. And then, when he asks you "What's the use of that", you must grab him by the shirtfront, and thrust him deep into the fire. Then he'll fly through the roof of the cottage.'

Alasdair of the Strong Arm did as requested, certain now that that wizened, strange creature was not his son, and as the fire began to roar, the voice called out, reedy and slim, 'What's the use of that?' at which the brave blacksmith seized the body that lay in Neil's bed and placed it firmly in the flames. There was a terrible scream, and the changeling flew straight through the roof, a sour yellow smoke all that remained of him.

And so Alasdair MacEachern cleared away the traces of the fire, and returned once more to the man of knowledge, for it was time to find his son, and he could delay no longer.

The wiseman bade him go to fetch three things: a Bible, a sword, and a crow-ing cock. He was to follow the stream that trickled through their land to the grassy green knoll where the fairies danced and played eternally. On the night of the next full moon, that hill would open, and it was through this door that Alasdair must go to seek his son.

It was many days before the moon had waned, and then waxed again, but it stood, a gleaming beacon in the sky at last, and Alasdair MacEachern col-lected together his sword and his Bible and his crowing cock and set out for the green knoll where the fairies danced. And as the moon rose high in the sky, and lit the shadowy land, a door burst open in the hill, spilling out laugh-ter and song and a bright light that blazed like the fire in the hearth of the blacksmith's cottage. And it was into that light and sound that the courageous Alasdair MacEachern stepped, firmly thrusting his sword into the frame of the door to stop it closing, for no fairy can touch the sword of a mortal man.

There, at a steaming forge, stood his son, as small and as wild-looking as the little folk themselves. He worked silently, absorbed in his labours, and started only when he heard the voice of his father.

'Release my son from this enchantment,' shouted Alasdair MacEachern, hold-ing the Bible high in the air, for fairies have no power over mortals who hold the good Lord's book, and they stood back now, cross and foiled.

'Return him to me, to his own land,' bawled the blacksmith, but the fairies be-gan to smirk, and they slowly crept around him in a circle, taunting him, pok-ing at him with blades of honed green grass. They began to dance, a slow and wiry gyration, moving to a weird song that tugged at the mind of the black-smith, that threatened to overcome him. He struggled to stay upright, and as he stabbed his arms out in front of him, he dropped his cock, who woke with a howl and gave one mighty crow that sent the little fairies shrieking from the doorway to the other side, sent them howling away from the cock and the blacksmith and his son, who they pushed now towards him, sending them all slipping towards the threshold of their world. For daylight was the curfew of the fairies, and it was with true fear that the crow of the red-combed cock was heard, for little people may never see the light of day per chance they turn at once to stone.

They struggled now, prodding the mortals from their world, and begging in an awkward chant for Alasdair MacEachern to release his dirk from their door. And as he drew it from the threshold, and stood once more in the land of mortals with his son, a small and crafty fairy thrust his face from the hill-side, and called out a curse that fell upon the son of the hapless blacksmith like the mist of a foggy night.

'May your son not speak until the day he breaks the curse.' The head popped back, and the fairy was gone, never to be seen again.

And so it was that Alasdair MacEachern and his son Neil went to live again in their familiar, cosy cottage next to the forge, and took up their work, their habits and their routines in place once more. Neil's tongue was frozen by the curse of the fairies, but his manner was unchanged, and this father and his son lived contentedly, for speech is not always necessary to those who live simply, with things and people to which they have grown accustomed.

One day, a year and a week from the fairy's fateful full moon, Alasdair set his son the task of forging the new claymore for the Chief of his clan. As his silent son held the metal to the fire, he started, and looked for one instant as wild as he had in the Land of the Light, for suddenly Neil had remembered, and in that flash of memory he recalled the intricate forging of the fairies' swords, how he'd learned to temper the blades of their glowing weapons with words of wisdom and charms, with magic and spells as well as with fire. Now he leapt into action, and worked with a ferocity and speed that set his father, Alasdair of the Strong Arm, reeling with shock and with fear.

And then the motion stopped, and holding up a sword that gleamed like the light of the full moon, he said quietly, 'There is a sword that will never fail the man who grasps it by the hilt.'

From that time onwards Neil spoke again, for unwittingly he had removed the curse of the fairies by fashioning a fairy sword to sever a fairy spell. Never again did he remember his days in the fairy kingdom, never again could he forge a fairy sword, but the Chief of his clan never lost a battle from that day, and the sword remained the greatest of his possessions.

Neil and his father, Alasdair MacEachern, returned to their cottage, the finest blacksmiths in all the land, their forge casting a glow that could be seen from hills all round, almost as far as the Land of Light, where the fairies kick up their heels in fury at the thought of that blacksmith and his clever son.

The Fairy Changeling

THERE ONCE WAS A WOMAN who lived on the sea, where the winds blew cold and damp. By day she combed the sands for seaweed, and by night she lay alone in her bed, weak and lonely, for her husband was a fisherman and by the light of the moon he trawled the rocky coasts, eking a cruel living, but one which kept them fed and warm in a cosy cottage.

The woman longed for a child, but it was many years before she was granted her wish, and when her baby finally came he was small and feeble. Her neighbours said he would die, or worse, be snatched by the fairies who loved a child so fair of complexion, so slight of build. He would be taken, they said, to the Land of Light where the fairies danced and sang and played all day, where they set traps and tricks for mortal folk who crossed their merry paths.

The fisherman's poor wife could not help but think that a life of laughter would bring roses to the cheeks of her white child, and she wished with all her being that he would be stolen by the fairies, and taken to a land where he could become strong. And so it was that the fisherman's wife set her child out on the rocks, on the edge of her land, and watched and waited. She slept for a few moments, but otherwise moved not, and still her baby lay there, swad-dled and spiritless, an invitation to the little folk which was not accepted.

At length she berated herself for the foolhardy actions, and brought her baby into the cottage once more. And there he surprised her by pulling himself up and demanding food, attaching himself to her teat with such relish that she drew back. He suckled the woman dry, and then demanded porridge, but still he lay small and wizened, more yellow than before, but so hungry that she could not feed him.

So the fisherman's wife placed her baby at her breast, and went to see the wiseman in the village, anxious about her small but starving baby, frightened by his curious change.

The wiseman listened carefully to her story, silently shaking his head. 'You have not your own bairn, but a fairy changeling,' he said finally.

The wife of the fisherman balked, for there in front of her was the very shape and likeness of her baby, and the cry was as shrill as ever. She refused to be-lieve him.

'Take him, then, to your cottage, and leave him in his cradle. Shut the door, but do not go. Spy upon him there and you will be sure.'

And so the fisherman's wife returned to her cottage, and laid the baby upon his bed, shutting the door firmly behind her, but skulking back to peer in the window. And suddenly her baby sat up and drew from under the mattress a chanter, which he began to play. And instead of her baby there was an old fairy bodach.

She fairly flew back to the wiseman, and implored him to help her get rid of the changeling, sickened at the thought of having suckled that gnarled old creature. Calmly the wiseman told her what to do.

The very next day, the wife of the fisherman took her changeling baby and laid him on a rock by the sea, busying herself by collecting seaweed as she did on every day that passed, and comforted by this routine, the baby, or the fairy bodach as she now knew he was, fell asleep. As he slept the tide drew in, licking at the rock on which he slept, until the waters began to dampen his wrappings, and he woke with a start. When he realized that he could not reach the fisherman's wife without swimming he rose to his full height, and a little fairy man once more he began to stamp his feet and howl, shaking his fist at the fisherman's wife who stood entranced as the waters threatened to engulf the fierce fairy.

And so it was that ten or twelve small fairies appeared to rescue their kin, but since fairies cannot swim, they danced helplessly on the shore while the water grew higher and higher about the rock. The fisherman's wife was smug, and she said, 'I shall leave him there, until you return my baby.'

And the fairies disappeared and returned with her baby, who had grown in his time away from his mother, and whose cheeks were roses, whose white skin held the bloom of good health. And she thanked the fairies, and returned their bodach to them.

So the fisherman's wife, flushed with her good fortune, went back to her cosy cottage, protected from the winds which blew cold and damp from the sea. She lived there with her blossoming baby, by day combing the sands for sea-weed, and at night nestling warm in her bed with her son, silently thanking the little people who had made him strong.

The Thirsty Ploughman

❦

IT WAS IN BERNERAY that two men from Brusda walked along a hot and sun-burnt field, parched from the fiery sun, from a long day of ploughing. Sweat glistened on their brows and they talked little, saving words for a time when their tongues were moister. Their feet were bare and despite the great heat they moved quickly, thirsting for a drink, for cool refreshment.

They passed across a rocky knoll and then they heard a woman, working at a churn. They looked at one another with relief.

'Ah, Donald,' said Ewan, the slighter of the two men, 'if the milkmaid had my thirst, what a drink of buttermilk she would drink.'

Donald was not sure. 'Ah, it's not buttermilk I would care for,' he said.

As they carried on over the dry brush that lined the hillock, the sound of the fresh milk splashing in the churn grew louder, more enticing, and both men licked their lips at the thought of it. There before them stood a fair maiden, her apron starched crisp white, holding a jug that foamed with pure butter-milk. She offered it to them then, Ewan first because he was the smaller of the two.

Ewan refused to drink because he knew neither the maiden nor the source of the buttermilk. He was afraid of what he did not know and though he thirsted for the cool milk, he would allow none to pass his lips.

Donald, who cared not for buttermilk, drank deeply from the jug, and wiping the frosting of white lather from his lip, he declared it the best he had ever tasted.

'Ah,' said the bonny maiden, whose face was cool with contempt, 'you who asked for the drink and did not accept it will have a short life. And you,' she gestured to Donald, 'you who took the drink, but did not ask for it, a long life and good living.'

She turned on her heel, and apron bright in the sunlight, left the men, one thirsty and one sated.

And so it was that Ewan returned home that night and took to his bed, never to waken, for the fear of God had been put into him that day by the maiden on the hill, who could be none other than a witch. And Donald lived a long and prosperous life, ploughing his field alone, but reaping better crops, and amassing great riches. He looked always across the knoll, listened intently for the sound of milk in the churn, but never again did he see the witch, or fairy, though he blessed her often.

Wee Johnnie in the Cradle

T HERE ONCE WAS A MAN and his wife who lived on a farm on the edge of a wood where fairies were known to lay their small hats. They were a young man and wife and they had not been married long before a child was born to them, a child they called Johnnie. Now wee Johnnie was an unhappy baby, and from the beginning he cried so loudly that the birds ceased their flight over the farmer's cottage, and the creatures of the woodland kept a surly distance. The man's wife longed for the days when she could tend the fields with her husband, and chat to him of things which those who are newly wed have to chat of, and to go to market, where they would share a dram and have a carry-on like they had in the days before wee Johnnie was born.

But Johnnie was there now, and their cosy cottage became messy and damp, and some days the hearth was not lit because the man and his wife were so intent on silencing the squalling boy, and some days they could not even look one another in the eye, so unhappy and disillusioned they had become.

And then, perchance, a kindly neighbour, a tailor by trade, took pity on the man and his wife, who grew ever thinner and ever more hostile as the cries of wee Johnnie grew wilder and lustier as he grew larger and stronger.

'I'll take yer bairn and ye can take yer wife to market,' he said to the farmer one day, and the man and his wife eagerly agreed and set off for the day.

They had not been gone longer than a minute or two, when the kindly tailor, who had placed himself beside the fire and was bracing himself for an afternoon of wailing, was startled from his reverie by a deep voice.

'Fetch me a glass o' that whiskey, there, in the press,' it said. And the tailor looked about him in amazement, the room empty but for the wee Johnnie in the cradle who was mercifully silent.

'I said to ye, fetch me a glass,' and up from the cradle of wee Johnnie popped wee Johnnie's head, and from the mouth on that head came that deep and bossy voice.

The tailor rose and did as he was bidden, and when the baby had drained the glass, and then another, and let out a belch that was very unbabyish indeed, he said to the wee bairn, 'You aren't Johnnie, are ye, ye are a fairy without a doubt.'

'And if I am,' said the fairy changeling, 'what will ye say to them, me mam and da?'

'I, I dunna know,' said the tailor carefully, settling himself back into his chair to watch the fairy more carefully.

'Get me some pipes,' said Johnnie the fairy, 'I like a bit of music with me drink.'

'I haven't any ... and I dunna play,' said the tailor, crossing himself and moving further from the loathsome baby.

'Fetch me a straw then,' he replied. And when the tailor complied, the fairy Johnnie played a song which was so exquisite, so effortlessly beautiful that the tailor was quite calmed. Never before had he heard music so haunting, and he would remember that melody until his dying day, although he could never repeat it himself or pass it on. But he was broken from his reverie, for wee Johnnie was speaking.

'Me mam and da, when will they be back?' he whispered.

The tailor looked startled, for the day had been pulled from under him, and it was time indeed for the farmer and his wife to return. He looked anxiously from the window and as they drew up he heard wee Johnnie begin to howl with all the vigour of a slaughtered beast, and he watched as a deep frown furrowed the brow of the farmer's wife, and a dull shadow cast itself across the face of her husband.

He must tell them, for the cruel fairy was manipulating them, taunting them with his tortuous cries. And their own wee bairn was somewhere lost to them.

He pulled the farmer aside as his wife went to tend to the wailing bairn, and told him of the fairy. A bemused look crossed his face and he struggled to keep his composure. 'My wife, she'll not believe it,' he said finally.

But the tailor had a plan. He told the farmer to pretend to leave for market the following day, and he, the tailor, would step in to look after the bairn once again. But the farmer and his wife were not really to leave, they should hide themselves outside the cottage walls and watch when the wee Johnnie thought them gone.

And so it happened that the next day the man and his wife set out for market again, but drove their horses only round the grassy bend, returning stealthily to look through the windows of their cottage. And there was wee Johnnie, sipping on a glass of their best whiskey, puffing idly on a straw pipe that played a song which was so exquisite, so effortlessly beautiful that they were quite calmed. Never before had they heard music so haunting, and they would remember that melody until their dying day, although they could never repeat it.

But when they heard that wee Johnnie's coarse voice demanding more drink, they were snapped from their reverie, and they flew into the cottage and thrust the changeling intruder on the burning griddle which the tailor had prepared for that purpose.

And the scream that ensued was not that of their own baby, and the puff of sickening smoke which burst from the fairy as he disappeared renewed their determination.

And then there was silence, an empty peace that caused the man and his wife to look at one another in dismay, for what had they done to cause their baby to be stolen from them, and where was their own wee Johnnie now?

Then a gurgle burst forth, and there was a movement in the corner of the room where the tiny cradle lay. They rushed to its side, and there lay Johnnie, brought back from his fairy confinement, smiling and waving tiny fat arms, with cheeks like pink buttons, and a smile so merry that the cottage of the man and his wife was warmed once again.

The tailor left them then, a grin on his face as he whistled to himself a tune which was so exquisite, so effortlessly beautiful that he was quite calmed.

The Fairy Dancers

❧

IT WAS CHRISTMAS EVE and by the Loch Etive sat two farmers, longing for a drink but with an empty barrel between them. And so it was decided, on that icy Christmas Eve, that these two farmers would walk the road to Kingshouse, their nearest inn, and they would buy a barrel of the best whiskey there, a three-gallon jar that would warm them through the frosty months to come.

So they set off along the winding road, and over the hills that glistened with snow, all frosted with ice, and came to the warm wooded inn at Kingshouse. It was there that a cup of tea was shared, and a wee dram or two, and so the two men were quite merry as they set off home again, the three-gallon jar heavy on the back of the youngest man, for they would take turns carrying its weight on the long journey down the winding road and over the hills.

And over the hills they went but they were stopped there, by the need for a taste of that whiskey, and for a smoke. Then the sound of a fantastic reel grew louder and louder, and a light shone brighter over the hills, towards the north.

'Och, it's just a wee star,' said one man, ready for his smoke and his tipple.

'Nah, it's a light, and there's a party there to be sure,' said the other, who was a great dancer and loved a reel more than any other.

So they crossed the brae to the north, towards the light, and the sound of pipes, which played a fine tune. There in front of them were dancers, women in silk dresses, bowing and twirling, and men in highland dress, with pipes playing an enchanted, fine tune that drew them towards the hill.

The younger man, who carried the jar, went first, and as he entered the great door in the hillside, and joined the merry throng, the door was closed. When the other farmer, slower than the first, reached the site, there was nothing to be found. For his friend had disappeared and there was no trace of him.

It was a cold and lonely walk home, and the farmer puzzled over what had occurred on that moonlit hill, with a magical reel playing from a light that shone in the darkness. He went first to the farm of the other man, and he told his wife what had happened, but as he talked, faces closed, and brows became furrowed, and it was clear that he was not believed, that no man could lose his friend on a hill just a few miles from home.

And so it was that the policemen were called from Inveraray, and they took him away and asked him questions that made his head spin, and caused him to slump over in exhaustion, and he wished more than anything for a drop of the whiskey that was hung on the other man's back. They kept him there, the police, and he was sent to trial, but he told them all the same thing, how a magical reel had played from a light that shone in the darkness, and how his friend had disappeared without trace.

He was sent back to that prison, and when they asked him again, he could only tell the truth of that fateful night, so they asked him no more, and sent him home, for he would not budge from his story, and that story never changed.

And it was near twelve months before this man had cause to travel past that hill again, and with him this time were some lads from the village who had set themselves the task of catching some fish for the Christmas feast. And with a basket full of fish, they stopped on their way back to their homes, with the need for a smoke and a taste of the whiskey that the farmer had tucked in his belt. And there again they heard that fantastic music, and saw the light beaming from the darkness of the hills.

But the lads from the village had heard too much of this madness, and they struggled home with the fish, ahead of the farmer who wanted more than anything to find his friend, and that barrel of whiskey. So the farmer climbed over the hills, towards that light, and he heard there the sound of pipes, which played a fine tune. There in front of him were dancers, women in silk dresses, bowing and twirling, and men in highland dress, with pipes playing an enchanted, fine tune that drew him towards the hill.

And he stuck his fishing hook in the threshold of the door, for no fairy can touch the metal of a mortal man, and he entered the room which spun with the music, and threatened to drag him into its midst. But this farmer never liked a dance, preferring instead a good smoke and a dram of whiskey, and he resisted the calls on his soul, and struggled through the crowd to find his friend the farmer, who danced in the middle of the reel like a man possessed.

'Och, lad, we've only just begun,' the dancer protested, as his friend dragged him away.

And since he had danced for near twelve months with that barrel on his back, he carried it home again, along the winding road and over the hills that glistened with snow, all frosted with ice. They came to the farm of the man who'd been dancing, and what a surprise met his poor lonely wife when she opened the door. For there was her husband, just skin and bones to be sure, but there nonetheless with his barrel of whiskey, just twelve months late.

And they sat up that night, the man and his friend, and each of their wives, and what a Christmas Eve they had with that barrel of whiskey, which had mellowed with the warmth of the fairy hill, and they drank it all, just twelve months late.

A Dead Wife Among the Fairies

❦

T HERE ONCE WAS A MAN who lived with a wife he loved. They had been married for many years, and they made their home in a lighthouse, on the rocky coast by the sea. The waves threw up a spray but never dampened them, for they were sealed tight in their little world inside that lighthouse, and they lived happily there together, needing little else but the other. And so they lived, working together and talking all the day, lighting their beacon in the mists and fogs which fell over the sea like a woollen blanket.

Then one day, the good wife died, and she was buried in the hillside, under the rocks. And on those rocks the man sat each day, never lighting his beacon when the mists and fogs fell over the sea, staring instead at the rock which marked her grave, which marked the end of his life too. And so it was that he became a little mad, and went to see a witch, a fairy midwife who practised the magic of the earth and who could tell him how to get her back, his wife that he loved so well.

He saw her in her cottage, over the hill and across the brae, and she shook her head, and warned him to leave the dead with the fairies, for after death there can be no real life on earth, where the light would turn into dust any mortal who tried to return. But for the poor widowed man there could be no real life either, and so he begged the fairy witch to tell him her secrets and at last she did.

He was to go, she said, to a cave at the brae of Versabreck, on the night of a full moon, and he should take with him a black cat, and a Bible, and a thick wooden staff. There he must cry for his wife, and read to her from the psalms, and when he heard her voice once more, he must throw in the black cat and wait quietly for her to appear. Now the fairy folk would never let a mortal who had died pass back to his own land, so they would rally round her, and fight to keep her in their dust-webbed cave, which led to the Land of Light. The staff was to beat them with, for they could be sent back into their cave by the force of his will.

The moon waned and then it waxed again, and soon the night of the full moon arrived. The man was shivering with the fear of seeing his wife once more, yet he longed to touch her body, to feel her warmth, to hear her tender voice, so he steeled his quivering nerves and set off for the cave at the brae of Versabreck, and under his arm he held a black cat, and a Bible and a thick wooden staff. There he cried for his wife, and he read to her from the psalms, and when he heard her voice once more, he threw in the black cat and waited quietly for her to appear.

Now the fairy folk fought for their mortal princess, and struggled to keep her in their dust-webbed cave, which led to the Land of Light, but he beat them with his staff, and sent them back into their cave by the force of his will.

And there was his wife, paler to be sure, and nothing more than skin and bones, but she smiled her same familiar smile, and although her body held no warmth and she smelled rather sour, he held her to him once again and heard her tender voice. And together they walked to their lighthouse home, snug in a warm embrace, and they lit their beacon in the mists and fogs which fell over the sea like a woollen blanket. When day broke, his wife was safe in the fairy cave again, for light would turn to dust any mortal who tried to return from the dead. And so her husband would watch carefully as the moon waned and then waxed, when they could meet again.

The Shepherd of Myddvai

❧

UP IN THE BLACK MOUNTAINS in Caermarthenshire lies the lake known as Lyn y Van Vach. To the margin of this lake the shepherd of Myddvai once led his lambs, and lay there whilst they sought pasture. Suddenly, from the dark waters of the lake, he saw three maidens rise. Shaking the bright drops from their hair and gliding to the shore, they wandered about amongst his flock. They had more than mortal beauty, and he was filled with love for her that came nearest to him. He offered her the bread he had with him, and she took it and tried it, but then sang to him before running off laughing to the lake:

> *Hard-baked is thy bread,*
> *'Tis not easy to catch me,*

Next day he took with him bread not so well done, and watched for the maidens. When they came ashore he offered his bread as before, and the maiden tasted it and sang:

> *Unbaked is thy bread,*
> *I will not have thee,*

and again disappeared in the waves.

A third time did the shepherd of Myddvai try to attract the maiden, and this time he offered her bread that he had found floating about near the shore. This pleased her, and she promised to become his wife if he were able to pick her out from among her sisters on the following day. When the time came the shepherd knew his love by the strap of her sandal. Then she told him she would be as good a wife to him as any earthly maiden could be unless he should strike her three times without cause. Of course he deemed that this could never be; and she, summoning from the lake three cows, two oxen, and a bull, as her marriage portion, was led homeward by him as his bride.

The years passed happily, and three children were born to the shepherd and the lake-maiden. But one day here were going to a christening, and she said to her husband it was far to walk, so he told her to go for the horses.

"I will," said she, "if you bring me my gloves which I've left in the house."

But when he came back with the gloves, he found she had not gone for the horses; so he tapped her lightly on the shoulder with the gloves, and said, "Go, go."

"That's one," said she.

Another time they were at a wedding, when suddenly the lake-maiden fell a-sobbing and a-weeping, amid the joy and mirth of all around her.

Her husband tapped her on the shoulder, and asked her, "Why do you weep?"

"Because they are entering into trouble; and trouble is upon you; for that is the second causeless blow you have given me. Be careful; the third is the last."

The husband was careful never to strike her again. But one day at a funeral she suddenly burst out into fits of laughter. Her husband forgot, and touched her rather roughly on the shoulder, saying, "Is this a time for laughter?"

"I laugh," she said, "because those that die go out of trouble, but your trouble has come. The last blow has been struck; our marriage is at an end, and so farewell." And with that she rose up and left the house and went to their home.

Then she, looking round upon her home, called to the cattle she had brought with her:

> *Brindle cow, white speckled,*
> *Spotted cow, bold freckled,*
> *Old white face, and gray Geringer,*
> *And the white bull from the king's coast,*
> *Grey ox, and black calf,*
> *All, all, follow me home.*

Now the black calf had just been slaughtered, and was hanging on the hook; but it got off the hook alive and well and followed her; and the oxen, though they were ploughing, trailed the plough with them and did her bidding. So she fled to the lake again, they following her, and with them plunged into the dark waters.

And to this day is the furrow seen which the plough left as it was dragged across the mountains to the tarn.

Only once did she come again, when her sons were grown to manhood, and then she gave them gifts of healing by which they won the name of Meddygon Myddvai, the physicians of Myddvai.

Brewery of Eggshells

❧

IN TRENEGLWYS there is a certain shepherd's cot known by the name of Twt y Cymrws because of the strange strife that occurred there. There once lived there a man and his wife, and they had twins whom the woman nursed tenderly. One day she was called away to the house of a neighbour at some distance. She did not much like going and leaving her little ones all alone in a solitary house, especially as she had heard tell of the good folk haunting the neighbourhood.

Well, she went and came back as soon as she could, but on her way back she was frightened to see some old elves of the blue petticoat crossing her path though it was midday. She rushed home, but found her two little ones in the cradle and everything seemed as it was before.

But after a time the good people began to suspect that something was wrong, for the twins didn't grow at all.

The man said: "They're not ours."

The woman said: "Whose else should they be?"

And so arose the great strife so that the neighbours named the cottage after it. It made the woman very sad, so one evening she made up her mind to go and see the Wise Man of Llanidloes, for he knew everything and would advise her what to do.

So she went to Llanidloes and told the case to the Wise Man. Now there was soon to be a harvest of rye and oats, so the Wise Man said to her, "When you are getting dinner for the reapers, clear out the shell of a hen's egg and boil some potage in it, and then take it to the door as if you meant it as a dinner for the reapers. Then listen if the twins say anything. If you hear them speaking of things beyond the understanding of children, go back and take them up and throw them into the waters of Lake Elvyn. But if you don't hear anything remarkable, do them no injury."

So when the day of the reap came the woman did all that the Wise Man ordered, and put the eggshell on the fire and took it off and carried it to the door, and there she stood and listened. Then she heard one of the children say to the other:

> *Acorn before oak I knew,*
> *An egg before a hen,*
> *But I never heard of an eggshell brew*
> *A dinner for harvest men.*

So she went back into the house, seized the children and threw them into the Llyn, and the goblins in their blue trousers came and saved their dwarfs and the mother had her own children back and so the great strife ended.

Guleesh

T HERE WAS ONCE A BOY in the County Mayo; Guleesh was his name. There was the finest rath a little way off from the gable of the house, and he was often in the habit of seating himself on the fine grass bank that was running round it. One night he stood, half leaning against the gable of the house, and looking up into the sky, and watching the beautiful white moon over his head. After he had been standing that way for a couple of hours, he said to himself: "My bitter grief that I am not gone away out of this place altogether. I'd sooner be any place in the world than here. Och, it's well for you, white moon," says he, "that's turning round, turning round, as you please yourself, and no man can put you back. I wish I was the same as you."

Hardly was the word out of his mouth when he heard a great noise coming like the sound of many people running together, and talking, and laughing, and making sport, and the sound went by him like a whirl of wind, and he was listening to it going into the rath. "Musha, by my soul," says he, "but ye're merry enough, and I'll follow ye."

What was in it but the fairy host, though he did not know at first that it was they who were in it, but he followed them into the rath. It's there he heard the fulparnee, and the folpornee, the rap-lay-hoota, and the roolya-boolya, that they had there, and every man of them crying out as loud as he could: "My horse, and bridle, and saddle! My horse, and bridle, and saddle!"

"By my hand," said Guleesh, "my boy, that's not bad. I'll imitate ye," and he cried out as well as they: "My horse, and bridle, and saddle! My horse, and bridle, and saddle!" And on the moment there was a fine horse with a bridle of gold, and a saddle of silver, standing before him. He leaped up on it, and the moment he was on its back he saw clearly that the rath was full of horses, and of little people going riding on them.

Said a man of them to him: "Are you coming with us tonight, Guleesh?"

"I am surely," said Guleesh.

"If you are, come along," said the little man, and out they went all together, riding like the wind, faster than the fastest horse ever you saw a-hunting, and faster than the fox and the hounds at his tail.

The cold winter's wind that was before them, they overtook her, and the cold winter's wind that was behind them, she did not overtake them. And stop nor stay of that full race, did they make none, until they came to the brink of the sea.

Then every one of them said: "Hie over cap! Hie over cap!" and that moment they were up in the air, and before Guleesh had time to remember where he was, they were down on dry land again, and were going like the wind.

At last they stood still, and a man of them said to Guleesh: "Guleesh, do you know where you are now?"

"Not a know," says Guleesh.

"You're in France, Guleesh," said he. "The daughter of the king of France is to be married tonight, the handsomest woman that the sun ever saw, and we must do our best to bring her with us; if we're only able to carry her off; and you must come with us that we may be able to put the young girl up behind you on the horse, when we'll be bringing her away, for it's not lawful for us to put her sitting behind ourselves. But you're flesh and blood, and she can take a good grip of you, so that she won't fall off the horse. Are you satisfied, Guleesh, and will you do what we're telling you?"

"Why shouldn't I be satisfied?" said Guleesh. "I'm satisfied, surely, and anything that ye will tell me to do I'll do it without doubt."

They got off their horses there, and a man of them said a word that Guleesh did not understand, and on the moment they were lifted up, and Guleesh found himself and his companions in the palace. There was a great feast going on there, and there was not a nobleman or a gentleman in the kingdom but was gathered there, dressed in silk and satin, and gold and silver, and the night was as bright as the day with all the lamps and candles that were lit, and Guleesh had to shut his two eyes at the brightness. When he opened them again and looked from him, he thought he never saw anything as fine as all he saw there. There were a hundred tables spread out, and their full of meat and drink on each table of them, flesh-meat, and cakes and sweetmeats, and wine and ale, and every drink that ever a man saw. The musicians were at the two ends of the hall, and they were playing the sweetest music that ever a man's ear heard, and there were young women and fine youths in the middle of the hall, dancing and turning, and going round so quickly and so lightly, that it put a soorawn in Guleesh's head to be looking at them. There were more there playing tricks, and more making fun and laughing, for such a feast as there was that day had not been in France for twenty years, because the old king had no children alive but only the one daughter, and she was to be married to the son of another king that night. Three days the feast was going on, and the third night she was to be married, and that was the night that Guleesh and the sheehogues came, hoping, if they could, to carry off with them the king's young daughter.

Guleesh and his companions were standing together at the head of the hall, where there was a fine altar dressed up, and two bishops behind it waiting to marry the girl, as soon as the right time should come. Now nobody could see the sheehogues, for they said a word as they came in, that made them all invisible, as if they had not been in it at all.

"Tell me which of them is the king's daughter," said Guleesh, when he was becoming a little used to the noise and the light.

"Don't you see her there away from you?" said the little man that he was talking to.

Guleesh looked where the little man was pointing with his finger, and there he saw the loveliest woman that was, he thought, upon the ridge of the world. The rose and the lily were fighting together in her face, and one could not tell which of them got the victory. Her arms and hands were like the lime, her mouth as red as a strawberry when it is ripe, her foot was as small and as light as another one's hand, her form was smooth and slender, and her hair was falling down from her head in buckles of gold. Her garments and dress were woven with gold and silver, and the bright stone that was in the ring on her hand was as shining as the sun.

Guleesh was nearly blinded with all the loveliness and beauty that was in her; but when he looked again, he saw that she was crying, and that there was the trace of tears in her eyes. "It can't be," said Guleesh, "that there's grief on her, when everybody round her is so full of sport and merriment."

"Musha, then, she is grieved," said the little man; "for it's against her own will she's marrying, and she has no love for the husband she is to marry. The king was going to give her to him three years ago, when she was only fifteen, but she said she was too young, and requested him to leave her as she was yet. The king gave her a year's grace, and when that year was up he gave her another year's grace, and then another; but a week or a day he would not give her longer, and she is eighteen years old tonight, and it's time for her to marry; but, indeed," says he, and he crooked his mouth in an ugly way—"indeed, it's no king's son she'll marry, if I can help it."

Guleesh pitied the handsome young lady greatly when he heard that, and he was heart-broken to think that it would be necessary for her to marry a man she did not like, or, what was worse, to take a nasty sheehogue for a husband. However, he did not say a word, though he could not help giving many a curse to the ill-luck that was laid out for himself, to be helping the people that were to snatch her away from her home and from her father.

He began thinking, then, what it was he ought to do to save her, but he could think of nothing. "Oh! if I could only give her some help and relief," said he, "I wouldn't care whether I were alive or dead; but I see nothing that I can do for her."

He was looking on when the king's son came up to her and asked her for a kiss, but she turned her head away from him. Guleesh had double pity for her then, when he saw the lad taking her by the soft white hand, and drawing her out to dance. They went round in the dance near where Guleesh was, and he could plainly see that there were tears in her eyes.

When the dancing was over, the old king, her father, and her mother the queen, came up and said that this was the right time to marry her, that the bishop was ready, and it was time to put the wedding-ring on her and give her to her husband.

The king took the youth by the hand, and the queen took her daughter, and they went up together to the altar, with the lords and great people following them.

When they came near the altar, and were no more than about four yards from it, the little sheehogue stretched out his foot before the girl, and she fell. Before she was able to rise again he threw something that was in his hand upon her, said a couple of words, and upon the moment the maiden was gone from amongst them. Nobody could see her, for that word made her invisible. The little man_een_ seized her and raised her up behind Guleesh, and the king nor no one else saw them, but out with them through the hall till they came to the door.

Oro! dear Mary! it's there the pity was, and the trouble, and the crying, and the wonder, and the searching, and the rookawn, when that lady disappeared from their eyes, and without their seeing what did it. Out of the door of the palace they went, without being stopped or hindered, for nobody saw them, and, "My horse, my bridle, and saddle!" says every man of them. "My horse, my bridle, and saddle!" says Guleesh; and on the moment the horse was standing ready caparisoned before him. "Now, jump up, Guleesh," said the little man, "and put the lady behind you, and we will be going; the morning is not far off from us now."

Guleesh raised her up on the horse's back, and leaped up himself before her, and, "Rise, horse," said he; and his horse, and the other horses with him, went in a full race until they came to the sea.

"Hie over cap!" said every man of them.

"Hie over cap!" said Guleesh; and on the moment the horse rose under him, and cut a leap in the clouds, and came down in Erin.

They did not stop there, but went of a race to the place where was Guleesh's house and the rath. And when they came as far as that, Guleesh turned and caught the young girl in his two arms, and leaped off the horse.

"I call and cross you to myself, in the name of God!" said he; and on the spot, before the word was out of his mouth, the horse fell down, and what was in it but the beam of a plough, of which they had made a horse; and every other horse they had, it was that way they made it. Some of them were riding on an old besom, and some on a broken stick, and more on a bohalawn or a hemlock-stalk.

The good people called out together when they heard what Guleesh said:

"Oh! Guleesh, you clown, you thief, that no good may happen you, why did you play that trick on us?"

But they had no power at all to carry off the girl, after Guleesh had consecrated her to himself.

"Oh! Guleesh, isn't that a nice turn you did us, and we so kind to you? What good have we now out of our journey to France. Never mind yet, you clown, but you'll pay us another time for this. Believe us, you'll repent it."

"He'll have no good to get out of the young girl," said the little man that was talking to him in the palace before that, and as he said the word he moved over to her and struck her a slap on the side of the head. "Now," says he, "she'll be without talk any more; now, Guleesh, what good will she be to you when she'll be dumb? It's time for us to go—but you'll remember us, Guleesh!"

When he said that he stretched out his two hands, and before Guleesh was able to give an answer, he and the rest of them were gone into the rath out of his sight, and he saw them no more.

He turned to the young woman and said to her: "Thanks be to God, they're gone. Would you not sooner stay with me than with them?" She gave him no answer. "There's trouble and grief on her yet," said Guleesh in his own mind, and he spoke to her again: "I am afraid that you must spend this night in my father's house, lady, and if there is anything that I can do for you, tell me, and I'll be your servant."

The beautiful girl remained silent, but there were tears in her eyes, and her face was white and red after each other.

"Lady," said Guleesh, "tell me what you would like me to do now. I never belonged at all to that lot of sheehogues who carried you away with them. I am the son of an honest farmer, and I went with them without knowing it. If I'll be able to send you back to your father I'll do it, and I pray you make any use of me now that you may wish."

He looked into her face, and he saw the mouth moving as if she was going to speak, but there came no word from it.

"It cannot be," said Guleesh, "that you are dumb. Did I not hear you speaking to the king's son in the palace tonight? Or has that devil made you really dumb, when he struck his nasty hand on your jaw?"

The girl raised her white smooth hand, and laid her finger on her tongue, to show him that she had lost her voice and power of speech, and the tears ran out of her two eyes like streams, and Guleesh's own eyes were not dry, for as rough as he was on the outside he had a soft heart, and could not stand the sight of the young girl, and she in that unhappy plight.

He began thinking with himself what he ought to do, and he did not like to bring her home with himself to his father's house, for he knew well that they would not believe him, that he had been in France and brought back with him the king of France's daughter, and he was afraid they might make a mock of the young lady or insult her.

As he was doubting what he ought to do, and hesitating, he chanced to remember the priest. "Glory be to God," said he, "I know now what I'll do; I'll bring her to the priest's house, and he won't refuse me to keep the lady and care for her." He turned to the lady again and told her that he was loth to take her to his father's house, but that there was an excellent priest very friendly to himself, who would take good care of her, if she wished to remain in his house; but that if there was any other place she would rather go, he said he would bring her to it.

She bent her head, to show him she was obliged, and gave him to understand that she was ready to follow him any place he was going. "We will go to the priest's house, then," said he; "he is under an obligation to me, and will do anything I ask him."

They went together accordingly to the priest's house, and the sun was just rising when they came to the door. Guleesh beat it hard, and as early as it was the priest was up, and opened the door himself. He wondered when he saw Guleesh and the girl, for he was certain that it was coming wanting to be married they were.

"Guleesh, Guleesh, isn't it the nice boy you are that you can't wait till ten o'clock or till twelve, but that you must be coming to me at this hour, looking for marriage, you and your sweetheart? You ought to know that I can't marry you at such a time, or, at all events, can't marry you lawfully. But ubbubboo!" said he, suddenly, as he looked again at the young girl, "in the name of God, who have you here? Who is she, or how did you get her?"

"Father," said Guleesh, "you can marry me, or anybody else, if you wish; but it's not looking for marriage I came to you now, but to ask you, if you please, to give a lodging in your house to this young lady."

The priest looked at him as though he had ten heads on him; but without putting any other question to him, he desired him to come in, himself and the maiden, and when they came in, he shut the door, brought them into the parlour, and put them sitting.

"Now, Guleesh," said he, "tell me truly who is this young lady, and whether you're out of your senses really, or are only making a joke of me."

"I'm not telling a word of lie, nor making a joke of you," said Guleesh; "but it was from the palace of the king of France I carried off this lady, and she is the daughter of the king of France."

He began his story then, and told the whole to the priest, and the priest was so much surprised that he could not help calling out at times, or clapping his hands together.

When Guleesh said from what he saw he thought the girl was not satisfied with the marriage that was going to take place in the palace before he and the sheehogues broke it up, there came a red blush into the girl's cheek, and he was more certain than ever that she had sooner be as she was—badly as she was—than be the married wife of the man she hated. When Guleesh said that he would be very thankful to the priest if he would keep her in his own house, the kind man said he would do that as long as Guleesh pleased, but that he did not know what they ought to do with her, because they had no means of sending her back to her father again.

Guleesh answered that he was uneasy about the same thing, and that he saw nothing to do but to keep quiet until they should find some opportunity of doing something better. They made it up then between themselves that the priest should let on that it was his brother's daughter he had, who was come on a visit to him from another county, and that he should tell everybody that she was dumb, and do his best to keep every one away from her. They told the young girl what it was they intended to do, and she showed by her eyes that she was obliged to them.

Guleesh went home then, and when his people asked him where he had been, he said that he had been asleep at the foot of the ditch, and had passed the night there.

There was great wonderment on the priest's neighbours at the girl who came so suddenly to his house without any one knowing where she was from, or what business she had there. Some of the people said that everything was not as it ought to be, and others, that Guleesh was not like the same man that was in it before, and that it was a great story, how he was drawing every day to the priest's house, and that the priest had a wish and a respect for him, a thing they could not clear up at all.

That was true for them, indeed, for it was seldom the day went by but Guleesh would go to the priest's house, and have a talk with him, and as often as he would come he used to hope to find the young lady well again, and with leave to speak; but, alas! she remained dumb and silent, without relief or cure. Since she had no other means of talking, she carried on a sort of conversation between herself and himself, by moving her hand and fingers, winking her eyes, opening and shutting her mouth, laughing or smiling, and a thousand other signs, so that it was not long until they understood each other very well. Guleesh was always thinking how he should send her back to her father; but there was no one to go with her, and he himself did not know what road to go, for he had never been out of his own country before the night he brought her away with him. Nor had the priest any better knowledge than he; but when Guleesh asked him, he wrote three or four letters to the king of France, and gave them to buyers and sellers of wares, who used to be going from place to place across the sea; but they all went astray, and never a one came to the king's hand.

This was the way they were for many months, and Guleesh was falling deeper and deeper in love with her every day, and it was plain to himself and the priest that she liked him. The boy feared greatly at last, lest the king should really hear where his daughter was, and take her back from himself, and he besought the priest to write no more, but to leave the matter to God.

So they passed the time for a year, until there came a day when Guleesh was lying by himself, on the grass, on the last day of the last month in autumn, and he was thinking over again in his own mind of everything that happened to him from the day that he went with the sheehogues across the sea. He remembered then, suddenly, that it was one November night that he was standing at the gable of the house, when the whirlwind came, and the sheehogues in it, and he said to himself: "We have November night again today, and I'll stand in the same place I was last year, until I see if the good people come again. Perhaps I might see or hear something that would be useful to me, and might bring back her talk again to Mary"—that was the name himself and the priest called the king's daughter, for neither of them knew her right name. He told his intention to the priest, and the priest gave him his blessing.

Guleesh accordingly went to the old rath when the night was darkening, and he stood with his bent elbow leaning on a grey old flag, waiting till the middle of the night should come. The moon rose slowly; and it was like a knob of fire behind him; and there was a white fog which was raised up over the fields of grass and all damp places, through the coolness of the night after a great heat in the day. The night was calm as is a lake when there is not a breath of wind to move a wave on it, and there was no sound to be heard but the cronawn of the insects that would go by from time to time, or the hoarse sudden scream of the wild-geese, as they passed from lake to lake, half a mile up in the air over his head; or the sharp whistle of the golden and green plover, rising and lying, lying and rising, as they do on a calm night. There were a thousand thousand bright stars shining over his head, and there was a little frost out, which left the grass under his foot white and crisp.

He stood there for an hour, for two hours, for three hours, and the frost increased greatly, so that he heard the breaking of the traneens under his foot as often as he moved. He was thinking, in his own mind, at last, that the sheehogues would not come that night, and that it was as good for him to return back again, when he heard a sound far away from him, coming towards him, and he recognised what it was at the first moment. The sound increased, and at first it was like the beating of waves on a stony shore, and then it was like the falling of a great waterfall, and at last it was like a loud storm in the tops of the trees, and then the whirlwind burst into the rath of one rout, and the sheehogues were in it.

It all went by him so suddenly that he lost his breath with it, but he came to himself on the spot, and put an ear on himself, listening to what they would say.

Scarcely had they gathered into the rath till they all began shouting, and screaming, and talking amongst themselves; and then each one of them cried out: "My horse, and bridle, and saddle! My horse, and bridle, and saddle!" and Guleesh took courage, and called out as loudly as any of them: "My horse, and bridle, and saddle! My horse, and bridle, and saddle!" But before the word was well out of his mouth, another man cried out: "Ora! Guleesh, my boy, are you here with us again? How are you getting on with your woman? There's no use in your calling for your horse tonight. I'll go bail you won't play such a trick on us again.

It was a good trick you played on us last year?"

"It was," said another man; "he won't do it again."

"Isn't he a prime lad, the same lad! to take a woman with him that never said as much to him as, 'How do you do?' since this time last year!" says the third man.

"Perhaps he likes to be looking at her," said another voice.

"And if the omadawn only knew that there's an herb growing up by his own door, and if he were to boil it and give it to her, she'd be well," said another voice.

"That's true for you."

"He is an omadawn."

"Don't bother your head with him; we'll be going."

"We'll leave the bodach as he is."

And with that they rose up into the air, and out with them with one roolya-boolya the way they came; and they left poor Guleesh standing where they found him, and the two eyes going out of his head, looking after them and wondering.

He did not stand long till he returned back, and he thinking in his own mind on all he saw and heard, and wondering whether there was really an herb at his own door that would bring back the talk to the king's daughter. "It can't be," says he to himself, "that they would tell it to me, if there was any virtue in it; but perhaps the sheehogue didn't observe himself when he let the word slip out of his mouth. I'll search well as soon as the sun rises, whether there's any plant growing beside the house except thistles and dockings."

He went home, and as tired as he was he did not sleep a wink until the sun rose on the morrow. He got up then, and it was the first thing he did to go out and search well through the grass round about the house, trying could he get any herb that he did not recognise. And, indeed, he was not long searching till he observed a large strange herb that was growing up just by the gable of the house.

He went over to it, and observed it closely, and saw that there were seven little branches coming out of the stalk, and seven leaves growing on every branch_een_ of them; and that there was a white sap in the leaves. "It's very wonderful," said he to himself, "that I never noticed this herb before. If there's any virtue in an herb at all, it ought to be in such a strange one as this."

He drew out his knife, cut the plant, and carried it into his own house; stripped the leaves off it and cut up the stalk; and there came a thick, white juice out of it, as there comes out of the sow-thistle when it is bruised, except that the juice was more like oil.

He put it in a little pot and a little water in it, and laid it on the fire until the water was boiling, and then he took a cup, filled it half up with the juice, and put it to his own mouth. It came into his head then that perhaps it was poison that was in it, and that the good people were only tempting him that he might kill himself with that trick, or put the girl to death without meaning it. He put down the cup again, raised a couple of drops on the top of his finger, and put it to his mouth. It was not bitter, and, indeed, had a sweet, agreeable taste. He grew bolder then, and drank the full of a thimble of it, and then as much again, and he never stopped till he had half the cup drunk. He fell asleep after that, and did not wake till it was night, and there was great hunger and great thirst on him.

He had to wait, then, till the day rose; but he determined, as soon as he should wake in the morning, that he would go to the king's daughter and give her a drink of the juice of the herb.

As soon as he got up in the morning, he went over to the priest's house with the drink in his hand, and he never felt himself so bold and valiant, and spirited and light, as he was that day, and he was quite certain that it was the drink he drank which made him so hearty.

When he came to the house, he found the priest and the young lady within, and they were wondering greatly why he had not visited them for two days.

He told them all his news, and said that he was certain that there was great power in that herb, and that it would do the lady no hurt, for he tried it himself and got good from it, and then he made her taste it, for he vowed and swore that there was no harm in it.

Guleesh handed her the cup, and she drank half of it, and then fell back on her bed and a heavy sleep came on her, and she never woke out of that sleep till the day on the morrow.

Guleesh and the priest sat up the entire night with her, waiting till she should awake, and they between hope and unhope, between expectation of saving her and fear of hurting her.

She awoke at last when the sun had gone half its way through the heavens. She rubbed her eyes and looked like a person who did not know where she was. She was like one astonished when she saw Guleesh and the priest in the same room with her, and she sat up doing her best to collect her thoughts.

The two men were in great anxiety waiting to see would she speak, or would she not speak, and when they remained silent for a couple of minutes, the priest said to her: "Did you sleep well, Mary?"

And she answered him: "I slept, thank you."

No sooner did Guleesh hear her talking than he put a shout of joy out of him, and ran over to her and fell on his two knees, and said: "A thousand thanks to God, who has given you back the talk; lady of my heart, speak again to me."

The lady answered him that she understood it was he who boiled that drink for her, and gave it to her; that she was obliged to him from her heart for all the kindness he showed her since the day she first came to Ireland, and that he might be certain that she never would forget it.

Guleesh was ready to die with satisfaction and delight. Then they brought her food, and she ate with a good appetite, and was merry and joyous, and never left off talking with the priest while she was eating.

After that Guleesh went home to his house, and stretched himself on the bed and fell asleep again, for the force of the herb was not all spent, and he passed another day and a night sleeping. When he woke up he went back to the priest's house, and found that the young lady was in the same state, and that she was asleep almost since the time that he left the house.

He went into her chamber with the priest, and they remained watching beside her till she awoke the second time, and she had her talk as well as ever, and Guleesh was greatly rejoiced. The priest put food on the table again, and they ate together, and Guleesh used after that to come to the house from day to day, and the friendship that was between him and the king's daughter increased, because she had no one to speak to except Guleesh and the priest, and she liked Guleesh best.

So they married one another, and that was the fine wedding they had, and if I were to be there then, I would not be here now; but I heard it from a birdeen that there was neither cark nor care, sickness nor sorrow, mishap nor misfortune on them till the hour of their death, and may the same be with me, and with us all!

The Field of Boliauns

ONE FINE DAY IN HARVEST—it was indeed Lady-day in harvest, that everybody knows to be one of the greatest holidays in the year—Tom Fitzpatrick was taking a ramble through the ground, and went along the sunny side of a hedge; when all of a sudden he heard a clacking sort of noise a little before him in the hedge. "Dear me," said Tom, "but isn't it surprising to hear the stonechatters singing so late in the season?" So Tom stole on, going on the tops of his toes to try if he could get a sight of what was making the noise, to see if he was right in his guess. The noise stopped; but as Tom looked sharply through the bushes, what should he see in a nook of the hedge but a brown pitcher, that might hold about a gallon and a half of liquor; and by-and-by a little wee teeny tiny bit of an old man, with a little motty of a cocked hat stuck upon the top of his head, a deeshy daushy leather apron hanging before him, pulled out a little wooden stool, and stood up upon it, and dipped a little piggin into the pitcher, and took out the full of it, and put it beside the stool, and then sat down under the pitcher, and began to work at putting a heel-piece on a bit of a brogue just fit for himself. "Well, by the powers," said Tom to himself, "I often heard tell of the Leprechauns, and, to tell God's truth, I never rightly believed in them—but here's one of them in real earnest. If I go knowingly to work, I'm a made man. They say a body must never take their eyes off them, or they'll escape."

Tom now stole on a little further, with his eye fixed on the little man just as a cat does with a mouse. So when he got up quite close to him, "God bless your work, neighbour," said Tom.

The little man raised up his head, and "Thank you kindly," said he.

"I wonder you'd be working on the holiday!" said Tom.

"That's my own business, not yours," was the reply.

"Well, may be you'd be civil enough to tell us what you've got in the pitcher there?" said Tom.

"That I will, with pleasure," said he; "it's good beer."

"Beer!" said Tom. "Thunder and fire! where did you get it?"

"Where did I get it, is it? Why, I made it. And what do you think I made it of?"

"Devil a one of me knows," said Tom; "but of malt, I suppose, what else?"

"There you're out. I made it of heath."

"Of heath!" said Tom, bursting out laughing; "sure you don't think me to be such a fool as to believe that?"

"Do as you please," said he, "but what I tell you is the truth. Did you never hear tell of the Danes?"

"Well, what about *them*?" said Tom.

"Why, all the about them there is, is that when they were here they taught us to make beer out of the heath, and the secret's in my family ever since."

"Will you give a body a taste of your beer?" said Tom.

"I'll tell you what it is, young man, it would be fitter for you to be looking after your father's property than to be bothering decent quiet people with your foolish questions. There now, while you're idling away your time here, there's the cows have broke into the oats, and are knocking the corn all about."

Tom was taken so by surprise with this that he was just on the very point of turning round when he recollected himself; so, afraid that the like might happen again, he made a grab at the Leprechaun, and caught him up in his hand; but in his hurry he overset the pitcher, and spilt all the beer, so that he could not get a taste of it to tell what sort it was. He then swore that he would kill him if he did not show him where his money was. Tom looked so wicked and so bloody-minded that the little man was quite frightened; so says he, "Come along with me a couple of fields off, and I'll show you a crock of gold."

So they went, and Tom held the Leprechaun fast in his hand, and never took his eyes from off him, though they had to cross hedges and ditches, and a crooked bit of bog, till at last they came to a great field all full of boliauns, and the Leprechaun pointed to a big boliaun, and says he, "Dig under that boliaun, and you'll get the great crock all full of guineas."

Tom in his hurry had never thought of bringing a spade with him, so he made up his mind to run home and fetch one; and that he might know the place again he took off one of his red garters, and tied it round the boliaun.

Then he said to the Leprechaun, "Swear ye'll not take that garter away from that boliaun." And the Leprechaun swore right away not to touch it.

"I suppose," said the Leprechaun, very civilly, "you have no further occasion for me?"

"No," says Tom; "you may go away now, if you please, and God speed you, and may good luck attend you wherever you go."

"Well, good-bye to you, Tom Fitzpatrick," said the Leprechaun; "and much good may it do you when you get it."

So Tom ran for dear life, till he came home and got a spade, and then away with him, as hard as he could go, back to the field of boliauns; but when he got there, lo and behold! not a boliaun in the field but had a red garter, the very model of his own, tied about it; and as to digging up the whole field, that was all nonsense, for there were more than forty good Irish acres in it. So Tom came home again with his spade on his shoulder, a little cooler than he went, and many's the hearty curse he gave the Leprechaun every time he thought of the neat turn he had served him.

Legends of Ghosts

IN SCOTLAND, stories of ghosts and evil-spirits form a rich and vibrant tradition, as alive today as it was centuries ago. It is one of the oldest genres of Scottish mythology and certainly the most enduring, for as little is known today as it ever was about where we go when we leave this earth. Our spirits may visit the realms of heaven, but we have religion to explain that. What of that time before the soul leaves the body? And what of the body in the ground? The dank, dark earth houses many secrets, and it is there that ghosts and other spirits are bred. The newly dead and the long-dead are the most frightening, for they are most venomous in their attacks on unsuspecting family, or even strangers. Beware of a fleeting glimpse of something unknown; watch out for that unexplained flash of light in a haunted house; take note when a chair moves suddenly in an empty room. And if a body is laid out for burial in a house near to you, sleep elsewhere, for the spirits of the dead can come back, in many strange forms. There's no doubt of that, as these stories will tell.

The Fiddler of Gord

❦

T HERE ONCE WAS A MAN who lived in Sandness, near Papa Stour. He was a fisherman by trade, but he was known across the lands for the tunes he played on his fine fiddle. Folk came for miles to hear his music, and he could dance and sing a bit, so making it a real evening for anyone who cared to join in.

Now one cold night he left his cottage home, which was nestled in the base of a knoll, sheltered from the winds which burst over the hills from the sea. He left that night grudgingly, for the fire was warm and the company merry, but the larders were empty and more fish must be got by morning. So out he went into the frosted air, which crisped his breath and crunched under his feet. And on to his cold, dark boat he climbed, then out to sea, where he settled himself under oilskins and drew out his fine fiddle and began to play. And the Fiddler of Gord, as the man was called, played for hours as the fish drew closer to hear the wondrous music, catching themselves in his nets, but fighting not at all, so comforted were they by the strains from his fiddle.

Then the fiddler headed homewards, his basket groaning with fresh fish, tastier for having expired happily. As he passed the grassy knoll that hid his sweet, snug cottage from the fierce winds, he heard a graceful melody, and stopping in his tracks and laying down his basket, he listened. There was a light which glinted and beckoned through the grass and he was drawn towards it, as the music grew louder.

A door had opened in the hill, and from inside came the enchanted music of the fairy folk, a melody so divine and simple that his heart grew larger in his breast and he pulsed with pure pleasure. The Fiddler of Gord entered the door that night, and it was shut firmly behind him.

The cottage, tucked into the base of the knoll, was quiet as the night grew longer and the fiddler had not returned, and finally, when it neared dawn, the youngest son was sent out with a lantern, and when he returned with the fiddler's basket of fish there was no doubt in their minds that he'd been blown down the cliffs into the sea. The family lived there for many years, but the fiddler did not return. Finally, they moved from that place to another, and a new family took over the wee cosy cottage tucked into the base of the knoll, and they made a happy home there, warmed by the hearth and protected from the angry winds by the arm of the hillock.

It was on one windy night, when the sky howled at the thundering clouds, that a knock was heard on the door of this warm cottage, and when the door was opened there appeared an old man, bent and cold, and he thrust his hands at the fire, laying his fiddle to one side. And as he looked around he realized that it was not his family who gazed at him with astonishment, but another, and they wore garments which spoke of ages to come, not those he had come to know.

The children who played at the feet of the chairs came to gawk, and he asked, with all the rage he could muster, 'Where is my family? This is my house' to which the new family all laughed and called him mad and a coot from the whiskey barrel.

But the old grandfather of the family stayed silent, and then, at length, he said quietly to their indignant guest, 'Where do you hail from, man?' And when the Fiddler of Gord explained, the grandfather nodded his head slowly and said, 'Yes, you did live here once, but a man of your name disappeared, gone a hundred years now.'

'Well, where are my folk then?' whispered the Fiddler of Gord, his face a mask of confusion and fear.

'Dead,' came the reply, and the room was quiet once more.

'And so I'll join them,' said the fiddler, and drawing himself up to his full height he left the glow of the hearth, and the warmth of the family, and he headed to the top of the hillock, where the winds blew cold and frosty, crisping his breath and crunching under his feet, and he was followed by the wee lad of the house, who hid behind a bush at the base of the hillock to watch.

And there, in a glorious symphony of sound the fiddler played a rich and moving song that tugged at the chords of the wee lad's heart and filled his eyes with burning tears. And those tears burnt the melody into his memory, and it remained there until he died. Then the fiddler looked over at the northern star and played the tune once again, and collapsed, his fiddle flying over the hilltop into the sea.

And when the bairn summoned the courage to creep over to the old man, he found there a body of one who had died near one hundred years earlier. So he crept away home again, all the while humming a song that would haunt him till his dying day, blinded by tears and seeing not the door of a magic kingdom which had opened to welcome him to its timeless light.

MacPhail of Uisinnis

MORE THAN THREE CENTURIES AGO there lived a man in Uisinnis, and his name was MacPhail. He was a big man, strong and silent, and he lived in a great stone house with his wife, his son, his son's wife, and their daughter. Now woe had fallen upon the family some thirteen years earlier when the daughter of MacPhail's son had been born dumb. Never a word had crossed the tongue of the young lass, but she was quiet and kind and well-liked by all.

The sad day came when old MacPhail died, and his body was dressed and laid at the end of their great stone house in preparation for burial. And his son, dressed in the black of mourning, drove off that day, to tend to the arrangements and gather together the old man's friends. He would be gone for a day, leaving the three women alone.

That night, as the moon hung high in the sky, lighting the path to the great stone house, and setting the rooms aglow with its beams, a scuffling was heard from the room with the body, and as the noise grew much louder, there came a shriek.

And from the mouth of the dumb girl who had never before spoken a word, came the cry, 'Granny, Granny. My grandfather is up, and he's coming to get you! He'll eat you, he will, but he won't touch me.'

And the old woman flew from her bed, and sure enough, there, striding down the hall was the man who had laid at the end of the hall, dead and about to be buried. And she slammed her door, and thrust the wardrobe against it, and the boxes and piles of mending. She screamed with fright, but the door was shut tight.

Then, at this, the old MacPhail bent down and began to dig. And he dug there for some time, his great hands heaving earth and rocks from under the doorframe, until a tunnel was bored straight under the door. And as he wedged his way into this space, and thrust his mighty shoulders up the other side, his face a mask of horrible pain and determination, a cock flew down from the rafters, on to the floor. And there he crowed three times, and returned to his loft.

And old MacPhail ceased his digging then, and he fell deep into the trough he had dug, stone dead.

His son returned to Uissinis the following morning, and there he found a wife and a mother who could hardly utter a word, and a daughter who could not stop speaking of the ghost that had come. And thinking them all quite mad, he was stopped short in his tracks by the sight of his father, his hands torn and bloodied, half of him in a hole under his mother's door, and half of him out.

Old MacPhail was buried the next day, but the hole he had dug beneath that doorway is still there, in the ruins of that ancient house, and there's been no one able to fill it. 'MacPhail's Pit' is its name, and the spirit of that man lies within it to this day.

Tarbh Na Leòid

ON THE ISLAND OF HEISKER, just west of Uist, lies an enchanted loch. Here lived a water-horse who was so terrible that everyone feared he would enter the village and destroy them all. And so it was that an old man in the village who knew of such things advised his neighbours to raise a bull, one to each household, and never let it out until it was needed.

For many years, the village was safe. Women washed their clothes at the loch in pairs, for everyone knew that the water-horse would only strike if you ventured to the loch alone. And every household had a bull, never let out in the event that it would be needed. But so it was one year, that the villagers had become a wee bit complacent about the water-horse, and women began to be a little less careful about doing their laundry in pairs. And one day, for whatever the reason, a woman washed alone there, and when she finished, she laid down on the banks of the river and slept there.

The sun was high in the sky, and she was warmed into a deep slumber. When she woke, she saw a magnificent man standing there, the sun glinting on his golden hair, and lighting his clear blue eyes. He spoke to her then, about the fineness of the afternoon, and she spoke back.

'You must be very tired, after all that washing,' he said kindly, and the woman blushed, for the men of Heisker never cared much about a woman's tiredness, or about the washing.

'I am indeed,' she stammered.

'Do you mind if I join you there?' He smiled at her. 'Because I am pretty tired myself.'

'Oh, no,' she said sweetly, and made room beside her.

Now that fine young man sat down beside her, and then spoke again.

'Do you mind if I lay my head in your lap?' he whispered, and the woman flushed again and shook her head.

And so it was that this young woman was sitting by the sunny banks of the loch with the head of a handsome young man in her lap. And as she gazed down, hardly believing her good fortune, she noticed sea-dirt in his hair, and weeds, and bits of water-moss. And only then did she notice his hooves, which lay crossed in slumber.

The water-horse.

And carefully, ever so gently, the woman took from her washing bag a pair of sharp scissors, and cutting a hole in her coat where the water-horse's head lay, she slipped out from under him, leaving a bit of her coat behind.

And then she ran back to the village, and as the fear struck her, she shrieked to the villagers, 'Help, it's the water-horse.'

There was a neighing behind her, and the sound of hooves on gravel, and she ran all the faster, calling for help.

Now the old man heard her first, and he called out to his neighbour, a man named MacLeod, whose bull was the closest. The bull was called Tarbh na Leòid, and he was a fierce creature, all the more so for being kept inside all his life.

'Let loose Tarbh na Leòid,' cried the woman, rushing into the village. 'Turn him loose!'

And so the bull was let loose, and he threw himself at the water-horse and there ensued a fight so horrific that the villagers could hardly watch. And it carried on for hours, and then days, and finally the bull beat that water-horse back to the loch, and they both disappeared.

The woman returned to her home, and she laid down on her bed, never to rise again. Nor did the bull or the water-horse, although it is said that the horn of Tarbh na Leòid rose to the surface of the water one fine day, many years later. It's still there, they say, guarding the path to the loch of the water-horse.

Origin and Didactic Legends

THE LEGENDS WHICH TELL of the genesis of the earth, of the countryside, and its inhabitants may seem wild and unlikely, but for many centuries they were used to account for landmarks, and the origins of creatures. For man has always longed to make sense of his beginnings, to give a formula to the chaos from which we began, and if a hill resembles the footprint of a giant, there's every reason to believe there was once one there. Didactic legends, too, seem far-fetched at times, but the moral is always clear – if you live by the rules, you are safe from the clutches of witches and fairy-folk; if you eat well, you'll have good luck. The simplicity of the message is engaging, but the strictures they put upon daily life were not, for men lived whole lives in fear because of a dirty deed done in childhood, or a curse flung casually by an unhappy neighbour. But so it was that all good boys ate their porridge, and hung a bit of rowan over a door, and treated their wives with kindness. For no one knew who might visit them next, and what that visit might mean. ✺

Dubh a' Ghiubhais

❧

I T WAS MANY HUNDREDS OF YEARS AGO, long before the days when stories were written down, that Scotland was covered in a great dark forest. This was a forest of fir trees, tall and fine as any to be seen, and there lived there a colony of people who made the trees their friends. Trees can be good friends indeed, for they spread their arms across the land, protecting it from the wind that blows from the stormy coasts, and the rain which is carried on its back. And they make homes for the wee folk, and animals of the forest, and wood for the houses and fires of the men who live there.

Now this fine forest was much admired, and there was one in particular who was very envious of Scotland's great dark trees. He was the king of Lochlann and he wanted more than anything to destroy them. He would pace round his castle, overcast and gloomy as the winter sky, and he would lament his unhappy lot, ridden right through with jealousy as hot as any good peat fire.

It was his daughter, the princess, who had watched this curious pacing for years on end who finally came to find out the cause of his unhappiness. He explained that he wished to find a way to destroy the trees of the Scottish forest; and that wee princess, she was a practical lass, and she said there was nothing for it but to do it herself.

And so it was that she bade her father leave to find a witch to put her in the shape of a bird, and when he'd done that, and when she'd become a beautiful, pure white bird, she set out over the grassy hills of Lochlann to the deep fir forests that carpeted the Scottish land. On the west coast of Scotland she came down, and there she struck a tree with a wand she had under her wing. With that single motion the tree would burst into flames and burn there, and it was not long before this beautiful white bird had burnt a great number of trees in that forest.

Now this beautiful white bird was no longer fair or pure; indeed, the smoke of the pinewood had cast an ugly black shadow across her feathers and she came to be known by the people of the country as the Dubh a' Ghiubhais, or Fir Black. And so it was that this Dubh a' Ghiubhais flew across the land, causing damage that robbed the wee folk of their homes and sent the animals scattering for shelter, and the men had no wood for their homes or their fires, and the trees could no longer spread their comforting arms across the land, protecting it from the wind that blows from the stormy coasts, bringing the rain on its back. And it was for this reason that the men of the land grouped together and decided that this bird must be stopped, for the Dubh a' Ghiubhais had brought sadness and rain to their sheltered lives.

It was not easy to catch the Dubh a' Ghiubhais, but it was heard, somewhere on the west coast of Scotland, that the bird had a soft, sweet heart in that blackened breast, and that a plan could be made to capture it.

And so it was that a man at Loch Broom hatched the plan, and on the very next morning spent a day at work in his barnyard, taking mother from her young all across the barn. For the piglets were taken wailing from their sows, the puppies barked as they were snatched from their mothers' teats, the foals were taken from mares, the lambs from sheep, the calves from the cows, the chickens from the hens, the kittens from the cats, and even the kids from the goats that grazed on the tender shoots of grass on the verge. And the uproar that followed was enough to churn the stomach of any man alive, for there were cries so piteous, so plaintive, so needing that the men and women for miles around hid themselves under soft down pillows in order to block out that dreadful sound.

It was not long before it reached the ears of the Dubh a' Ghiubhais, who was passing on her fiery course of devastation. And her soft, sweet heart nearly burst with pity for these poor creatures. She flew at once to the ground, and drawing her wand from beneath her wing she made as if to set the animals free when a small sharp arrow stung her breast, piercing her heart and bringing a clean, cold death. And the man at Loch Broom picked up his quiver and slinging it over his shoulder, bent over to collect the dead bird.

And so it was that the Dubh a' Ghiubhais was hung from a tree, where folk gathered round to cheer her death. News of what had happened reached her father, the king of Lochlann, and he was torn with grief and guilt. He sent his hardiest crew in a great long boat to bring the body of his dear daughter home. But there were fearful gales which pitched and jolted the ships that carried the funeral pyre, and although the brave sailors tried three times, they could get no further than the mouth of the Little Loch Broom.

And so it was that the Dubh a' Ghiubhais was buried beneath the tree where she hung, at Kildonan, at the bend of the loch at Little Loch Broom. She rests there still, a single fir tree growing atop her grave, which lies beneath a grassy green hillock.

The Pabbay Mother's Ghost

THERE ONCE WAS A MAN WHO LIVED in a cottage in Pabbay, a kindly man who knew a woman's needs and saw to them in the course of every day. And so it was that when this kindly man's wife was in childbed, he made for her a great steaming bowl of porridge with butter. For the oats and butter in the porridge would make her strong, and the baby would be born without a murmur.

This man sat by the fireside that night, stirring the porridge and reaching across occasionally to mop the brow of his sweet, dear wife. And then a woman came in and sat by him on his bench, and she asked quietly for a bowl of the steaming porridge with butter. The man handed her the bowl without a word and carried on stirring, reaching across occasionally to mop the brow of his sweet, dear wife. And when the woman returned her bowl empty he filled it once more, and then again, until the woman had three great pots of porridge with butter. But still the man made no sound, passing another bowl across to his wife now and then, reaching across occasionally to mop her sweet, dear brow.

And then the woman stood up, and she said to the man, as he stirred his porridge, 'There, that's what I should have had when I was in childbed myself, for I am strong now, and my baby would have been born without a murmur. It was hunger that was the cause of my death, but now, as long as a drop of your blood remains, no woman shall ever die in childbed if anyone who tends her with porridge and butter is related to you.'

So the woman left the cottage in Pabbay, and it was not long before the man's baby was born without a murmur, and his sweet, dear wife sat up strong and healthy in the childbed. And from that time on, not a wife or child of his, or a wife or child of his children died, for like their forefather, they knew a woman's needs and saw to them in the course of every day.

Luran

THERE ONCE WAS A CROFTER and his wife, and they lived in a glen far from the prying eyes of neighbours. They were quiet folk, but they lived well, with a herd of cattle to be envied, and a good bit of land. Their house was snug and warm in the coldest months, they had cream and milk and butter, and they wanted for nothing, in that glen, far from the prying eyes of neighbours.

Now that crofter was a healthy man, and he liked nothing more than a good meal, particularly if it was a feast of his favourite oakcakes, smeared with butter and dipped again in cream. And he partook of this kind of meal on most days so he grew rather heavy and clumsy. But their house was safe from any kind of danger, being far from the prying eyes of neighbours, and he grew perhaps a little too satisfied, and a little too complacent in his happy home.

For it was a cold Hallowe'en evening that strange things began to happen on the land of that satisfied crofter, and although everyone living near the fairy folk knows that Hallowe'en evening is their time for mischief, the crofter had not had cause to worry before this particular Hallowe'en night.

It was just as he was settling himself and his wife into their beds that they heard the howling of their guard dog, and a rumpus going on in the henhouse. And then they heard the cattle lowing, and everyone knows that cattle never low in the dead of night, so the crofter and his wife grew alarmed. Then he put back on his outdoor clothes, and he lit a lantern and headed towards the barnyard.

There, an astonishing sight met his eyes, for the barnyard was empty, his cattle gone, his pig sty clean, his henhouse bare. And the crofter sat down and held his head in his hands, and he asked himself how such a thing could happen to a house tucked so neatly in the glen, far from the prying eyes of neighbours. And then he started, for there was the sound of a lowing cow just over the knoll, and when he looked more closely there were tracks heading there too.

And so it was that the crofter plucked up his courage that Hallowe'en night, and went over that knoll, into the realm of the fairies. He crept there silently, until he heard voices. Then he stopped and he listened.

'Luran didn't run,' came a voice.

'Didn't run at all,' said another.

'Couldn't run at all,' giggled the first, and then there was a great deal of scuffling and laughter.

'If only his bread were not so hard,' said the other, 'but if Luran were fed on porridge, Luran would outrun the deer.'

And the crofter heard this conversation, and filled with fear (for everyone knows that fairies who speak English are the most dangerous of all) he peeked over the hilltop. There sat two smug fairies and just beyond them were his cattle, and all the livestock of the barnyard. He sat back again, Luran the satisfied crofter, and he began to think.

And when he returned home to greet his anxious wife, he was still thinking, and again in the morning when she offered him his favourite meal of oatcakes, smeared in butter and dipped again in cream. And so it was that Luran held up his hand and said to his wife, 'You'll have to give me porridge and milk every day.'

As the days shortened and then lengthened again, Luran grew long and lean, and a fine, fit sight of a man he was. He worked on his farm and he raised more cattle, and on that house in the glen, far from the prying eyes of neighbours, Luran plotted his revenge.

It was twelve months now, and Luran was ready. Hallowe'en night found the crofter hidden in the stable of cattle, peering restlessly across their troughs. He was soon rewarded, for in popped the same two fairies who had visited there before, and as they led the first cattle away from his barn, Luran leapt up and chased those fairies over the knoll. And when he caught them, not far from the top, they gazed at him in surprise, and danced a fairy dance of approval.

So the crofter returned to his cosy house, leading his cattle back to the stable. And never again did those fairies trouble that house, tucked in the glen, far from the prying eyes of neighbours, for the master of that house ate nothing but porridge and milk, as all good men should.

The Hugboy

THERE ONCE WAS A GIANT, a hugboy he was called, and he lived with his wife somewhere near Caithness. Now they fought a great deal, that hugboy and his wife, and when they stamped their feet and howled, the little folk scurried for cover, for it was likely that a boulder or two could be thrown in their direction, or a mighty foot placed firmly upon a house or farm. Some say it was at that time that the fairy folk went to live inside the hills, for only then were they safe from the rages of the hugboy and his wife.

Well, so it happened, one dark day, that the hugboy fell out with his wife, and having had enough of his tempers, and with one of her own to match, she set out from home, never to return.

The hugboy was furious, for he chased her north, stepping through the Pentland Firth, and when he caught sight of her once more he threw a great stone at her. She was nearly flying now, so furious and fast she was making away from the hugboy, and up Ireland Brae she ran as he threw another great boulder that missed its mark. But that stone still lies in the field above Ramsquoy, and his great fierce fingermarks are in it still. She ran still further, the wife of the hugboy, for there is another stone he threw at her in the Lylie Banks at Skaill in Sandwick.

But that's where he lost her, and the hugboy stopped his chase and set about finding some turf to build himself a new home, so far had he come from his old one. He stomped further north, scooping up handfuls of turf and placing them in his great straw basket. One handful carved out the Loch of Harry, and another made the Loch of Stenness. And then going back to lay the foundations of his great new house, he tripped, and stubbed his toe, whereupon a great bit of turf fell off that is now Graemsay. His toe fell off, too, and it forms a hillock that is mossed but cannot hide the fact that it was once a part of the hapless hugboy.

It was here that his great basket gave way, tipping its contents over the land. Now that giant had never had such a bad day, and in disgust he left the contents of his basket strewn as they lay, and that is what became the hills of Hoy. He turned towards home now, rubbing his sore head, stopping occasionally to adjust a sandal over his sore foot, and lamented his unhappy lot. For who could be so unlucky as to have lost a wife and a toe in one day.

The Three Questions of King James

THERE ONCE WAS A SCOTTISH PRIEST, a man adored by his flock, but not by the King himself; King James he was, and not an easy man to please. Well, this priest had crossed the path of the King and in the course of doing so had managed to offend him. And so it was decreed that the priest would be hung by his neck at the palace at Scone.

The poor kind priest had accepted his lot, when word came that there had been a partial reprieve. For if that priest would come along to

Scone, and sit there with the King, and answer three questions that the King would put to him, he would be free to go home, to preach among his flock once more.

Now questions are difficult things, for there are some that have no answers at all, and some that can be put in a way that even the wisest man on earth could find no answer. And although the priest was a clever man, and he knew from the top to the bottom his great black Bible, he knew there would be traps, for who would let a man free on the back of three easy questions.

So he mulled over this dilemma, and he hummed and he hawed, and it was many days that he paced round his country cottage, and tapped his head, and sighed.

And then his brother, who lived with him and who was known to all as the simpleton he was, said, 'What is making you so catty?'

'Och, what use is it telling you, you're a simpleton no doubt.'

'Ahh, but can I not hear your problem? Maybe I can help?'

Now the priest thought little of this offer of help, but he was at the end of his frayed wits and he poured out his story to the simpleton man. He explained he was to be executed, and that there would be three questions put to him which could save his life.

'Hmmm,' said his brother, 'there are, you know, questions that just can't be answered.'

'I know it, I know it,' said the priest, shrugging unhappily. 'What am I to do?'

Now the priest was a good man, and even his simpleton brother could see this. 'I am going in your place,' he said firmly.

'Oh no. How can a fool like you answer questions that may not have answers?' asked the priest.

'Well it seems to me that if you are killed I will die too, for how can a simpleton live on his own. If I am executed in your place, what is the difference?'

So the priest agreed finally that his brother should go in his place, and so he draped his habit over the simpleton and handed him his staff. A prayer was said on his head and then the simpleton set off for Scone.

When he arrived, he was greeted by a man in a fine uniform, gold and blue and red, and he gravely ushered the priest's brother into the grand hall, for they had been expecting him, and the King was waiting. So the priest's brother was taken then to the King's room, where he sat on a throne that was more opulent than anything the young man had seen before. The room was hung with gold and jewels that winked and sparkled as the candles flickered in the breeze of his entrance. And the young man was enchanted by this fine sight, and he turned eyes at the stiff-faced King which shone as rich and true as any gem.

Now the king had chosen questions which were designed to trap the priest, for he cared not if he lived or died, and he settled back to watch the holy man's discomfort.

'You know why you are here,' he said gravely.

'Oh, yes,' said the simpleton in the priest's disguise.

'Well, then, let us begin. First question: where is the centre of the world?'

'Why, it's right here!' And the simpleton stamped the floor with his great staff.

'Oh!' The King looked surprised. 'I must let you have that one. Yes, I believe that you are right. For the world is a ball, and anywhere can be its centre. Yes, yes ...' he stroked his great beard, 'I'll let you have that one.' And then he continued, 'Next question: What am I worth sitting here, in all this,' he gestured round the room. 'Just what am I worth in money?'

'Well,' said the simpleton without hesitation, 'you are not worth anything more than thirty pieces of silver.'

'Why do you say that?' said the King with some consternation.

'Because the greatest man ever to enter the world was sold for only thirty shillings,' said the simpleton simply.

'Quite right,' blustered the king. 'I'll give you that one, too. Then the third question – and if you can answer this you'll be a free man ...

Do you know what I am thinking now?'

And with that the King sat back, for there was no way that even a man of the cloth could know the kingly thoughts of a monarch.

But the simpleton blazed on. 'Why yes, I do,' he said.

'What's that, then?' said the King, sitting up with amazement.

'You think you are talking to a priest, and you are talking to a fool, his brother,' he said then.

And so it was that the stony King James rose from his throne to shake the hand of a simpleton, and then he laughed out loud.

'Be free man,' he said. Anyone who has a brother like that, and that brother a simpleton, deserves to be free. Away you go.'

King O'Toole and his Goose

OCH, I thought all the world, far and near, had heerd o' King O'Toole—well, well, but the darkness of mankind is untellible! Well, sir, you must know, as you didn't hear it afore, that there was a king, called King O'Toole, who was a fine old king in the old ancient times, long ago; and it was he that owned the churches in the early days. The king, you see, was the right sort; he was the real boy, and loved sport as he loved his life, and hunting in particular; and from the rising o' the sun, up he got, and away he went over the mountains after the deer; and fine times they were.

Well, it was all mighty good, as long as the king had his health; but, you see, in course of time the king grew old, by raison he was stiff in his limbs, and when he got stricken in years, his heart failed him, and he was lost entirely for want o' diversion, because he couldn't go a-hunting no longer; and, by dad, the poor king was obliged at last to get a goose to divert him. Oh, you may laugh, if you like, but it's truth I'm telling you; and the way the goose diverted him was this-a-way: You see, the goose used to swim across the lake, and go diving for trout, and catch fish on a Friday for the king, and flew every other day round about the lake, diverting the poor king. All went on mighty well until, by dad, the goose got stricken in years like her master, and couldn't divert him no longer, and then it was that the poor king was lost entirely. The king was walkin' one mornin' by the edge of the lake, lamentin' his cruel fate, and thinking of drowning himself, that could get no diversion in life, when all of a sudden, turning round the corner, who should he meet but a mighty decent young man coming up to him.

"God save you," says the king to the young man.

"God save you kindly, King O'Toole," says the young man.

"True for you," says the king. "I am King O'Toole," says he, "prince and plennypennytinchery of these parts," says he; "but how came ye to know that?" says he.

"Oh, never mind," says St. Kavin.

You see it was Saint Kavin, sure enough—the saint himself in disguise, and nobody else. "Oh, never mind," says he, "I know more than that. May I make bold to ask how is your goose, King O'Toole?" says he.

"Blur-an-agers, how came ye to know about my goose?" says the king.

"Oh, no matter; I was given to understand it," says Saint Kavin.

After some more talk the king says, "What are you?"

"I'm an honest man," says Saint Kavin.

"Well, honest man," says the king, "and how is it you make your money so aisy?"

"By makin' old things as good as new," says Saint Kavin.

"Is it a tinker you are?" says the king.

"No," says the saint; "I'm no tinker by trade, King O'Toole; I've a better trade than a tinker," says he—"what would you say," says he, "if I made your old goose as good as new?"

My dear, at the word of making his goose as good as new, you'd think the poor old king's eyes were ready to jump out of his head. With that the king whistled, and down came the poor goose, just like a hound, waddling up to the poor cripple, her master, and as like him as two peas. The minute the saint clapt his eyes on the goose, "I'll do the job for you," says he, "King O'Toole."

"By Jaminee!" says King O'Toole, "if you do, I'll say you're the cleverest fellow in the seven parishes."

"Oh, by dad," says St. Kavin, "you must say more nor that—my horn's not so soft all out," says he, "as to repair your old goose for nothing; what'll you gi' me if I do the job for you?—that's the chat," says St. Kavin.

"I'll give you whatever you ask," says the king; "isn't that fair?"

"Divil a fairer," says the saint; "that's the way to do business. Now," says he, "this is the bargain I'll make with you, King O'Toole: will you gi' me all the ground the goose flies over, the first offer, after I make her as good as new?"

"I will," says the king.

"You won't go back o' your word?" says St. Kavin.

"Honour bright!" says King O'Toole, holding out his fist.

"Honour bright!" says St. Kavin, back agin, "it's a bargain. Come here!" says he to the poor old goose—"come here, you unfortunate ould cripple, and it's I that'll make you the sporting bird." With that, my dear, he took up the goose by the two wings—"Criss o' my cross an you," says he, markin' her to grace with the blessed sign at the same minute—and throwing her up in the air, "whew," says he, jist givin' her a blast to help her; and with that, my jewel, she took to her heels, flyin' like one o' the eagles themselves, and cutting as many capers as a swallow before a shower of rain.

Well, my dear, it was a beautiful sight to see the king standing with his mouth open, looking at his poor old goose flying as light as a lark, and better than ever she was: and when she lit at his feet, patted her on the head, and "Ma vourneen," says he, "but you are the darlint o' the world."

"And what do you say to me," says 'Saint Kavin, "for making her the like?"

"By Jabers," says the king, "I say nothing beats the art o' man, barring the bees."

"And do you say no more nor that?" says Saint Kavin.

"And that I'm beholden to you," says the king.

"But will you gi'e me all the ground the goose flew over?" says Saint Kavin.

"I will," says King O'Toole, "and you're welcome to it," says he, "though it's the last acre I have to give."

"But you'll keep your word true?" says the saint.

"As true as the sun," says the king.

"It's well for you, King O'Toole, that you said that word," says he; "for if you didn't say that word, the devil the bit o' your goose would ever fly agin."

When the king was as good as his word, Saint Kavin was pleased with him, and then it was that he made himself known to the king. "And," says he, "King O'Toole, you're a decent man, for I only came here to try you. You don't know me," says he, "because I'm disguised."

"Musha! then," says the king, "who are you?"

"I'm Saint Kavin," said the saint, blessing himself.

"Oh, queen of heaven!" says the king, making the sign of the cross between his eyes, and falling down on his knees before the saint; "is it the great Saint Kavin," says he, "that I've been discoursing all this time without knowing it," says he, "all as one as if he was a lump of a gossoon?—and so you're a saint?" says the king.

"I am," says Saint Kavin.

"By Jabers, I thought I was only talking to a dacent boy," says the king.

"Well, you know the difference now," says the saint. "I'm Saint Kavin," says he, "the greatest of all the saints."

And so the king had his goose as good as new, to divert him as long as he lived: and the saint supported him after he came into his property, as I told you, until the day of his death—and that was soon after; for the poor goose thought he was catching a trout one Friday; but, my jewel, it was a mistake he made—and instead of a trout, it was a thieving horse-eel; and instead of the goose killing a trout for the king's supper—by dad, the eel killed the king's goose—and small blame to him; but he didn't ate her, because he darn't ate what Saint Kavin had laid his blessed hands on.

The Tale of Ivan

❦

THERE WERE FORMERLY A MAN AND A WOMAN living in the parish of Llanlavan, in the place which is called Hwrdh. And work became scarce, so the man said to his wife, "I will go search for work, and you may live here." So he took fair leave, and travelled far toward the East, and at last came to the house of a farmer and asked for work.

"What work can ye do?" said the farmer. "I can do all kinds of work," said Ivan. Then they agreed upon three pounds for the year's wages.

When the end of the year came his master showed him the three pounds. "See, Ivan," said he, "here's your wage; but if you will give it me back I'll give you a piece of advice instead."

"Give me my wage," said Ivan.

"No, I'll not," said the master; "I'll explain my advice."

"Tell it me, then," said Ivan.

Then said the master, "Never leave the old road for the sake of a new one."

After that they agreed for another year at the old wages, and at the end of it Ivan took instead a piece of advice, and this was it: "Never lodge where an old man is married to a young woman."

The same thing happened at the end of the third year, when the piece of advice was: "Honesty is the best policy."

But Ivan would not stay longer, but wanted to go back to his wife.

"Don't go today," said his master; "my wife bakes tomorrow, and she shall make thee a cake to take home to thy good woman."

And when Ivan was going to leave, "Here," said his master, "here is a cake for thee to take home to thy wife, and, when ye are most joyous together, then break the cake, and not sooner."

So he took fair leave of them and travelled towards home, and at last he came to Wayn Her, and there he met three merchants from Tre Rhyn, of his own parish, coming home from Exeter Fair. "Oho! Ivan," said they, "come with us; glad are we to see you. Where have you been so long?"

"I have been in service," said Ivan, "and now I'm going home to my wife."

"Oh, come with us! you'll be right welcome." But when they took the new road Ivan kept to the old one. And robbers fell upon them before they had gone far from Ivan as they were going by the fields of the houses in the meadow. They began to cry out, "Thieves!" and Ivan shouted out "Thieves!" too. And when the robbers heard Ivan's shout they ran away, and the merchants went by the new road and Ivan by the old one till they met again at Market-Jew.

"Oh, Ivan," said the merchants, "we are beholding to you; but for you we would have been lost men. Come lodge with us at our cost, and welcome."

When they came to the place where they used to lodge, Ivan said, "I must see the host."

"The host," they cried; "what do you want with the host? Here is the hostess, and she's young and pretty. If you want to see the host you'll find him in the kitchen."

So he went into the kitchen to see the host; he found him a weak old man turning the spit.

"Oh! oh!" quoth Ivan, "I'll not lodge here, but will go next door."

"Not yet," said the merchants, "sup with us, and welcome."

Now it happened that the hostess had plotted with a certain monk in Market-Jew to murder the old man in his bed that night while the rest were asleep, and they agreed to lay it on the lodgers.

So while Ivan was in bed next door, there was a hole in the pine-end of the house, and he saw a light through it. So he got up and looked, and heard the monk speaking. "I had better cover this hole," said he, "or people in the next house may see our deeds." So he stood with his back against it while the hostess killed the old man.

But meanwhile Ivan out with his knife, and putting it through the hole, cut a round piece off the monk's robe. The very next morning the hostess raised the cry that her husband was murdered, and as there was neither man nor child in the house but the merchants, she declared they ought to be hanged for it.

So they were taken and carried to prison, till a last Ivan came to them. "Alas! alas! Ivan," cried they, "bad luck sticks to us; our host was killed last night, and we shall be hanged for it."

"Ah, tell the justices," said Ivan, "to summon the real murderers."

"Who knows," they replied, "who committed the crime?"

"Who committed the crime!" said Ivan. "If I cannot prove who committed the crime, hang me in your stead."

So he told all he knew, and brought out the piece of cloth from the monk's robe, and with that the merchants were set at liberty, and the hostess and the monk were seized and hanged.

Then they came all together out of Market-Jew, and they said to him: "Come as far as Coed Carrn y Wylfa, the Wood of the Heap of Stones of Watching, in the parish of Burman." Then their two roads separated, and though the merchants wished Ivan to go with them, he would not go with them, but went straight home to his wife.

And when his wife saw him she said: "Home in the nick of time. Here's a purse of gold that I've found; it has no name, but sure it belongs to the great lord yonder. I was just thinking what to do when you came."

Then Ivan thought of the third counsel, and he said "Let us go and give it to the great lord."

So they went up to the castle, but the great lord was not in it, so they left the purse with the servant that minded the gate, and then they went home again and lived in quiet for a time.

But one day the great lord stopped at their house for a drink of water, and Ivan's wife said to him: "I hope your lordship found your lordship's purse quite safe with all its money in it."

"What purse is that you are talking about?" said the lord.

"Sure, it's your lordship's purse that I left at the castle," said Ivan.

"Come with me and we will see into the matter," said the lord.

So Ivan and his wife went up to the castle, and there they pointed out the man to whom they had given the purse, and he had to give it up and was sent away from the castle. And the lord was so pleased with Ivan that he made him his servant in the stead of the thief.

"Honesty's the best policy!" quoth Ivan, as he skipped about in his new quarters. "How joyful I am!"

Then he thought of his old master's cake that he was to eat when he was most joyful, and when he broke it, to and behold, inside it was his wages for the three years he had been with him.

Legends for Children

THE MYTHS AND LEGENDS told to children over the centuries were largely fictional, and they were developed to instil in children the kind of morality and superstition they would need to live a life of good fortune and good will. The legends were often violent, and many of the events that occurred were so frightening that a child would be shocked into a rigid belief, and good behaviour. For what child would not go straight to bed each night when he heard of the old fairy wife who comes with her brownie child? But there is a certain perverse morality there, too, designed to appeal to children. Bad mothers are punished, sometimes with death, and children can reign supreme in the fantasy world of the imagination. For when animals can talk, and a tall tale has a moral, anything is possible, and that magic is as strong today.

The Little Bird

❧

A FAMILY ONCE LIVED IN THE WOODS, a man and a woman with their three small children. Now two of these children were boys, but the third was a wee slight girl with a smile that lit the hearts of all who met her. Her face was fair and her eyes held the promise of many dreams, but her mother, who had no time for those dreams, threw up her hands in despair at her fairylike daughter.

Their cottage was set deep in the woods, and it was a walk indeed to fetch milk from the farm down the hillock. But that wee slight girl was sent on that walk, with her mother's good jug, every day from the time she could toddle, and so it was that she would make that walk again on this particular day.

Now the girl had just counted five years, and on the table, laid there surely by the wee folk, was a bright shiny skipping rope, with handles as red as the flowers that gazed into the stream. And the girl wanted nothing more than to skip with that new rope, and to hold those red handles, but it was time, as it always was in the middle of the morning, to fetch the milk from the farm down the hillock.

'Can I take my skipping-rope with me?' she asked, her eyes shining with excitement.

But her mother, who had no time for that excitement, threw up her hands in despair at her fairylike daughter. 'No, ye can't,' she said sourly, and turned back to her cooking.

'But I won't spill the milk, Mummy, I promise,' said the wee girl.

And because her mother was not the sort who liked a good chat, or indeed a wee girl with eyes that shone with the promise of dreams, she said tersely, 'Well, then. Ye can take the skipping-rope, but if ye spills so much as a drop of the milk, I'll kill ye.'

And so it was that the little girl took her new skipping-rope, and skipped pertly down the lane, over the hillock to the farm, the milk jug clasped tightly in a hand that also clutched the shiny red handles of the skipping-rope. She stopped at the farm, and her jug was filled, and her skipping-rope admired, and away she went home again, skipping with the jug in one hand.

But things being as they are with matters that involve milk jugs and skipping-ropes, it was not long before that jug was dropped and broken, and the wee girl sat sadly in its midst and sobbed.

Now the girl was a familiar figure down this forest road, and soon enough a woman came along who recognized her, and who knew of the girl's mother, who was a very stern woman indeed, having no time for the dreams that shone in the eyes of her wee lass. So this kindly woman took it upon herself to right the young thing, and she said to her then, 'Now come along with me. I've got a jug just the twin of yours there.'

Then the new jug was filled, and with her skipping rope folded carefully and tucked under an arm, the little girl went home without spilling even a drop of milk.

But her mother, whose eyes shone not with dreams but with spite, said, 'Where did ye get the jug?'

And the little girl said, 'It's our jug, Mummy, just the same as ye gave me.'

But she said, 'No, this one is different. My jug had a blue stripe and this one has a red one.'

And with that she killed the wee girl, wrapping that skipping-rope around her thin neck until she was blue and still, and then she baked her in a pie. And being near to dinnertime, it was not long before her father came in, and he asked for the wee girl, for he had a soft spot for her fairylike ways, and those eyes that shone with the promise of dreams reminded him of another wee child with those same bright eyes, and that child had been himself.

His wife shook her head. 'Och, she's out playing, let her be.'

'Should we not call her for her dinner?' asked her husband, surprised at this sudden leniency.

'Na, let her go then.'

So the man tucked into the pie, with morsels of meat so tender that he ate greedily. And then, as he cut into an even larger piece, he found a finger, with a small silver ring.

He looked at his wife in horror, and he said, 'This is my daughter's ring. Why is she in this pie?'

And his wife said then that she had killed her, for she'd broken their milk jug and spilled the milk.

'Now what have you done?' he cried, and made as if to kill his wife himself. But now that the lass was gone there wouldn't be a woman around the house to keep it spic and span, and to make great succulent pies, so he thought again, and said, 'Och, I'll let ye live.'

When the two sons came in they too were distressed by the death of their wee sister, and none could eat his dinner that day.

Time went by, and nothing changed in the cottage set deep in the woods, except they had a visitor, in the shape of a small brown bird, who peeped into the windows of the house for hours of each day, and who had eyes that shone with the promise of dreams. But with the windows misted with the heat of the fire, the boys and their father couldn't see those eyes, and so they would shoo away the wee bird.

But everyday, there it would be again, peeping in the windows of the house.

By the time Christmas came round, the boys had grown to love the wee bird who sat on the sill, and they fed it with crumbs and bits of seed. They were doing just that, on Christmas Eve, when a voice startled them from their play. It boomed down the chimney and when the two boys reached the hearth it grew quieter, almost plaintive.

'Brother, look up and see what I've got,' and so the first brother looked up and was met by a shower of toys and sweets.

And then came the voice once again, 'Brother, look up and see what I've got,' and when the next brother looked up, he too was met by a shower of toys and sweets.

Then, 'Father, Father, look up and see what I've got,' and down the chimney came a fine new suit, and a bag of tobacco, and as he was admiring that suit, a letter dropped down the chimney, and on it was written the words, 'Open this letter two hours after Christmas night.'

And into the silence came the voice once more, 'Mother, look up and see what I've got,' and when the mother looked up she dropped upon her head a great stone and killed her dead.

When the two hours had passed, the father opened the letter, which said, 'Dear Father, this is your daughter. The spell is broken. Once I have killed my mother, I shall return on New Year's Eve.'

The days to New Year's Eve passed slowly, and the father and his boys were filled with fear of what might greet them, for the wee girl had been long dead, and cut into a pie at that. But on that New Year's Eve there was no sign of her, and they grew more and more worried and frightened. And then, there was a tap tap tap at the window, a pecking sound that was familiar to them all.

'Och, it's only the wee bird,' said a brother to the other, but they opened the window anyhow, and prepared to feed it some crumbs. It was then that the bird hopped into the kitchen, and turning to them with eyes that shone with the promise of dreams, said, 'It's me, I'm home.'

They all stood aghast, the father and his two boys, and then the father spoke tentatively, reaching out to stroke the smooth feathers of the little bird, 'But you're a bird now.'

'Yes,' said the little bird, 'but if you take my mother's pinkie ring and give it to me now, I'll come back as a girl.'

This they did, though it meant digging up the body of the wicked mother from her newly turned grave. But they returned with the ring, and presented it to the bird, who turned at once into a little girl.

And the girl drew herself up tall, and took the ring that had belonged to her mother, and the ring that had once been hers, and laid them safely away in a box, a reminder of what can happen to girls with skipping ropes, and mothers with no time for fairylike ways or dreams.

The Fox, The Wolf and The Butter

ONG, LONG AGO, when a fox could befriend a wolf without fear of becoming his midday meal, and when all animals and folk in the woods spoke Gaelic, there was a wee den set deep in the forest, and it was the home of a fox and a wolf who lived there together. Now this fox and this wolf were friends, and firm friends they were, but there would always be that shadow of mistrust that hung between them, for a fox is a wily creature, and it was then, too, even in the days when a fox could befriend a wolf without fear of becoming his midday meal.

The fox and the wolf walked together each day, along the path overhung by fronded green firs, and over the hills, to the beach. And there they would comb the shores for debris that had blown in from the sea. Often it was, too, that they'd find a choice bit of fish for their dinner, or a bit of salt pork that had fallen over the side of a poor seaman's ship.

And so it was one day that they walked together, along the path overhung by fronded green firs, and over the hills to the beach. And there they came across a great cask of pure white butter, cold and creamy and freshly churned. And what delight lit their beady eyes, and their tongues fairly dripped with anticipation of this creamy treat, all cold and freshly churned. They danced about it then, and said to the other, 'We'll hide it now, till we get a chance to take it home.'

And so the fox and the wolf struggled with this great cask, up the hill and partway along that path overhung by fronded green firs, where they dug a great hole and buried it. And then they went home.

When they woke the next morning, the wolf yawned, and licked his lips, and thought of all that lovely pure white butter, and he said to the fox, 'Shall we bring it a little further today?'

But the fox shook his head. 'Oh no,' he said, 'not today. I am going away today.'

The wolf looked surprised. 'Where are you going?' he asked.

'I am going,' said the fox, 'to a Christening. And then I'll be back.'

So the fox went off and he was gone for near a whole day. And when he came back he was smiling and content, and he laid himself down on a cosy bit of the den as if to sleep.

'So you're back,' said the wolf to the fox.

'Yes,' he said.

'What name was the babe given?' asked the wolf.

'We called him Mu Bheul (About the Mouth),' said the fox, to which the wolf nodded sagely.

The fox and wolf settled down for the night, and the next morning the fox rose and made as if to leave. Now it was one thing for the fox to set out alone of a morning, but quite another for him to do it twice, and the wolf felt a funny kind of suspicion, as the shadow of mistrust that hung between them grew ever so slightly larger.

And he said to the fox, 'Shall we bring it a little further today, the cask of butter?'

But the fox shook his head. 'Oh no,' he said, 'not today. I am going away today.'

The wolf looked wary. 'Where are you going?' he asked.

'I am going,' said the fox, 'to a Christening. And then I'll be back.'

So the fox went off and he was gone for near a whole day. And when he came back he was smiling and content, and he laid himself down on a cosy bit of the den as if to sleep.

'So you're back,' said the wolf to the fox.

'Yes,' he said.

'What name was the babe given today?' asked the wolf.

'We called him Mu Leth (About Half),' said he.

'I see,' said the wolf, although he didn't, and as he settled down for the night he felt that shadow of mistrust growing larger still.

But the wolf wakened fresh and ready for the day, the thought of all that pure, creamy butter making him salivate. And he stood and stretched, and looked for his friend, the fox. But he was not there. So he looked around, outside the den, and the fox was just setting off down the path overhung by fronded green firs, and he called out then, 'Fox, where are you going? Shall we bring it a little further today, the cask of butter?'

But the fox shook his head. 'Oh no,' he said, 'not today. I am going away again today.'

The wolf just looked. 'Where are you going today?' he asked.

'I am going,' said the fox, 'to a Christening. And then I'll be back.'

So the fox went off and he was gone for near a whole day. And when he came back he was smiling and content, licking his chops and smacking his lips. And he laid himself down on a cosy bit of the den as if to sleep.

'So you're back,' said the wolf to the fox.

'Yes,' he said.

'What name was the babe given today?' asked the wolf.

'We called him Sgrìobadgh a' Mhàis (Scraping the Bottom),' said he.

'I see,' said the wolf, although he didn't again, and as he settled down for the night that shadow of mistrust was firmly between them.

But he woke again the next morning fresh and hungry, and the thought of that creamy butter made him nearly swoon with expectation. And he said to the fox, his tongue dripping so that he could hardly speak, 'Shall we get it today, the cask of butter we hid?'

And the fox said, 'Yes indeed.'

And so it was that the fox and the wolf set off down the path, overhung by fronded green firs, almost to the hills whereupon lay the shore. And they reached the spot where the great cask of butter was hidden, cold, creamy and freshly churned. They uncovered it then, and lifting off the lid, eager for a succulent pawful, they discovered it ... empty.

It was awful. They jigged and railed and danced a furious reel round that empty cask. And the fox was so puzzled, and so too was the wolf, for neither knew who had taken their butter.

'Well,' said the fox at last, when they lay down spent from their angry dance, 'this is very queer. For not another creature knew of this cask but you and I, dear wolf. And this terribly queer affair means only one thing to me, and that is this: that it was you or me who took that butter. And that is what I think:

> *If I ate the butter, and it was I*
> *Chiorram chiotam, chiorram, chatam, chiorram chiù*
> *But if you ate the butter and it was you,*
> *A galling plague on your grey belly in the dust.*

There was no great harm in the curse of the fox, for his words were empty, but the curse he had laid on the wolf was poison indeed, for his belly was empty and the butter was gone.

The Ainsel

❧

DEEP IN THE HEART of the Border country, where the wind howls with cold, lived a wee boy called Parcie. He lived with his mother in a small, snug cottage where the fire burned bright and bathed the stone clad walls in a soft, cosy glow. They lived alone there for his father was long since gone, but they managed with little, living simply and happily among the trees and the wood folk who inhabited them.

Now like most small boys, Parcie plotted all day in order to avoid being sent to bed each night. He longed to sit by the hearth with his mother, watching the burning embers cast intriguing shadows which danced and performed a story that seemed to Parcie like it could go on forever. But each night it was cut short, as was the sound of his mother's mellifluous voice as she sang to him of fairies and sea-folk, and told of stories and legends of long ago. For it was it at this point that Parcie's mother would close up her bag of mending.

'It's time for your bed, Parcie,' she would say, always the same thing, and Parcie would be packed neatly into his tiny box-bed where the fairies had laid a nest of golden slumberdust so potent that his eyes were shut and he was fast asleep as soon as his head touched his soft pillow. And there he'd sleep all the night, until the next morning he struggled to hatch a plan to stay awake all night, to carry on and on the drowsy contentment of the evening.

But one night Parcie's tired mother could argue no further and when the fire began to sink down into black-red embers, and she said,

'It's time for your bed, Parcie' he would not go. And so she picked up her mending, and tidied it away, setting a bowl of cool, fresh cream by the doorstep as she went along the corridor to her own bed.

'I hope to God the old fairy wife does not get to you, lad, but it will be your own fault if she does,' whispered his mother as she disappeared into her room.

And suddenly the warm red room took on a more sinister cast, and the shadows no longer told a story but taunted him, warning him, tempting him until he was a jumble of fear and confusion. And just as he steeled himself to dash to his warm box-bed, filled with golden slumberdust, a tiny brownie leapt from the chimney and landed on his foot.

Now brownies were common in the days when Parcie lived in the stone cottage with his mother, and they came each day to every house that had the courtesy and the foresight to leave a bowl of cool, fresh cream by the doorstep. And if some foolish occupant forgot that cream one night, she would be sure to find a tumultuous mess the next day. For brownies came to tidy everything away, neat and clean, collecting specks of dust and laying things just so, so that in the morning the lucky household gleamed with shining surfaces and possessions all in order.

But Parcie knew nothing of the magic that dropped through the chimney each night and he was surprised and rather pleased to see this tiny fairy. The brownie was not, however, so pleased to see Parcie, for he was an efficient wee brownie and he liked to have his work done quickly, in order to get to the lovely bowl of cool, fresh cream which awaited him by the doorstep.

'What's your name?' asked Parcie, grinning.

'Ainsel (own self),' replied the brownie, smiling back despite himself. 'And you?'

'My Ainsel,' said Parcie, joining in the joke.

And so Parcie and the brownie played a little together, and Parcie watched with interest while the brownie tidied and cleaned their cottage in a whirlwind of activity. And then, as he neared the grate to sweep away some dust that had come loose from the hearth, Parcie took an inopportune moment to poke the fire, and what should fly out upon the poor brownie but a red-hot ember which burnt him so badly that he howled with pain.

And then, into the snuffling silence that followed, a deep frightening voice boomed down the chimney. It was the old fairy wife who Parcie's mother had warned of, and she flew into a rage when she heard her dear brownie's tears.

'Tell me who hurt ye,' she shouted down the chimney, 'I'll get him, so I will.'

And the brownie called out tearfully, 'It was My Ainsel'. Parcie lost no time in hurling himself from the room and into his box-bed where the golden slumberdust did not cast its magic over the terrified boy, for he laid awake and shaking for a long time after his head touched his soft pillow.

But the old fairy wife was not concerned about Parcie, for she called out, 'What's the fuss, if you did it yer ainsel' and muttering she thrust a long brown arm down the chimney and plucked the sniffling brownie from the fireside.

Now what do you think Parcie's mother thought the next morning when she found her cottage spic and span, but the bowl of cream still standing untouched, cool and fresh by the doorstep. How perplexed she was when the brownie stopped visiting her cottage, although she always left a bowl of cream to tempt him. But in the heart of the Border country, where the wind howls with cold, bad is almost always balanced by good, and so it was then when from that night onwards, Parcie's mother never again had to say to him, 'Parcie, it's time for your bed,' for at the first sudden movement of the shadows, when the fire began to sink down into black-red embers, he was sound asleep in his tiny box-bed, deep in the sleep of the golden slumberdust.

Gold-Tree and Silver-Tree

❧

ONCE UPON A TIME there was a king who had a wife, whose name was Silver-tree, and a daughter, whose name was Gold-tree. One day, Gold-tree and Silver-tree went to a glen, where there was a well, and in it there was a trout.

Said Silver-tree, "Troutie, bonny little fellow, am not I the most beautiful queen in the world?"

"Oh! indeed you are not."

"Who then?"

"Why, Gold-tree, your daughter."

Silver-tree went home, blind with rage. She lay down on the bed, and vowed she would never be well until she could get the heart and the liver of Gold-tree, her daughter, to eat.

At nightfall the king came home, and it was told him that Silver-tree, his wife, was very ill. He went where she was, and asked her what was wrong with her.

"Oh! only a thing—which you may heal if you like."

"Oh! indeed there is nothing at all which I could do for you that I would not do."

"If I get the heart and liver of Gold-tree, my daughter, to eat, I shall be well."

Now it happened about this time that the son of a great king had come from abroad to ask Gold-tree for marrying. The king now agreed to this, and they went abroad.

The king then went and sent his lads to the hunting-hill for a he-goat, and he gave its heart and its liver to his wife to eat; and she rose well and healthy.

A year after this Silver-tree went to the glen, where there was the well in which there was the trout.

"Troutie, bonny little fellow," said she, "am not I the most beautiful queen in the world?"

"Oh! indeed you are not."

"Who then?"

"Why, Gold-tree, your daughter."

"Oh! well, it is long since she was living. It is a year since I ate her heart and liver."

"Oh! indeed she is not dead. She is married to a great prince abroad."

Silver-tree went home, and begged the king to put the long-ship in order, and said, "I am going to see my dear Gold-tree, for it is so long since I saw her." The long-ship was put in order, and they went away.

It was Silver-tree herself that was at the helm, and she steered the ship so well that they were not long at all before they arrived.

The prince was out hunting on the hills. Gold-tree knew the long-ship of her father coming.

"Oh!" said she to the servants, "my mother is coming, and she will kill me."

"She shall not kill you at all; we will lock you in a room where she cannot get near you."

This is how it was done; and when Silver-tree came ashore, she began to cry out:

"Come to meet your own mother, when she comes to see you," Gold-tree said that she could not, that she was locked in the room, and that she could not get out of it.

"Will you not put out," said Silver-tree, "your little finger through the key-hole, so that your own mother may give a kiss to it?"

She put out her little finger, and Silver-tree went and put a poisoned stab in it, and Gold-tree fell dead.

When the prince came home, and found Gold-tree dead, he was in great sorrow, and when he saw how beautiful she was, he did not bury her at all, but he locked her in a room where nobody would get near her.

In the course of time he married again, and the whole house was under the hand of this wife but one room, and he himself always kept the key of that room. On a certain day of the days he forgot to take the key with him, and the second wife got into the room. What did she see there but the most beautiful woman that she ever saw.

She began to turn and try to wake her, and she noticed the poisoned stab in her finger. She took the stab out, and Gold-tree rose alive, as beautiful as she was ever.

At the fall of night the prince came home from the hunting-hill, looking very downcast.

"What gift," said his wife, "would you give me that I could make you laugh?"

"Oh! indeed, nothing could make me laugh, except Gold-tree were to come alive again."

"Well, you'll find her alive down there in the room."

When the prince saw Gold-tree alive he made great rejoicings, and he began to kiss her, and kiss her, and kiss her. Said the second wife, "Since she is the first one you had it is better for you to stick to her, and I will go away."

"Oh! indeed you shall not go away, but I shall have both of you."

At the end of the year, Silver-tree went to the glen, where there was the well, in which there was the trout.

"Troutie, bonny little fellow," said she, "am not I the most beautiful queen in the world?"

"Oh! indeed you are not."

"Who then?"

"Why, Gold-tree, your daughter."

"Oh! well, she is not alive. It is a year since I put the poisoned stab in her finger."

"Oh! indeed she is not dead at all, at all."

Silver-tree, went home, and begged the king to put the long-ship in order, for that she was going to see her dear Gold-tree, as it was so long since she saw her. The long-ship was put in order, and they went away. It was Silver-tree herself that was at the helm, and she steered the ship so well that they were not long at all before they arrived.

The prince was out hunting on the hills. Gold-tree knew her father's ship coming.

"Oh!" said she, "my mother is coming, and she will kill me."

"Not at all," said the second wife; "we will go down to meet her."

Silver-tree came ashore. "Come down, Gold-tree, love," said she, "for your own mother has come to you with a precious drink."

"It is a custom in this country," said the second wife, "that the person who offers a drink takes a draught out of it first."

Silver-tree put her mouth to it, and the second wife went and struck it so that some of it went down her throat, and she fell dead. They had only to carry her home a dead corpse and bury her.

The prince and his two wives lived long after this, pleased and peaceful.